BACK IN THE GAME

In a low tone, the intruder said: "You have a gun, Professor Cassidy. Please get it."

"My gun's not for hire, Armand," said Cassidy. "Look," he added gently, "I'm a professor of medieval history."

"And much more," said Armand. "Covert operations in Guatemala, Hungary, the Congo. . . ."

"I've been out of that outfit for years. I was fired."

"I know." Armand raised the gun to shoulder level again—and there was distinct menace in the gesture. "'Never take a chance with a man holding a gun.' You wrote that, Cassidy. It's in your resume."

That was a stunner. The resume was at Langley, theoretically impervious even to Senatorial snoops, an exception to the Freedom of Information Act.

That winning smile again on Armand's face: "Please get your gun, Professor. I don't want to shoot you."

Books by John Crosby

Contract on the President
An Affair of Strangers
Nightfall
The Company of Friends
Dear Judgment
Party of the Year
Penelope Now
Men in Arms
Take No Prisoners*

*Published by
WARNER BOOKS

TAKE NO PRISONERS

JOHN CROSBY

WARNER BOOKS

A Warner Communications Company

Warner Books, Inc.
75 Rockefeller Plaza
New York, N.Y. 10019

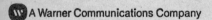 A Warner Communications Company

Printed in the United States of America

First Printing: October, 1985

10 9 8 7 6 5 4 3 2 1

To Ellie

"We have profaned graves and mosques. We have sent to their death on mere hearsay and without trial people whose guilt is extremely doubtful. We have killed off on mere suspicion whole populations who have since been found innocent. We have surpassed in barbarity the barbarians we came to civilize—and we complain of having no success with them. . . ."

> — from the report of the Commission on Africa to King Louis Philippe of France in 1833, concerning the war against the Berbers

1

The man was standing in the vestibule just outside the door to Cassidy's first-floor apartment, gun in hand. A slender fellow of perhaps forty with a distinctly boyish look about him, wearing a gray flannel suit as if he were born in it.

When Cassidy stepped into the vestibule, the man pointed the gun at him and said: "I'm frightfully sorry about this but I must ask you to step back inside." With a winning smile. Cassidy could never remember anyone pointing a gun at him before with such a winning smile.

The gun struck a wildly discordant note. It was a 9mm Frank with a silencer, a professional killer's gun. Professional killers didn't wear gray flannel suits. Or say: "I'm sorry."

"I'm sorry too," said Cassidy, not to be outdone in courtesy, "because you're making me late for class. I'm a professor of medieval history at the New School for Social Research."

"And a very good one, Professor Cassidy," said the man

flashing that winning smile again. "You have the most *marvelous* reputation, Professor, for making your students *think* and so few professors do that. I am sorry to trouble you—" waving the gun at him again apologetically—"but it's a matter of life and death. My life and my death."

All this in a soft, well-educated—perhaps overeducated—voice. Groton? Groton was one of the few schools left that overeducated the young. (Though why he persisted in thinking of this chap as young, Cassidy didn't know. He was a very young forty.)

Cassidy stepped backward into the apartment and the man with the winning (and very boyish) smile followed him and closed the door.

"You know my name," said Cassidy, "but I don't know yours."

"Armand," said the man. "I've always hated it."

"Why?" asked Cassidy mildly. "It's not such a bad name."

Armand had lost interest in his name and was gazing about Cassidy's big high-ceilinged room with its twelve-foot windows, the bookshelves which lined the walls, the two fireplaces. "What a charming room, Professor!"

"Rent controlled," said Cassidy. "Otherwise I couldn't afford it. Should I hold up my hands?"

"Oh, no, no! Nothing like that!" Armand waved the gun at him negligently. "Just stand over there, please, and don't move."

"Oh, I wouldn't do a thing like that."

Armand was walking around inspecting the firedogs in the fireplace, the library ladder that ran the length of the booklined room on its brass rail, Cassidy's unmade bed, the high Japanese screen behind which lay Lucia's bed, also unmade.

"I knew you'd be in a charming apartment like this," said the man with that winning smile again. "I just knew it." He gazed at Cassidy adoringly, golden streaks in those eyes.

2

"Why don't you put the gun down and tell me what this is all about?" asked Cassidy.

"Oh, I couldn't do that. You wouldn't pay any attention to me if I didn't have the gun, nobody ever does. It won't take a minute, Professor. Well, perhaps a few minutes." Glancing all around him now, definitely looking for something.

He found it. Cassidy's little black book with all the telephone numbers in it. He pointed the gun at it because it was across the bed from him, reposing on Cassidy's night table. "If you'd just hand me that black book, Professor."

"I don't want to do that," said Cassidy flatly. There were telephone numbers in that book he wouldn't like anyone to know—or to know that he knew. The people whose numbers they were would like it even less.

Armand raised the gun shoulder high and held it in both hands pointed at Cassidy's chest. "I've killed a man, you know," he said, a note of high glee in his overeducated voice, as if this were a game. "I wouldn't like to kill you, Professor, and I assure you I wouldn't do such a thing unless you *forced* me to. I'll count to three."

"Don't bother," said Cassidy. He picked up his black book and tossed it across the bed to Armand, thinking he might drop the gun to catch it. He didn't. He caught the book and laid it on top of the gun, flipping through the pages.

Cassidy let out a long sigh and tried to relax. *"I've killed a man, you know."* Was this to be taken seriously? From this childlike, apologetic charmer? There was—in this man's tone, in his golden gaze—a nursery aspect that bothered Cassidy. As if the man were in his private fantasy land.

With a professional killer's silenced gun.

A dangerous weapon to be in the hands of a man floating on his private cloud. A pity, Cassidy was thinking. Nice fellow if it weren't for that damned gun.

Armand had found the number he was looking for (and there were numbers in there that the KGB would give its eyeteeth to know) and was dialing it. Cassidy counted the digits—eleven—which meant it was long-distance, running his telephone bill up even higher than it already was. Silence in the room so intense that Cassidy could hear the number ringing wherever it was.

Armand's eyes full of their glinting golden lights from his own interior sunshine.

Somebody had answered and Armand said: "Victor! Surprise! It's me! Just fancy that, Victor."

Cassidy was wondering when if ever he'd heard somebody say: "Just fancy that!" This kid was not off the streets.

Armand was saying, voice full of glee: "Yes, I'm quite alive—and isn't that a shock, Victor? Things aren't working out as you planned at all well. And what is more, things are going to get very much worse. I'm on my way to the *New York Times* and I'm going to tell them everything—and I've got the documentation to prove it."

Victor, Cassidy was thinking. There were no Victors in that black book that he could remember.

Armand had stopped talking now and was listening. Victor on the other end was doing a lot of talking. Cassidy could hear the low, urgent hum of it. On Armand's face was a bemused smile, in the eyes those golden glints. . . .

"No, Victor, I'm not coming to see you. I don't want to see you ever again. You tried to kill me." Armand saying that in his nursery style. "Oh, it was you all right, Victor. I'm not such a fool as all that. . . ."

Victor was again doing a lot of talking. It was none of Cassidy's business, but he felt he had to butt in.

"He's stalling you, Armand. If he keeps that up long enough, Victor'll trace that call and I don't think you'd like that. Nor would I because, after all, it's my phone."

"Good-bye, Victor," said Armand—and hung up. The glee had gone out of Armand's face. He looked woebegone, almost as if he were about to burst into tears.

4

In a low tone, he said: "You have a gun, Professor Cassidy. Please get it."

Now what sort of lunacy was this? If I got my gun, I could shoot this fellow. But Cassidy didn't want to shoot Armand.

"My gun's not for hire, Armand," said Cassidy.

Armand said: "My life and my sacred honor are at risk. . . ."

Even at Groton they didn't talk like that. People didn't even write sentences like that anymore.

"Look, I'm a professor of medieval history," said Cassidy gently.

"And much more," said Armand. "Covert operations in Guatemala, Hungary, the Congo. . . ."

"I've been out of that outfit for years. I was fired."

"I know." Armand raised the gun to shoulder level again—and there was a distinct menace in the gesture. "Never take a chance with a man with a gun. You wrote that, Cassidy. It's in your résumé."

That was a stunner. The résumé was at Langley, theoretically impervious even to senatorial snoops, an exception to the Freedom of Information Act.

That winning smile again on Armand's face: "*Please* get your gun, Professor. I don't want to shoot you."

Cassidy took his time. He pushed the library ladder the length of the room on its brass track to the far end where the Greek histories lay in their special place of honor near the ceiling where they could look down on all the other centuries.

The gun lay behind Thucydides' *History of the Peloponnesian War*— a .357 magnum fully loaded. Ordinarily Cassidy would never leave a loaded gun anywhere within reach of his thirteen-year-old daughter, but he knew Lucia would never, *never*, look behind a volume of Thucydides. Lucia had no use for history. History, she liked to tell her father, the historian, started thirteen years earlier—the day she was born. Before that, nothing mattered.

The ladder rested now at the foot of the big room, almost thirty feet from Armand. Outside the window Cassidy could see the white pillars of the Catholic church across the street. Inside the room there was total silence. The silence and the distance were important. If it weren't for the silence and the distance, neither of them would have survived.

Cassidy climbed the ladder to the second step from the top, which was as high as he liked to go on that ladder, pulled out Thucydides, and reached in for the gun. He pulled out the gun, replaced Thucydides, and sat down on the top step with the gun in his hand, pushing the safety to off, not knowing quite what he planned to do. He certainly didn't want to shoot Armand, but perhaps with his own gun in hand he might talk Armand into dropping the 9mm.

The decision was taken out of his hands. The front door burst open and into the room burst a huge apelike figure, his right shoulder held low. Clearly the man who had broken the door.

Behind the apelike fellow came another man—skinny, Hispanic, ferocious. Ferocity was this man's purpose in life, his sole purpose, as if there were no other. It was what he was for. The man came in quickly, high stepping, almost prancing, the gun outstretched in both hands. Even in the microsecond before he fired it, Cassidy noted that it was a 9mm silenced Frank—same gun Armand had.

Armand moved quickly, swinging his gun away from Cassidy in an arc toward the Hispanic—but not swiftly enough. The man shot twice—*phhfp pfffhp*—and Armand pitched backward, spouting blood from head and neck.

The high-stepping Hispanic moved in quickly for the coup de grace, but he never got it off.

High on the ladder thirty feet away, Cassidy snap-shot—all he had time for—and the .357 bullet caught the Hispanic in the shoulder, sent the gun flying across the room, and spun him around into the wall.

The man's mouth fell open in a snarl and he turned on Cassidy (noticing him for the first time), a look of pure, undistilled malevolence sharp as an ice pick in a brown face of demonic intensity. Before Cassidy could shoot again, the Hispanic, quick as a ferret, was out the door—the apelike one shambling after him.

Armand's eyes popped open, his face twisted in a little sad smile. "I'm sorry!" he said.

"You must stop apologizing all the time," said Cassidy and came off the ladder fast.

By the time he got to him, Armand's eyes had closed, but he still had a bit of pulse. Cassidy stemmed the flow of blood by pressing down hard on the skull with his left hand even while dialing St. Vincent's Hospital around the corner. "Send an ambulance quick," he bawled to Emergency. "A man's been shot. He's bleeding to death."

The medics were very fast for a change because the hospital was so close. Even before they got there, Cassidy had retrieved his private black telephone book with all those very private numbers in it from Armand's inside pocket. His right hand came out of the pocket covered with blood. Stuck to the black book was a brown manila envelope, also covered in blood.

" . . . and I've got the documentation to prove it."

Imprinted on the brown manila envelope was a beautiful set of Cassidy's fingerprints, implicating him even more deeply in something he had no wish to be connected to. Cassidy stuffed the bloodstained envelope in the bookcase behind Emily Dickinson's collected works.

Only then did he call Lieutenant Fletcher at the Fourteenth Street Station.

Before Lucia got home from school, roughly ten minutes later, the medics had pumped Armand full of synthetic blood and taken him to St. Vincent's.

2

Lieutenant Fletcher was two hundred pounds of pure skepticism. "If I can believe my ears," he was saying, "this man came in here flourishing a nine-millimeter Frank in order to get—a *telephone number*?"

Cassidy was stretched out on his dirty white sofa enjoying Fletcher's incredulity. "A mother's boy, Fletch," he said. "I might even hazard the opinion that he is an only child." Lucia was curled up on the arm of the sofa. Time and again Cassidy had told her that if she continued to put her weight on the arm of the sofa that way she'd break it. It did no good.

"You were always good at character analysis, Professor, but let's get back to the facts. The man got a number of someone named Victor out of your black book which, you say, has nobody named Victor in it. . . ."

"Maybe it's his middle name, Lieutenant. I don't know all of their middle names." Lucia, taking it all in with her big round eyes and her pointed ears, loving it all.

". . . then these two hoods break in and gun the guy down

for reasons not apparent to the naked eye. You'll have to do better than this, Cassidy."

Fletcher picked up the phone and dialed a number.

"Are you accusing me of lying, Lieutenant?" said Cassidy.

"Leaving things out. You're holding back, Professor." Into the phone the detective said: "Hi, this is Lieutenant Fletcher, Fourteenth Street Station, shield number 3487, I'm calling from 342-8976. Somebody made a long-distance call from this number—uh—when, Professor? What time?"

"Three. Three-ten."

"Three. Three-ten." Into the phone. "Yeah, I'll wait."

He waited. Fletcher's partner, Jim Hazelwood, was on all fours by the bed, looking for whatever he could find. The fingerprint men were dusting the door for fingerprints and not getting any.

Cassidy said: "I'm not giving you any information, Lieutenant, because nobody gave me any. The gunsels didn't utter a single word. Armand had very little to say except that he hated that name. That should tell you something, Lieutenant. A psychiatrist could write a whole book on that remark alone. Why did he feel called upon to tell me *that*? Why don't you ask him, Lieutenant."

"He's in a coma," said Fletcher, who had just come from the hospital. "The docs don't know whether he'll ever come out of it or if he does whether he'll have enough brain to ask questions. That leaves you, Cassidy. If you don't cooperate, I may have to run you in for illegal possession, shooting with intent to do grievous bodily harm, conspiracy . . ."

The operator seemed to be taking a very long time.

Cassidy said: "What did you get out of the man's wallet—like his last name?"

"Shotover. Armand Shotover. Sounds very upper case, like he should be Armand Shotover IV. That name ring any bells?"

As a matter of fact, it did—but so far in Cassidy's cranium he could summon up nothing.

"His driver's license gave his address as Route 1, Box 62, Marietta, Virginia. That mean anything?"

"No," said Cassidy. "How much money in the wallet?"

"Aaah," said Fletcher with a wolfish smile.

"Now you're holding back."

"Confidential material of ongoing investigation. . . ." Into the phone, "Yeah, I'm here." He listened, mouth open, growling. "How about local calls—any of those? Yeah, thanks." Fletcher hung up and faced Cassidy. "There have been *no* phone calls emanating from this phone either local or long-distance in two hours, Cassidy."

Cassidy sat up straight. "Fletch, I swear to God. He dialed a long-distance number. He got his party. I heard the guy talking to him—a long time, five minutes. I could hear it. I couldn't hear what the man on the other end was saying, but I could hear his voice. The call's been scrubbed."

"Who would scrub it, Cassidy? Who *could* scrub it."

Who, indeed? Cassidy put his feet on the floor and massaged his face. There was only one outfit he could think of, and he hated the thought. . . .

Fletcher reached across Cassidy to the night table and picked up Cassidy's black book. "We'll be taking this along to the station house, Cassidy."

"Why?" said Cassidy violently. "If there were no calls . . ."

Fletcher smiled. "You ought to know police procedure better than that. I'm going to call every name in the book and ask the guy who answers if his name is Victor. Very boring, but the police are anything if not thorough."

"You don't even think there was a phone call. . . ."

"Maybe I do believe there was one," said Fletcher.

Cassidy was on his feet now "Fletch, you can't do that to me. There are people in that book—top intelligence people not only here but in France, England, Italy, well, you name

11

it. They're *all* in there. Those are *private* numbers, Lieutenant. Some of those people are so private their very existence is not known. You could get somebody killed. If you call them, they'll be on my neck; they'll never talk to me again. . . ."

"Why should you care? You're not in the outfit anymore."

Why did he? But he did. The black book was his last hold on an organization that had been his life for twenty years. Besides, there were men in the book who were his friends and had been his colleagues in operations that would not bear scrutiny. Certainly not by a cop.

"I just don't know any other way to run Victor down," said Lieutenant Fletcher silkily. "Unless you'd cooperate a little more, Professor."

"Goddamn it, Lieutenant." Cassidy breaking his ironclad rule never to swear in front of Lucia. "I don't want to get mixed up in this. I never want to see that little spic with the gun again. He's bloody dangerous, and I got a thirteen-year-old child to support."

"Well then . . ." said Fletcher. And put the book in his pocket.

"You bastard," said Cassidy.

"That's what they all say," agreed Lieutenant Fletcher. "My best friends and frequently my wife."

Half an hour later Cassidy and Lucia were on their way to Deborah's, Cassidy bearing a single suitcase. Deborah lived just two blocks away, on the other side of Fifth, the rich side.

Lucia was complaining bitterly: "Every time things get interesting I get moved out of the flat over to Deborah's."

"This time I'm coming too. It's very nice of Deborah to put us up on a moment's notice."

"She's crazy about you. Haven't you noticed?"

"You're to do your homework the minute you get there," said Cassidy.

"You can *both* help me with my irregular verbs. Two teachers helping me with my irregular verbs. What a lark!"

Deborah met them at the front door with her wide smile and her ample thighs (too ample, by Cassidy's lights), helped Lucia with her irregular verbs, put supper on the table, and didn't ask any questions.

Lucia asked the questions. "It's real fun being here, the three of us, but *why*?"

"Each venture," said Cassidy, "is a beginning, a raid on the inarticulate with shabby equipment always deteriorating in the general mess of imprecision of feeling."

"Now what does *that* mean?" cried Lucia.

Deborah knew. She'd been Cassidy's student at the New School before she became a history teacher herself. "When he wants to throw dust in your eyes, he quotes T. S. Eliot to change the subject. That's from the *Four Quartets*."

"I just wanted to see if your tiny mind retained anything at all I taught you."

In his breast pocket was the heavy manila envelope he'd taken out of Armand Shotover's coat, which was what the gunsels had come for (besides blowing Armand away, which they hadn't accomplished either). The gunsels would be back for the envelope. That's why he and Lucia were at Deborah's, but if Lucia knew that she'd be so wild with excitement she wouldn't sleep.

He hadn't shared the manila envelope with Lieutenant Fletcher. All he'd promised was cooperation—but not until he got Lucia safely in bed.

After that event took place, Deborah watched nervously as he reloaded the .357 and put it in his shoulder holster. "When will you be back?" she asked.

"Don't wait up."

He kissed her lightly on the lips. It was the least he could do in return for such a nice supper and the fact she asked so few questions.

The Catholic church was always open late at the back of the building where the fathers ran a little cafeteria for the pot smokers and the intellectuals. Through the cafeteria Cassidy knew the way to the stairs which led to the long, low room under the eaves where the fathers kept the basketballs, the cheerleaders' costumes, and the referees' whistles. (They got around to religion in that building now and then.)

It was dimly lit in the cafeteria and Cassidy hoped to slip through and up the stairs unnoticed. Father Flaherty was at a table with three longhairs, talking with his rich, fruity voice about the 1953 Dodgers—Peewee Reese, Jackie Robinson, Gil Hodges, Duke Snider. He was reciting the great names and the batting averages and the fielding averages like a litany—but he caught sight of Cassidy and was instantly at his side, smelling of Carstairs.

"I saw the ambulance and the police cars, Professor. Is there anything I can help with?"

Last thing in the world Cassidy wanted. But he couldn't say that. "If you'd just keep those acidheads out of my hair, Father," said Cassidy, "I'd appreciate it. I want to use the room under the eaves for an ongoing investigation." Stealing Fletcher's phrase. Father Flaherty would love to be part of an ongoing investigation. "I may be up there very late. I promise I won't get the church mixed up in anything." Which the church—or at least Father Flaherty—would love to get mixed up in.

"Just keep talking baseball to those infidels; you'll be doing a very great favor," said Cassidy and slipped up the stairs, hoping that would settle Father Flaherty but not counting on it. Flaherty liked to butt into everything (so long as it wasn't theological).

It was a thickly cluttered, musty room under the eaves. Cassidy could stand up straight only in the very middle of it.

On the Thirteenth Street side was a large round window extending clear to the floor through which came a glow from the street lights below. Cassidy picked his way through the debris and sat cross-legged next to the window, which over-looked his apartment. He put the camera, a Kluge which took such pretty pictures in the dark, on top of a chest containing baseball uniforms.

Positioning himself a few feet back from the window, he peered out, looking for the stakeout. There was Fletcher's beat-up Chrysler, probably a '69, forty feet from his front door. Fletcher and Hazelwood would be in there, probably in the back seat. Cassidy hoped they'd brought some extra soldiers. He had tried hard to impress on Fletcher just how dangerous a man the gunsel was, but he was afraid he hadn't succeeded. Fletcher was a hard man to worry.

It was a good stakeout, though. The street looked empty and asleep, which was the way it should look. Twenty past twelve. The gunsels wouldn't hit the place until much later.

He rested his back against the wooden case that con-tained the baseball uniforms and pulled out the manila envelope which held his fingerprints so beautifully embossed in blood. He removed the thick rubber band from it and took out the document, which was thick and looked as if it had been folded up for years.

DEED OF TRUST

Cassidy fought his way through the verbiage.

This DEED OF TRUST is made this 27th day of May 1981 among the Grantor, Armand Shotover (herein Borrower), and Philip J. Cantor, trustee of Commonwealth Bank & Trust, a corporation organized and existing under the laws of Virginia whose address is Marietta, Virginia, in the County of Alester.

15

Borrower in consideration of the indebtedness herein recited and the trust herein created irrevocably grants and conveys to Trustee in trust ...

Lawyers! thought Cassidy.

... with powers of sale the following described property located in the County of Alester, Virginia: all that certain tract or parcel of land with improvements thereon and appurtenances thereunto belonging situated in the Hunter's Ridge Magisterial District of Alester, Virginia, on the north side of State Route 822 containing 27,642 acres.

Cassidy put his tongue between his lips and contemplated the ceiling—27,642 acres. Not in Colorado or one of those wide-open states but in little old Virginia where 27,642 acres was a pretty hefty tract or parcel of land.

Reference is made here to the attached plat for further and more particular description of the property hereby conveyed and for matters affecting same. . . .

Cassidy looked at the attached map. Roughly in the center was the drawing of the main house, which looked enormous. Scattered around were the subsidiary buildings, all labeled—stables, barns, stud farm, swimming pool; the acreage was labeled too—fields, pastures, woods—and one long rectangle—airstrip.

Airstrip!

Cassidy went back to the main body of the deed of trust.

To secure to Lender (a) the repayment of the indebtedness evidenced by borrower's note dated

16

May 17, 1981 (Herein Note), in the principal sum
of One Million Five Hundred Thousand Dollars.

Wouldn't you know the lawyers would capitalize One
Million Five Hundred Thousand Dollars. As well they
might. It was a nice round sum for the mild little overeducated Armand Shotover, who now lay gravely wounded in
St. Vincent's Hospital.

Cassidy remembered that "aah" of Lieutenant Fletcher's
when he asked how much money in his wallet. Certainly not
One Million Five Hundred Thousand Dollars but maybe a
few princely thousand-dollar bills.

A whopping loan on the old homestead, but still a frightfully respectable piece of paper no different from a million
other deeds of trust. What had a mortgage on the old home
to do with that ferocity with a gun? It seemed as out of place
as the 9mm silenced gun in the hands of Armand Shotover.
The whole affair was shot through with implausibilities.

So thinking, Cassidy lowered his head, shut his eyes, and
dozed.

The dreams were bad. They always were when he fell
asleep in a sitting position. He was back in Bulgaria trying
to flag down a Toonerville Trolley of a train coming right at
him—and not succeeding. He had to be somewhere immediately and he wasn't getting there. An old much-repeated
dream. . . .

"Horatio, I think you're missing it." Father Flaherty
whispering it in his ear, shaking him violently.

Cassidy came awake with a thump, wondering where he
was, and *why* he was, resonant with alarm.

"The street's alive with malefactors," whispered Father
Flaherty. His prose style, even when whispering, was always
baroque.

"Sssh," said Cassidy because the silence was awful. He
grabbed for the camera.

Thirteenth Street was crawling with shadowy figures who

were avoiding the street lights, pairs of them in doorways, standing next to cars so that their outlines would disappear, trying to be invisible and not succeeding because the street lighting on Thirteenth was just too good. Cassidy stayed well back from the window and counted bodies in twos (because they were everywhere paired and what did *that* mean?)—two, four, six, eight—my God, *twenty*. Capone hadn't needed that many for the St. Valentine's Day Massacre! Twenty hoods scattered from Sixth to Seventh and maybe more on those avenues.

No cars. Cassidy ran his eyes down the street; the parked cars seemed to be unchanged. If they'd come in cars they were not on Thirteenth Street.

All the soldiers wearing long shapeless trench coats. Very odd, because the weather was warm.

Two of them now climbing the brownstone steps at 124—Cassidy's steps—and bending over the front door of the building, which was not Cassidy's front door but an outer door. His own apartment front door was just inside the vestibule.

Cassidy was snapping pictures now, bringing them in as tight as possible with the marvelous little camera, but he doubted he was getting anything. The hoods were holding their faces away from the light, their bodies all hunched up as if they'd been instructed about cameras.

Cassidy praying to the God he didn't believe in that Fletcher had enough sense to stay out of this. He couldn't fight this mob with anything short of the whole Fourteenth Street Station. Cassidy wished now he'd taken the radio Fletcher had tried to thrust on him. His view was much better than anything Fletcher had from that beat-up Chrysler. Did Fletcher have any idea how many were out there?

What in hell was at stake here that would justify so much firepower?

The two men on the brownstone steps at 124 had jimmied the front door now and disappeared inside.

Cassidy looked at his watch. Two A.M. He'd slept two hours. Disgraceful.

A dim slatted glow came through the venetian blinds in Cassidy's apartment. They'd be looking for him and for Lucia by flashlight, and if they'd been there . . . Now the hoods had turned on the lights. They'd be working the place over now. The mess. The god-awful mess.

"What are they doin' to your place, Cassidy?" whispered Father Flaherty.

"Sssh," said Cassidy. The silence was frightening. He'd never known New York that quiet.

Stay low, Fletcher, he prayed. Stay out of it, we can't win this one.

The shadowy figures were frozen in stone. No movement and no sound.

Cassidy used the viewfinder on the Kluge to zero in on the beat-up Chrysler. He could see nothing at all. No movement inside and that was good. Stay out of it, Fletch! Way Out!

A match flared. Someone had disobeyed orders to light a cigarette, and in the flare Cassidy got a good picture of the sharp brown Hispanic face—young, cruel, handsome—before the man's partner smothered the flame and tossed the cigarette in the gutter.

Cassidy could see movement inside his apartment. They'd be turning the place upside down, pulling out all his precious books, dumping them on the floor, every drawer upside down. It would take weeks to clean it up.

Father Flaherty stretched out on the floor next to him, his mouth working. Praying, of course, in his baroque style. Oh blessed celestial Father of us all is the way he usually started off. Very musical. . . .

Half an hour dragged past like eternity.

The sound when it came was distant. *Ush ush ush ush*

ush. Unmistakable even at a distance. A chopper. And choppers were not usually abroad at 2 A.M. over Manhattan.

Cassidy watched the hoods to see if they'd heard. They had. One of them ran up the steps at 124 and darted inside.

The chopper was getting closer now, *chuff chuff chuff*, verging into *ack ack ack*—the louder, harsher vowels of sound.

Fletcher buried in the Chrysler had a radio. Had he summoned a police helicopter? It would take more than one with this crowd.

The door of 124 opened and out came two hoods and turned their faces to the sky in the direction of the approaching helicopter, which was coming north, up from the bay. The faces were in the light, and Cassidy snapped the upturned brown faces—one of them the demonic face of that ferocious one who had shot Armand.

The chopper was getting close now, and Cassidy was wondering what else Fletcher had summoned. There could be a half dozen squad cars approaching too, silently, on Sixth or Seventh. Or both.

The demonic one was signaling now to his soldiers. Holding up one arm with clenched fist and crossing it like a T with the other. Whatever that meant.

The soldiers were fumbling under those ridiculous trench coats, bringing out long, lumpy objects. In the darkness Cassidy couldn't make out what the objects were.

The copter was now overhead, making its hideous racket. It turned its searchlight on, transforming night into day. Other searchlights came from Sixth and Seventh Avenue and the squad cars came roaring up and stopped—two blocking the Sixth Avenue entrance to Thirteenth Street, two more the Seventh Avenue entrance.

Beautifully timed strike.

In the brilliant white light Cassidy saw what the hoods had brought out from under their trench coats.

"Rockets," he screamed. No point in silence now, the

20

chopper drowning out everything. The hoods were operating in pairs—one man with the missile, the other with the long portable tube on his shoulder.

The bullhorn voice came like thunder: "Everybody freeze. Drop the weapons or we'll fire."

All those idiot things a cop had to say before taking action because the loony judges said they had to.

The hoods, with no such constraints, fired when ready— one SAM slamming into the helicopter, which exploded almost directly over the church and came down slantwise in a ball of fire that blanketed four parked cars.

Even before the chopper hit the street, the other SAMs were launched point-blank into the four police cars, which blew up with great woomphs of flame.

Machine guns started, *ratatatatatatata* . . .

Cassidy could see them chattering their death song in the hands of the hoods—West German MP5s (and where had they got those?).

"Oh, my God," said Father Flaherty, for once his prose style stripped to the essentials, "it's Armageddon!"

"Keep your head down, Father."

The hoods moving in on foot toward the police cars— *ratatatatata* . . . finishing things off. . . . Well trained. Now moving off toward Seventh, the whole bloody lot. Past the beat-up Chrysler, which now had a line of bullet holes in it from front to rear.

Cassidy was on his feet, dashing down the stairs, through the cafeteria, down the alley, and out into Thirteenth Street, Father Flaherty behind him.

The chopper burning merrily on the four unfortunate cars. Windows along the street going up now, from them issuing short sharp bleats with that peculiar timbre of fright in the upper registers. The heat was terrible.

Dead cops spilled out all over Thirteenth Street.

Cassidy ignored them and headed for the Chrysler, but before he got there, he saw the rear door of the Chrysler on the sidewalk side open slowly. Fletcher slumped out, limping, face alight.

He was wearing a flak jacket which had a line of holes the MP5 bullets had stitched into the fabric.

"What possessed you to wear the flak jacket, Lieutenant?" said Cassidy.

"You did," said Fletcher, low, very low. "You said he was dangerous. I couldn't persuade Hazelwood to wear one."

Hazelwood was lying faceup on the back seat, eyes open, mouth wide as if emitting exclamation marks.

Father Flaherty went down on his knees to perform last rites in the light of the burning chopper.

Cassidy and Fletcher started toward Seventh Avenue, slowly; they had no desire to catch the hoods.

"Didn't we get any of them?"

They found one—Hispanic, young, brown faced, dead in the middle of a litter of dead cops at the head of the street.

Cassidy took a picture of him with his Kluge.

The other soldiers had vanished.

"Where did they go?" said Fletcher. "And how?"

"Subway," said Cassidy. "There's an entrance right around the corner. Change at Forty-second Street and you can go anywhere you want to in New York."

"Jesus, Cassidy. Rockets! Machine guns! What the hell do they *want*?"

"I wish I knew," said Cassidy.

3

Cassidy broke away at 4 A.M., the detectives as weary of the questioning as he was. Two uniformed cops were at the foot of the brownstone steps, two others up in the vestibule in front of his door. The burnt helicopter, the wrecked police cars, and the bodies were gone, but the street was still a litter of smashed glass and burned cars.

Cassidy showed his driver's license to the uniformed cop. "It's my apartment," he said. They let him in reluctantly past his splintered door (and what's the landlord going to say about *that*?). Books covered the floor, every inch, not a single one left on the shelves. Cassidy leaned down and picked up the Bible he'd been given at his first communion and had hardly opened since. He opened it now at random and read: "And David smote them from the twilight even unto the evening of the next day and there escaped not a man of them." An ill omen.

He picked his way to the telephone and dialed the number from memory because the detectives had taken away his black book. The most secret of all Alison's four secret numbers. It rang by the bedside in Alison's elegant town house in Georgetown.

"Yeah," said Alison. He never said "hello" on that phone. Just "Yeah."

"Me," said Cassidy.

"It's four in the morning, you fink!"

Cassidy grinned, enjoying himself for the first time that night. "I'm in no mood for your endearments, Hugh. They've taken my little black book with all those lovely phone numbers, including this one."

"Who?"

"The police." Cassidy gave him a fast rundown. "Eleven dead cops. The uproar is going to shake things right up to the White House. You're in it up to your ass, Alison."

Alison was wide awake now, "It wasn't a Company matter, I swear, Horatio. I'm horrified! Who would do such a thing?"

"Somebody scrubbed that long-distance call from my apartment and I don't know anyone who can scrub a call off the phone company's books that fast except the CIA, do you?" Alison, third man in the Agency.

Silence on the other end. Cassidy could picture Alison in his silk Sulka pajamas in the French Provincial bed, his rich wife, Grace, asleep beside him. (Did they still sleep together? Probably not.) Nothing Cassidy liked better than to shake Alison, the unflappable survivor of a dozen CIA shakeouts, the everlasting survivor.

"You've got to get on the horn, Alison, and stop them. Fletcher is threatening to call every number in that book. Besides your four numbers, there are Illitch's in Moscow, Pyotr in Stockholm, Georges in Prague . . ."

"Don't enumerate, Cassidy. Not even on this phone!"

Cassidy grinning like a schoolgirl. He really had Alison on the hip now. "Fletcher is going to ask each one of them if his cryptonym is Victor. By the way, who *is* Victor?"

"I don't *know*!" Explosive, that denial.

Cassidy pushed hard. "Hispanics, Alison. What dirty work is the Company up to in the pampas?"

Alison was hissing now like a snake. "I'll be on your doorstep as soon as I can get there."

"That's not good enough, Hugh, you've got to get on the phone this minute before they blow your network from Belgrade to Vladivostok. There are good men there, Alison; you're risking their necks."

Not that Alison ever gave a damn about any neck but his own, but if the agent's necks went, his would be next. Cassidy never knew how Alison pulled off these things, but he did. He pulled wires no one else knew existed. Ongoing investigations were stopped in their tracks. Silence descended on district attorneys, police commissioners, mayors, governors. It was black magic. Very black. Cassidy didn't approve of Alison's black magic, but in this case . . .

He pushed the books off his bed, took off his shoes, and pulled the covers over him. God rest their souls, he prayed, not believing in either prayer or God but thinking he had to say a word for those who had died that night. He had one last thought.

DEED OF TRUST.

Where on earth . . .? The cops had searched him and searched the flat but not found it, and he'd not told them. Aaah, yes, he'd left it on the floor in the low room under the eaves of the Catholic church. Must remember to pick it up.

Alison shook Cassidy awake at 11 A.M., Cassidy blinking, groaning, bleary eyed. Alison stood beside him in his beautifully cut Italian suit with the thin lapels, leaning on his black stick from Kismet with the silver top under which lay a single-shot .38-caliber pistol.

Alison looking around at the mess. "So this is where you live, Horatio? How . . . picturesque!"

"Not all of us have rich wives, Hugh!" rasped Cassidy. He rolled into a sitting position on the bed and put on his shoes. "What do you suppose they were looking for?"

25

Alison's face was impassive. "We'll go to Spumi's for refreshment," he said, which was as close as Alison ever came to answering questions.

Spumi's Bar and Restaurant lay directly below Cassidy's apartment, its entrance under the brownstone steps. It wasn't officially open yet, but Cassidy was an old customer and he bent the rules. Henry, the bartender and owner, was behind the bar, polishing glasses gloomily.

"Police lines," he said. "There won't be four customers in here today. Vot haff you done, Cassidy, to bring this curse down on our heads?"

"Forty years in America and you still don't understand Americans," said Cassidy. "They'll be flying in from Duluth just to have a drink at your famous bar on the street where all those cops were killed. They'll write songs about our street, Henry. Could we get a coffee and Perrier in the back room right now?"

"Perrier?" said Henry.

"Mr. Alison doesn't drink anything stronger than Perrier for fear it will cloud his judgment."

The two men threaded their way through the waiters who were setting up the tables for lunch.

"Always the needle," complained Alison. "I've come all the way from Washington to get you out of this mess, Cassidy, and all I get in return is hostility."

Cassidy said: "*Naked* hostility—the best kind. It's the undercover hostility that kills you, Hugh."

They sat in the back room, which was very dark.

"The man came in spouting my résumé, which is buried in Langley under ten miles of secrecy. Who would know about my résumé, Hugh? My address? My black book? Unless he's one of your villains?"

Silence deep as a well. Alison hated to divulge *anything*. Finally he said: "Armand Shotover hasn't been in the Company for years."

Cassidy grunted and sipped his coffee. He doubted that

anyone ever quite left the CIA (unless, like himself, he was fired). They all hung on somewhere—as consultants, nonresident experts, associates, until death sent them down to the netherworld where they still hung out together whispering dirty secrets in the corner.

"What was his specialty?" asked Cassidy.

"I can't tell you that."

"If you want any favors, you'll have to." Alison wouldn't be there unless he had favors to ask. He never gave away anything for nothing.

He gave Cassidy the long, level look which was the Alison trademark and took his time. Finally: "Colombia. Venezuela."

"Aaaah," said Cassidy.

"Why do you say aaaah in that sinister way?"

"Money," said Cassidy. "This thing stinks to high heaven of money. Twenty men just to turn my apartment upside down. Carrying rockets which cost seventy-five thousand dollars apiece and on the black market three times that much. German submachine guns. Who's got that kind of dough? The cocaine trade, that's who. They don't know the rules of the game, Hugh. Your Mafia hood would never kill a cop, much less eleven cops, but these maniacs couldn't care less. What's cooking in the Andes, kid?"

Alison wrinkled his nose as if the word *kid* had a bad smell. "I want to see the photographs you took."

"How do you know I took photographs?"

But of course, he'd been in touch with the cops. Anyway, Alison never answered questions; he *asked* questions as if that was what he was for, a new kind of subspecies that devoured information and would die if deprived of it for even a day.

"With a Kluge you stole from the Agency," said Alison smoothly. "That was very naughty of you, Cassidy. I could play very rough about that if I chose but I won't if you'll give them over."

"The cops have them, all of them." Cassidy was tired of getting pushed around—first by the cops, now by Alison. "What do you want them for, Hugh? One Hispanic looks much like another. What's the scam?"

"My sole concern is Armand. He was once one of us. One must observe rules of civilized conduct."

"Civilized conduct, yes. The CIA is world-renowned for spreading civilization to the far corners of the tortured earth."

Alison sipped his Perrier, not blinking an eyelash. He pulled out his gold money clip from Cartier's and detached the wad of bills from it and began counting out hundreds.

"No," said Cassidy violently. "I don't want to have anything more to do with this thing. I never want to see that spic again as long as I live. He's a killer and a maniac and I am a registered coward. Also, I have a thirteen-year-old daughter and these lunatics kill children just for the fun of it."

"You could take Lucia along with you," said Alison, still counting out hundred-dollar bills. "It would be a nice trip for her, and Shotover Hall is one of the most beautiful homes in America. Designed by Thomas Jefferson. . . ."

"Shotover Hall," said Cassidy. That was why the bell had rung dimly in the back of his mind. So Armand was one of those Shotovers. Famous mansion, reeking of history, but just what history Cassidy didn't know. It was historic for being historic. One of those.

"Shotover Hall," said Alison bitchily, "would be a refreshing change from . . ." He pointed upward in the general direction of Cassidy's messy apartment. "While you're away we can send some of our people down to straighten the place and fix the door . . ."

And go through the place with a fine-tooth comb, thought Cassidy, looking for whatever the hoods were looking for and not finding.

"It's just for a few days until we get another man in place. . . ."

In place. One of those Company terms. You were never on the job, you were *in place*—as if you were one of the pieces on a chessboard. It was all assuming shape.

"Replacing a man who's retired with a man who's been fired. Ah, Hugh. When the Senate committee comes sniffing around asking what you're up to in the rain forest, you can say with a straight face you haven't a single agent on the premises. Ex-agents are not considered people. We are nonpeople you use to get your dirty laundry washed. . . ."

Alison erupted. "Don't use that word!"

"Which word? Dirty? Or laundry? Oh, *laundry* is the word! That's what you're up to. . . ."

"If you want to get your black book back . . ." Alison furious now, gimlet eyed.

The set-to ended right there because Fletcher loomed unexpectedly in the murk of the back room, standing next to the table looking down on the pile of hundred-dollar bills with the ingrained suspicion of all cops that piles of hundred-dollar bills are automatically dishonest and should be cause for immediate arrest.

"You look like a skull, Fletcher," complained Cassidy, "and in this dim light it's enough to unseat a man's reason." He pointed to Alison with one scornful finger. "This is Hugh Alison, Lieutenant. He works for Uncle Sammy, if you know what I mean, and I think that you do."

Fletcher said: "They want you downtown, Cassidy. You too, Mr. Alison."

"Who's they?"

"All your favorite people, Cassidy—the Mayor, the District Attorney, the assistant attorney general for this district, the Police Commissioner, the FBI, the Secret Service, Internal Revenue. Let's see—have I left anyone out? Oh, yes, Alan Muir. . . ."

"Who's he?"

"Drug Enforcement Agency."

"Aaah," said Cassidy, "the plot thins. How about the Governor? He couldn't make it?"

"He sent his regrets. Come on, Horatio. You too, Mr. Alison, since it's your party."

Alison reacted as if stung. "There'll be media there. I'm not to be photographed, I'm not to be mentioned at all in connection with this."

"No media," said Fletcher in a tone that Cassidy had never before heard from Fletcher—a mixture of awe and disgust, if such a thing was possible. "You fixed things good, Mr. Alison. They brought all these big shots in the rear door and they're meeting in a room in the City Hall basement no one knew existed."

The room had been designed as a bomb shelter long ago when bomb shelters were considered feasible. Its principal article of furniture was a long table around which the survivors were expected to discuss their future as if they had one.

Almost every chair was full of bureaucracy. Cassidy recognized the District Attorney, the FBI, the Police Commissioner, and the Mayor, but none of the others. Mayor Forbush, a loud-talking extrovert who was his own greatest admirer, was at the head of the table in full cry. " . . . police force that I personally have brought to the highest peak of efficiency of any in the land ambushed, betrayed . . ."

On the table in front of the Mayor was Cassidy's black book and the photographs Cassidy had taken with the Kluge. Alison stepped forward and put the black book in his breast pocket. His book, Cassidy reflected bitterly, kept vanishing into other people's pockets.

"This has been marked Security Four," Alison explained. "It's the highest security classification in the nation. If any of you have looked at it, I ask you to forget what you've seen. If any copies have been made, I must demand you turn them over to me now."

That brought forth a babble of protest from almost everyone—District Attorney, FBI, Secret Service, all of them—but the Police Commissioner dominated the outcry and took over. His name was Henry Jefferson and he was black and enormous and looked as if fires smoldered in him thousands of feet deep that would never be extinguished. "That book the only evidence we got of the greatest crime ever committed against a police force in this country. You telling me we can't use it?"

"Yes," said Alison in his thin-lipped way, "I'm saying exactly that. We are at war, Mr. Jefferson, with an enemy of our country so devious and so evil that our every move, our methods, our agents must remain totally secret or we are undone. If these names and these numbers fall into the wrong hands, we could be set back ten years—and we haven't got another ten years to undo the damage. We could lose the war."

Cassidy was amazed. It was bullshit, all of it, but very high quality bullshit and it was delivered with stunning panache and authority. Alison, the survivor.

"Well . . ." sputtered Mayor Forbush, "well . . . you leave us no recourse . . ."

He was drowned out by the others—the FBI, the District Attorney, the Assistant Attorney General, the DEA—all of them furious. The assassination of eleven cops was the most marvelous excuse to summon the press and the TV cameras before which to spout indignation, to tear the hair, to show the muscles. It was a lovely catastrophe for rounding up votes, increasing appropriations, putting names and faces on the front pages and the TV. And here this man was telling them they must back off!

The Police Commissioner stopped the uproar with a wave of his monstrous black hand. "You mean these men are not to be brought to justice?" he asked.

"We'll bring them to justice, all right," said Alison, "much more effectively than you or your courts will."

Your courts, Cassidy was thinking. He's saying *your* rather than *our* courts. Much as Cassidy hated to admit it, Alison was right. What all these people wanted was not justice but the *machinery* of justice—the hoopla, the razzmatazz, the publicity, the attitudinizing. They'd all fight for a little bit of turf on this lovely catastrophe; the intramural warfare between one bureaucrat and another would occupy ten times the effort and the money spent on finding the criminals. Even if they caught the malefactors (which Cassidy doubted), the magnificent nonsense known as American jurisprudence would defeat the ends of justice. Some idiot judge would discover that a T had not been crossed on the original complaint and would throw the whole prosecution out of court.

What am I doing here? thought Cassidy. I should be in my class teaching medieval history, where life was stark and beautiful and simple and the only complexity was how many angels could dance on the point of a pin—arguments exactly as ridiculous as those used in American courts every day. How many hundreds of years would it be before the American legal system in the late twentieth century would be seen to be the exact equivalent in sheer breathtaking idiocy to medieval theology?

"Does that mean we can't question Mr. Cassidy about his role in this affair?" asked the District Attorney, a man named Henry Bates whom Cassidy had tangled with before and didn't like.

Cassidy said: "I was questioned for two hours last night, Mr. Bates. I think I said 'I don't know' about a thousand times. You want to hear it all again? I was held up as I was leaving my apartment to go to class by a man I don't know, who then called a number I don't know that he found in my black book and talked to a man I don't know. Two men I don't know came in and shot the first man I don't know. How much else can I tell you?"

The District Attorney said: "We've heard all this, Mr.

Cassidy. The trouble is we don't believe it. Three guns were found in your apartment for none of which do you have a permit."

"Only one was mine."

· "That's your story. One of the guns—a nine-millimeter Frank—is the same gun that killed a man in Grand Central Station at noon yesterday."

"What?" Cassidy was startled.

Fletcher said: "We got another body, Cassidy. As if we didn't have enough bodies."

A whole new ball game, Cassidy was thinking. To Fletcher he said: "Hispanic?"

"Yes."

"Which nine-millimeter gun—Armand's or the spic's?" He'd labeled them carefully for Fletcher.

"Armand's."

"Well! Well!" said Cassidy softly. He'd underestimated the little overeducated one.

Alison was looking over the photographs that Cassidy had taken with the Kluge, most of them dark and meaningless, but three of them—one of the demonic Hispanic with uplifted face looking at the approaching helicopter, one of the dead Hispanic at the head of the street, and one the handsome face of the man who'd lit a cigarette—were quite clear.

The Police Commissioner said: "Copies of those pictures are in the hands of the FBI and dozens of them have been shown to our police informers—especially those who know drugs or Hispanics. The fingerprints of the dead man have been through our computer and the FBI's. These men have no police record. Customs and Immigration don't have anything on them. Very peculiar we shouldn't get any kind of fix on these people. Does that suggest anything to you, Mr. Cassidy?"

Cassidy made a face. "Why are you asking *me*, Commissioner, when you got all these experts here?"

"Because it started in your apartment. You're the only person we got to ask questions of. You're the center of this investigation."

"No," said Alison firmly. "Mr. Cassidy's name, like my name and the CIA's must be kept out of this thing altogether. Mr. Cassidy's on special mission for the President of the United States."

Cassidy kept his fact straight with great effort. I am? Since when?

The meeting broke up shortly after that because there was little to be said after the name of the Great White Face had been dropped in their midst.

Cassidy managed to get Fletcher into a corner for a moment to ask about Armand's condition.

"He's not in our hands anymore," said Fletcher bitterly. He pointed at Alison. "Armand's been whisked away by that spook pal of yours to some private CIA hospital in a CIA helicopter. I tell you, Cassidy, if the police had the facilities the CIA has we'd clean up this city in five days."

"Oh, no, you wouldn't," said Cassidy. "You'd just make everything much worse."

In the end Cassidy didn't get to see the Great White Face who told such good jokes with the Irish accent and smiled so becomingly—that's what we elect them for, their smile, their dental work, so much more important than their policies. Instead, he saw Harriet Van Fleet, who was the President's right hand (and much more, some said, but of course there were always those rumors). She was a broth of a woman, slim as a pencil and, so they said, hard as granite, a hawk who put the Joint Chiefs to shame for their cowardice, and number one in the White House triad who really ran the Great White Face.

Cassidy had heard much about her, none of it good. She was younger than he'd been led to expect, had a nice smile, but was very brief and to the point. "The vital interests of this country are at stake—the Panama Canal, access to the Pacific. We are in danger of being cut off from our allies in South America. This is a pincer operation by the communist nations in Central America which would wall us off from our friends in South America," and so forth. Cassidy didn't believe any of it. He got to the point.

"What were they doing in New York?"

"That's what you're to find out, isn't it? Shotover Hall is a communication point of great importance to the President and it must stay under cover or it would be swarmed over by the press and lose all of its usefulness. I'm sure you understand." Cassidy didn't, but what could he say to this formidably pretty lady who was supposed to be bedding the Great White Face himself and even in the midst of sexual transports to be urging him to greater feats of arms. . . .

4

Cassidy sat in the little church cafeteria, sipping coffee and wondering if he wasn't being very foolish. "I don't want you to stick your neck out, Father. If you'd just keep an eye open . . ."

"I'll not sleep," said Father Flaherty, bursting with the joy of it.

The last thing in the world Cassidy wanted. "No, no, Father. Please, not an excess of zeal. That would do more harm than good. Just go about your ordinary duties. If you *happen* to be out on the street playing stickball with your juvenile deliquents or when you're directing the street play that you do so well"—Father Flaherty's duties were multifarious, few of them religious—"if anyone goes into the house besides my landlord whom you know . . ."

With the utmost reluctance he handed over the Kluge. "A jewel of a camera. You can hardly go wrong with it. Just take a quick picture—bang, like that—and then slip it back under your cassock."

Father Flaherty glowed with an inner light. "It will be

with the greatest pleasure. I will avoid zeal, but you cannot ask me to avoid the pleasure."

"It could be dangerous. If you attract any attention to yourself, you could get killed."

"Dying for my country," said Father Flaherty, radiant with happiness.

"It would be much better if you lived for your country. That way we'd get the pictures."

Father Flaherty bellowed with laughter. "Don't worry, Cassidy, I'll still be alive to dance on your grave."

"You'll have to take your turn, Father. The crowd waiting to dance on my grave will stretch clear around the block."

Cassidy drove the CIA Mercedes through northern New Jersey, a treeless wasteland of mists and fumes, oil refineries, and garbage, Lucia seated beside him, her plain face alight with wonder.

"No school," she bleated. "Wow!"

"I'm going to inflict Latin, math, English, and French on you every day," said Cassidy. "So watch it! I'll be much tougher than your teachers."

"Yeah," said Lucia, who knew better than that. She put her head on his shoulder. "I know all about Shotover Hall. It was designed by Thomas Jefferson and it's one of the few houses still in the hands of the same family, the Shotovers, who didn't quite sign the Declaration of Independence but did a lot of other things."

"Like what?" asked Cassidy.

"Well . . . one of the early ones was a Senator, and they were in shipping and then banking and then . . ." She fell silent, thinking. "Well, things like . . . charity and, you know, social things. One of them was master of the hounds, but then that was awhile ago. . . . The more recent ones, golly, I don't know, but they're prominent. . . ."

Prominent for being prominent. It was a classic progression of the American dream—from the Senate to shipping to banking to fox hunting to—nothing—if you can call the CIA nothing.

"Where did you learn all this?" asked Cassidy.

"The *Dictionary of American Biography* in the school library. Everyone visited that house, Daddy—John Quincy Adams, General Sheridan, Jefferson, of course . . ."

Jefferson would be horrified, Cassidy was thinking, at the uses it was being put to by the CIA.

". . . but why are we being invited there?"

"It's because you got an A in Latin. It came to the attention of Amanda Shotover, and she insisted you come down and ride her horses."

"I hate it when you evade questions, Professor." Lucia called him Professor when she was displeased, Daddy when she wasn't.

"I'm evading the question because I don't know the answers, Contessa." Contessa was Cassidy's riposte to Professor. Lucia had once been an Italian contessa. She'd been bequested to Cassidy by a dying principessa; he'd adopted her and she was now an American girl and hated to be called Contessa.

"I haven't ridden a horse since Italy," said Lucia soberly. "I used to ride every day when the weather was fine." She said this as if she didn't believe it, as if her own past was not the realm of possibility. Hers was an upside-down life, like a film run backward. She'd been an unhappy Italian contessa, a poor little rich girl; she had achieved poverty only after many tribulations and much misery and was now happy as a puppy. It violated all the rules of Hollywood narrative, but there it was.

"Do we get to keep the car?"

"No," said Cassidy.

It was a James Bond car, full of electronic wonders that connected him by radio to Langley, which would call in the Army, Navy, Air Force if he needed the Army, Navy, or Air

39

Force. There were concealed apertures in which rested machine guns, night glasses, explosives. Just in case . . .

"In case of what?" Cassidy had asked Alison before they left. "I thought this was supposed to be a restful week in the country, smelling the flowers."

"You never know," said Alison.

"I'm taking Lucia down there to get her out of the line of fire, not to get her into another line of fire."

"Nothing will happen," said Alison smoothly. "Relax."

"I don't even know what the mission is."

"Something you do very well, Cassidy—wait." Alison's speech reminded Cassidy of modern poetry. The important bits were what was left out. You had to fill in the spaces yourself. "Harburg is due back in three days. You knew Harburg—in Guatemala, didn't you?"

Cassidy smiled. Not only in Guatemala. Also Bulgaria and China, after each of which Harburg was going to quit— and here he was, still in the CIA soup. "Yeah," said Cassidy.

Alison examined his nails which were, as always, beautifully trimmed. "The radio is in Armand's room. Don't tamper with the wave length; it's preset. But the codes . . ." He sighed. "It's not one of ours. He and Harburg had their own code; they worked it out together when they were in the Company."

"Where is Harburg coming back from?"

"Balisario." As if it were of no importance. "Someone has broken the code, Cassidy. That's the only explanation."

"Explanation for what?"

"All of it."

"You mean the cop massacre, the shooting of Armand?" said Cassidy.

"You're leaving out the most important bit—why was he in *your* apartment?"

"Oh, I'm not leaving that out. That's uppermost in my mind, Hugh. Right there is the heart of the matter. Tell me this, the someone who broke the code, is he on their side or our side?"

Alison looked at his nails again and avoided the question as if it were a rattlesnake. "You must express my heartfelt sympathy to Amanda Shotover, who is a dear friend. Explain that I had nothing to do with this unfortunate occurrence and we are doing everything in our power to save the life of her son. She's a great lady, Horatio."

Alison collected great ladies, at least those who permitted themselves to be collected. A form of snobbery. Cassidy sometimes wondered if Alison's CIA career was not itself pure snobbery. I-know-something-you-don't-know.

They were out of the ugliness of New Jersey now and into Virginia, driving through the breathtaking countryside.

"How lovely!" gasped Lucia.

"That's what New Jersey is for—to make you appreciate the beauty of Virginia," explained Cassidy.

"I've never seen so many horses," said Lucia. "I'm going to get you on a horse, Daddy."

"Not me. I'm scared to death of horses. I don't think they've got them perfected yet."

"You're not scared of anything. You're the bravest man I know."

"That's because you don't know very many. I'm terrified of everything—the future, the present, my own nature . . ."

"You belittle yourself very well, Daddy. It's your way of attracting attention."

"I thought I was being modest."

"You're not at all modest, really. And you have nothing to be modest about. You're quite a fellow, Daddy. I'm very pleased with you—most of the time."

"You'll turn my head if you keep this up, and I need my head straight in this business."

Lucia leaped on that. "What business? You're on some spook mission again. I know! And you won't tell me what it is!"

I don't know what it is myself. He didn't say it.

The driveway was a mile long, a beautifully swept dirt road with long, slow curves under towering Norway maples. The fields on one side were full of horses, on the other side, of Jersey cows, all of them kept in by an old-fashioned split pine fence, the palings laid over one another as the earliest settlers had done. There was something almost ostentatious in the avoidance of macadam, gravel, nails, or anything resembling the twentieth or even the nineteenth century. It was an eighteenth-century driveway and it must have cost a fortune to keep it up.

The vast house was of red brick, as were most of Jefferson's houses, the round fanlight windows, the hallmark of a Jefferson house, set high under the white portico. Even before Cassidy had turned off the engine, a white-haired black man in a white coat came down the steps and opened the front door of the car as if he'd been waiting.

"Good evening, Professor Cassidy. Good evening, Miss Lucia." It was four o'clock but that in Virginia was evening. The black man's voice was deep and slow, soft as honey and his movements had the elegance of a courtier at the court of Charles X.

"Mrs. Shotover is expecting you. This way."

They glided through an enormous sitting room containing a sea of deep sofas in flowered chintz, the wall covered with hunting scenes from England, men on horseback, men with guns and dogs at their feet, stags at bay, fox hunts. Over the fireplace was a full-length portrait of Thomas Jefferson. No American has been painted more often than Jefferson and hardly any two portraits look alike, as if Jefferson had stand-ins sit for the portraits while he went about his busy life, tobacco farming, designing buildings, writing the Declaration of Independence, inventing clocks, being President.

Behind the sitting room was the music room, dominated by a gold concert grand piano, the walls covered by prints of ancient Rome, this room full of little gold chairs. Connected to it by two large sliding doors on either side of the fireplace was the library, leatherbound books from floor to ceiling, deeply carpeted (unlike the music room whose floor was covered only with clear varnish). Behind that lay the gun room. Cases of rifles, shotguns, pistols. Even in their glass cases they looked dusty and unused.

Everything, in fact, looked unused.

A glass door led from the gun room to the glassed-in side porch, which was full of green plants hanging from the ceiling or in huge pots around the room. There sat Amanda Shotover in a painted wicker chair watching "The World Walks In" on television. She turned off the set when they entered, and rose, all four feet six of her.

"How nice of you to come, Professor Cassidy. And Lucia. You sit right here next to me, Lucia, where I can enjoy you, and you, Professor Cassidy, sit right there." She was one of these fierce aristocrats who manages everything swiftly and well. "You've caught me in my one remaining vice—soap opera." She turned to the butler with a merry gleam in her eyes. "Robert has caught his wife in the arms of the stable boy, Geoffrey. There'll be hell to pay tomorrow." Geoffrey's black face split in a great smile and he rubbed his hands together gleefully. A private joke between mistress and servant.

Only after the butler had left the room did she say: "How is my son, Professor? Have they sent you down here to tell me he's dead?"

"He's alive," said Cassidy. There was no sense in trying to con this fierce old lady. "He's in a coma. There's hope. Not much, but some."

"My three other sons are dead," said Amanda Shotover, not pitying herself, just giving the facts, "from this war and that—World War II, Korea, Vietnam. Armand is all I have left. If I have him left."

She was, of course, much too old to be Armand's mother. He must have been the baby of the family, which accounted

43

for a certain softness and sweetness in him, that constant apology for having been shot.

Cassidy delivered the speech he'd been told to give. "Mr. Alison asked me to express his deep regret. None of us has any idea . . ."

The old lady cut him short, her piercing blue eyes contemptuous. "Alison said that, did he? He got my son into this, and he's trying to wash his hands of it. How very like him!"

Clearly Amanda Shotover had not allowed herself to be added to Alison's collection of great ladies.

Geoffrey came in wheeling the tea wagon, which carried a silver tea set, cakes, and sliced hot breads on Minton china. The old lady became a hostess. "Lucia, we'll serve you first because you look famished. That cake? Or that one? Tell me about yourself. What grade are you in? Eighth? And are you the brightest in your class? Second brightest? Oh, good! I like bright children. The dumb ones are so difficult to talk to. There you are. Eat hearty because dinner is not until eight."

Geoffrey appeared. "I've put Miss Lucia in Mister George's old room at the head of the stairs and the Professor in Mister Armand's room, as you suggested."

That was almost too convenient.

Cassidy looked at the piercing old lady for a moment. She was handing Lucia another piece of cake. Without glancing at him, she said, "If you're looking for something, Professor, I thought you might as well start at the source. Then you won't have to sneak around behind our backs."

5

It was an immense bedroom, high ceilinged and perfectly proportioned, with two great windows which looked out on the south lawn and the front of the house. (Eighteenth-century architects made the windows of their great houses enormous to disguise the scale of the house, the White House, which is much bigger than it looks, being the most conspicuous example.)

It was 11 P.M. The household had retired early after a plain, robust dinner of roast chicken, roast potatoes, salad, and stewed pears, during most of which the old lady kept up a sprightly conversation with Lucia entirely about horses, a subject that bored Cassidy out of his wits, though he was dazzled by his daughter's command of it. Before the pair got into the horse talk, Cassidy had made one conversational effort. He had asked Amanda Shotover if she didn't want to be with her son in New York. Her answer stopped him in his tracks. "I *am* with my son, Professor. I'm with all of them, all of the time."

After that he left the talk to the females while doing a

little mental arithmetic. The son killed in World War II would have to be—if he were alive—in his sixties; the one killed in Korea would probably have been—what? fifty or maybe fifty-five. Those were old wars. The one killed in Nam could have been Armand's age. Armand was fortyish, and why hadn't he been in Nam? He looked much too young to have been whelped by this formidable old lady, who looked eighty-five.

After dinner the old lady excused herself and went to her room. Cassidy tore his daughter away from the TV set, deposited her in bed, kissed her good night, ran his fingertips lightly over her velvety cheek, and left her for his own huge old-fashioned room.

There was nothing old-fashioned about the radio. It looked like a typewriter with a regular keyboard. The messages came in at high speed and were decoded by the machine. Messages went out at even higher speed so the enemy couldn't get a fix on you—*blip*, like that, each blip being two hundred fifty words. Cassidy remembered his instructor always said if you can't say it in 250 words, don't bother.

Cassidy sat down at the desk and fingered the machine. He'd been told to do nothing. Wait. But waiting was foreign to his nature and also quite contrary to what Alison expected. Something was clearly wrong in this setup, and Alison hoped Cassidy would find out what. But Alison didn't want to give instructions. In case of success, Alison would take credit. In case of failure—or some kind of disaster—Alison would wash his hands of the whole operation and give Cassidy hell for having started it.

Cassidy was there as a lightning rod, and of course they'd be watching him like a hawk. It was an old Company device, using the outworn ones, the expendables like himself to draw the fire. But what kind of fire and for what? Alison would sell his own grandmother into white slavery, but he certainly hadn't planned that massacre in New York. Something got out of hand. Perhaps Armand. . . .

And who was Victor?

Cassidy took out the black book (which he'd wrested from Alison only by threatening not to go to Virginia unless he got it) and started at the beginning with the As. Joe Aaron. It wasn't Joe because Joe was long dead in Biafra, blown in half by a mine. A slender, laughing Jew, full of jokes, one hundred percent alive until the land mine had ripped him apart. Cassidy hadn't drawn a line through Aaron for the same reason the old lady had said she was with her sons. One didn't draw lines through Joe Aaron. He lived on.

Next Abe Zweig (Cassidy frequently put them under first name if that's how he thought of them). No, Victor wasn't Abe. Abe was alive somewhere in China, probably Canton, swindling the natives, drinking too much, throwing up every morning because he said it kept his weight down.

It was old home week. A class reunion. All the old chums. Except that some of them were not chums. Eleu Assad was certainly no chum. Last time he'd seen Eleu the man had tried to knife him. And where was Eleu now? Dead, probably, in Beirut.

Cassidy picked up the pace. It had to be someone with a connection—some sort of leaning—toward South America. This was a South American caper. He was sure of that. Look for the probabilities first, though it wasn't always the probabilities you scored with. There were people on both sides of the game—Them and Us—and it could be either. With modern dialing it could be anywhere—London, Paris, even behind the Iron Curtain. Someone like Rodney Peters buried under the cultural attaché label in Vienna? Perhaps in Balisario itself? No. The telephone didn't work that well in Central America. Nothing worked in Central America except the machine guns.

After an hour Cassidy gave up, marking the spot in the black book where he'd got to. There were other things to do.

He took out the deed of trust and looked at it. No point in reading it. Deeds of trust were all pretty much alike, twenty-two pages of whereases. Why would Armand be carrying such a thing? You didn't go around carrying your deed of trust unless you were calling on your banker. Or your lawyer.

He put the deed on the typewriterlike radio and looked at it.

Codes.

Cassidy started with the bed, tearing off blankets and sheets, feeling between mattress and bedsprings, slipping under the bed and looking at the joints, the supports. It wouldn't be sewed inside the mattress because it had to be where Armand could get to it. After the bed, Cassidy started on the big walk-in closet stuffed with Armand's clothes, of which he had far too many—riding clothes, shooting clothes, sports jackets, formal wear, business suits—and shoes to match all of them. He went through the shoes, the pockets, felt the linings, looked on the shelves between the folds of the extra blankets.

Nothing.

Next the desk. The central drawer was full of notebooks, all empty of contents. Nice notebooks with ring bindings and not a word in them. Why? There were pencils, pens, all very neatly kept (although the maid might have done that). Armand was prepared to transcribe interesting bits from South America—but where were the interesting bits? The side drawers were full of books—archeology, the history of art—and Cassidy leafed through these looking for clues. Or pencil marks. Or something.

Nothing.

At the bottom was a little slim volume: Thomas de Quincey's *Confessions of an Opium Eater*. Cassidy leafed through it and here struck pay dirt. A bit anyway. Armand had underlined a few things—"the secret of happiness ... happiness might now be bought for a penny." In pencil in

48

the margin Armand had written, "Happiness much cheaper 1821." Toward the end of the De Quincey *Confessions* happiness had turned largely to horror.

Here Armand had underlined: "I fled from the wrath of Brama through all the forests of Asia; Vishnu hated me; Shiva lay in wait for me. I was buried for a thousand years in stone coffins, with mummies and sphinxes, in narrow chambers at the heart of eternal pyramids I was kissed with cancerous kisses by crocodiles; and laid, confounded with all unutterable and slimy things, amongst reeds and Nilotic mud."

Cassidy started on the huge painted bureau, which was so big it looked as if it had been built right in the room. He went drawer by drawer through Armand's incredible collection of shirts, socks, underpants, taking everything out and feeling in around the empty drawers for hidden spaces, putting everything back after he'd done with it.

Then he had another idea. He took the drawers out of the bureau again and reached his arm in the apertures, feeling for the back of the bureau. Aaaah! He found a notebook attached to the rear of the piece of furniture by Scotch tape.

Very neat, like everything in Armand's room.

On the first page, printed in what Cassidy now recognized as Armand's neat print style, was:

Day 1—all easements, rights, appurtenances
Day 2—rents subject however to the rights
Henceforth by count. Always full word.

Now what did that mean? And where had he seen those phrases before?

Cassidy picked up the deed of trust and glanced at the first pages. "All that certain tract or parcel. . . . Reference is made here to. . . . This conveyance is made subject to . . ." etc., etc.

"Together with all the improvements now or hereafter

erected on the property, and *all easements, rights, appurtenances, rents subject however to the rights* and authorities given herein to Lender. . ."

Cassidy counted the letters in the Day 1 message—thirty-one—then the letters in the Day 2 message—thirty-one.

Well! Well!

Twenty-six letters in the alphabet. Each day they would move on in the deed of trust by a full word. That meant the code would change every day—these letters substituted for the alphabet.

Cassidy leafed through the notebook—pages of messages from Harburg about transfers of money from and to Swiss bank accounts, vast sums, with the bank account numbers, no names. Where did all that bread come from? The CIA? Cocaine? Along with the messages were sketches which must have been sent by mail of Roberto Garcia' house—upstairs, downstairs, cellars—where the famous dungeon was.

Some of the messages were in another code, one code implanted on top of another:

"BANANAS WILL COME BY PIGEON PATRICIA MUST CHECK WITH ELEANOR FULL LIST SIXTY YARDS CALICO BUTTONS PROVIDED RYE ON WHEAT JASPER."

Was Harburg Jasper?

Cassidy looked through the notebook. On the very next page to the coding instructions were what looked like messages—but whether ingoing or outgoing he couldn't tell.

Cassidy searched for the key to code two and didn't find it. A simple code, almost simpleminded. They must have kept the keys in their heads. Bananas would be—what? Cocaine? Pigeons would be aircraft. Patricia and Eleanor were cryptograms for some links in the chain of communications. Sixty yards of calico. A yard was a thousand, sixty yards sixty thousand? Maybe it was payment for the courier. Buttons was the gang word for *pistoleros*, hit men, gunsels. Cassidy had no idea what rye on wheat stood for, but probably a date and maybe a destination. Miami, the fourteenth. Something like that.

He ran his eye over some of the messages of which there were dozens, each labeled Day 1 or 2 or 3 or whatever number so Armand would know which code words would be used, both incoming and outgoing.

Cassidy looked at his watch. Two A.M. Enough!

He was very tired.

But not too tired for a last bit of play (which he was to regret).

He composed a message which might just amuse George Harburg, who was down there somewhere preparing to come home but not yet on his way. He hadn't seen old George in twelve years, but they'd once been very close on a mission in Bulgaria.

BANANAS OVERRIPE. ELEANOR COME HOME SOONEST JELLYROLL.

Jellyroll had been Cassidy's cryptonym in Bulgaria.

He had to encode that, and that meant he had to count all those words to Day 28. However, when he looked closely at the deed of trust he found the counting had been done for him. Armand had counted out twenty-eight twenty-six-word segments, putting after each one a tiny, almost invisible pencil mark. Cassidy counted out twenty-eight of these little clumps of lawyer prose, which brought him up to: "nonuniform covenants with limited variations," a lovely legalism. That meant the first letter in the coded alphabet would be N for A and the second O for B—and so on. Cassidy fed twenty-six letters of that bit of the deed of trust into the coding aperture and then typed out the message. The machine would code it automatically, and if Harburg's machine was preset, it would decode it automatically. He pushed the TRANSMIT button. *Blip,* said the machine, and out went his twice-coded message, winging its way to Balisario.

Cassidy went to bed.

6

The man with the demonic face was sitting at the bar in Diablo's, drinking coffee and reading his newspaper. Pedro, who was only sixteen, was behind the bar, washing dishes and keeping quiet. He had once attempted conversation with Arguello (which was the name of the man with the demonic face) and had never repeated that mistake. Arguello did not like to be bothered when he was having breakfast and reading his paper. He was full of fury, that Arguello. All the time, especially now with his arm in a sling.

Martinez came down the wooden stairs into the bar and sat next to Arguello, even though Pedro tried, by rolling his eyes heavenward, to warn him Arguello was in a black mood.

Arguello put down his paper and looked Martinez in the eye with his furious look, which didn't deter Martinez, who said, "A message on the machine. I think you'd better come."

Without a word Arguello put down the newspaper and

followed Martinez up the unpainted wooden stairs, which creaked abominably with every footstep. The room was up three flights, at the very top where radio reception was best, at the end of a long corridor, it too, full of dust and smelling of rancid oil.

A very plain room with a bed in one corner and a table in another. On the table was the machine, an exact replica of the one in Armand's room. The message was on the roll of paper. "I wanted you to see it just as it came in," said Martinez. The message said: "BANANAS OVERRIPE. ELEANOR COME HOME SOONEST JELLYROLL." In English, which the two men spoke imperfectly, Arguello looked at the message as if it were an adder: "When did this come in?"

"Some time last night."

"It don't make sense, that message. 'Bananas overripe.' Bananas is cocaine. What is overripe, what that mean in Spanish?"

"*Excessivamente maduro.*"

"Cocaine does not get *excessivamente maduro*. And this '*Eleanor come home.*' Eleanor is Miami. How does Miami come home?"

Martinez shrugged. "It is signed Jellyroll. Who is that? The machine decodes only the right code. The wrong code come out gibberish."

Arguello tore the message off the machine. "Come."

The two men went down the creaking stairs out into the brilliant sunshine of Balisario, which was a city founded in 1649 by some very cruel Spaniards. It was full of smells and three-hundred-year-old churches. The colors of the stone-and-adobe houses were yellow and ochre and there were many wrought-iron balconies; also much poverty and still much cruelty.

Roberto Garcia's house was on Avenida Estrada, the biggest boulevard, behind a high stone wall painted pink and surmounted by broken glass and barbed wire. The gate was very fancy and looked like wrought iron but was actually high-tensile steel painted black and very strong. The guard, who resided in a little stone house behind bulletproof glass, waved them through because he knew them well. The two men found Roberto Garcia alone at breakfast in his beautiful long dining room which would seat fifty people and was hung with Spanish paintings of Roberto's ancestors.

Roberto was an immensely assured, quiet man with gray hair and a squarecut body. He was eating a melon, drinking coffee, and reading the *Nación*, which printed nothing but lies, but, as Roberto liked to tell people, you could always read between the lies. (A joke that came off only in English. Roberto was witty in both languages.)

"So early in the morning, Chico," said Roberto amiably. "It must be bad news." He folded his paper carefully and put it beside him on the table. He did not ask the men to sit down because he was the *comendador* and they were soldiers. It would just make the men uncomfortable to sit down with the *comendador*.

Roberto read the message and smiled. "Very amusing," he said. "Which means it could not have been sent by Victor because Victor has no sense of humor."

"The man who sent it must know the other code because it came in code. There has been no message on that machine since Armand was killed."

Roberto sipped his coffee and let the silence sit there like a presence in the beautiful dining room. Finally he said: "I have news for you, Chico. Armand is not dead. Badly wounded, but alive. Not dead."

"Hoo!" spat Arguello. An expostulation. "Who says?"

"True, Chico. We have sources." The *comendador* directed his gaze fully at Arguello, who was, he knew, the best in his line, which was killing. "Did you have to kill eleven cops, Chico?"

"I was told to take strong measures," cried Arguello

55

passionately. "The strongest. 'Let nothing stand in your way'—you said that."

Roberto made a little grimace. He had indeed said that. 'Well, I didn't mean kill eleven police, Chico. The Americans are wild with anger. The Americans take death very seriously, Chico, especially dead police. They are very peculiar, the Americans. Not like us. They do not take seriously the things we take seriously—chastity, honor, manhood, God. On the other hand, death bothers them—I don't know *why*. Everyone dies. They should know that, but they don't. They get very upset when a few cops get killed. I'm telling you all this, Chico, because you have to go back there, and I don't want any more dead cops."

"I go back! Why?"

Roberto sipped his coffee and took his time. "Twenty-six million dollars, Chico. Where is it?"

"I told you, *comendador*. We searched Cassidy's *cuarto*. We turn it upside. There is not twenty-six million there. There is not twenty-six pesos there."

The *comendador* had heard all this before. It didn't explain what he wanted explained. He sipped his coffee and allowed Arguello to feel guilty. Finally he said: "How is the arm, Chico? Painful?"

"It's all right."

"No, it's not all right, Chico. If you have to wear a sling, you can't handle a gun, can you? Someone must go back to America and get the twenty-six million. What does the doctor say? When can the sling come off?"

"Three days. I take it off now if you like."

"No, no, we'll follow doctor's orders."

Arguello burst out: "We search Cassidy's apartment. The money is not there. Maybe the police . . ."

"We have informers with the police. The police know nothing about twenty-six million dollars. They would be boasting to the papers if they had it. They know nothing about it."

Roberto fell silent, turning the paper with the message over and over in his hand. He read the message again thoughtfully.

"This man Cassidy, has he a sense of humor?"

"How would I know?"

"An Irish. They are all comedians," said the *comendador*. "I think maybe Cassidy sent this amusing message." He thought it over with a little smile on his face. "We must reply to this *amusing* message with a little amusement of our own."

"What can we say to that nonsense?"

"Let me work on it. Meanwhile, you take care of that arm, Chico, because you must go back—the usual—Panama to Florida to Virginia."

"Are we all right in Virginia? Armand is not there anymore."

"Kaska is still at Shotover Hall, looking after things," said Roberto.

Garcia dismissed the two men pleasantly after inquiring solicitously about Martinez' health, his children, his dog, Roberto's manners were always very fine. After they left, Roberto Garcia finished his coffee and his newspaper. He took the cup into the big kitchen flooded with morning light and handed it to Ernestina, a wiry black girl whose health and happiness he also inquired about, as he did every morning, listening intently to her answering recital of woes, clucking sympathetically.

The stairs to the cellar were in the kitchen next to the big stove. Roberto went down into the cellar, which smelled of earth and vegetables, down the long corridor to the big wooden door. He knocked three times and the guard unlocked the door and let him through. This led to another long corridor, and here the smells were not so nice—sewer smells and rotting vegetation. At the end of this corridor deep in the earth was a steel door with a panel. The *comendador* knocked and the panel opened. "Good morning, Juan. How are you?"

The guard let him into the small cell. Harburg lay on the bed, his chest and legs bound to the mattress, his feet in dirty bandages. On his face a stubble of beard many days old.

"Señor Harburg," said Roberto genially. "How goes it this morning?" Roberto had spent time in the United States and he prided himself on his command of the vernacular.

Harburg turned his red-rimmed eyes to the *comendador* for a moment, then closed the eyes and turned his head away.

"Answer the *comendador*," shouted the guard and kicked Harburg in the head.

Harburg didn't even open his eyes.

"Wire him up, Juan," said Roberto. "I have a few questions."

Harburg's eyes flew open. He tried to arise, but the cords on his chest held him tight so he could barely get his shoulders off the mattress. "You bastard! What do you want now? I've told you all I know. You'll get nothing but screams—I'm almost out of screams." The last bit spoken low, almost to himself.

Roberto drew up a wooden chair and sat down while the guard attached the wires to the genitals. "You've told us very little, George, considering the amount of electricity we've expended on you. Do you know how expensive electricity is in Balisario?"

"Ready when you are," said the guard.

"What I'm interested in today, George, is a man named Cassidy who has been dispatched to Shotover Hall for some reason or other. He's a comedian who sends comical radio messages, and I must reply—comically, of course. Tell me about this Cassidy, George. Who is his control and why are they sending him, exactly?"

"I don't know any Cassidy. For God's sake, Garcia, don't

58

you know how an intelligence operation runs? They tell me only . . ."

The words became a shrill, piercing scream as Juan turned on the juice. Roberto listened to the scream, appreciating it as if it were Beethoven.

"You haven't run out of screams at all, George. That was a very good *high* scream. The high scream is the Stradivarius of screams, thrilling to the connoisseur. Now tell me who is Cassidy's control? Is it Victor? Another touch, Juan, of the precious electricity."

This time the scream was lower and ended in a choking gurgle.

"Oh, I didn't like the sound of that," said Garcia. "I think you gave him a little too much. George, speak to me!"

Harburg was still as a plank, his eyes wide open.

Roberto listened to the chest, felt the pulse. "What a shame! A very good man, Juan. He told us nothing. I shall miss him."

He rose from the chair. "He's to go into the river tonight, Juan, but only after curfew when everyone's off the street. The crocodiles will handle the disposal problem. You're to say nothing at all to anyone about Harburg—not to your wife, mistress, mother, your best friend. You understand."

"I understand."

Roberto walked back down the smelly corridor, feeling the sadness that always enveloped him at these moments. He got very close to the tortured ones, an emotional bond that nothing else quite gave him. The kill was always a marvelous moment, but like an orgasm, there was always the postcoital *tristesse* which sometimes enveloped him for hours.

He went to his office to compose a reply to Cassidy, addressing him, of course, as Jellyroll. It took him a long time, because the reply must be comical and he didn't feel comical.

After that he called El Presidente at the palace and did

his best to soothe him. It was El Presidente who would get most of the twenty-six million if and when they ever got it. El Presidente was still furious. It took all of Roberto's charm to calm him.

7

Lucia wore jeans, a plaid shirt, and sneakers, her hair in a long pigtail down her back. Amanda Shotover looked at her sorrowfully. "We have trunks full of riding clothes," she said. "All sizes."

"Tomorrow," said Lucia crisply. "We can do all that tomorrow, Mrs. Shotover." She was cinching the saddle herself, fending off Joseph, the black groom, who had worked in that stable for more than forty-five years and was helping her more than she wanted to be helped. "No, no, I can do it!" cried Lucia, taking the chin strap out of his hands and tightening it.

The horse looked enormous to Cassidy. Far too big for his thirteen-year-old.

Joseph said softly: "This horse Sandpiper gentle as a kitten. She take good care your little girl, Professor."

"I don't need taking care of," cried Lucia and hauled herself up into the saddle of the enormous horse, ignoring Joseph's clasped hands.

Anne Falk was already astride her horse, Faun, standing

quietly a few feet away. She had been at the table when Cassidy—far later than the others—sat down for breakfast. Amanda had introduced her: "Anne Falk. My companion." Coming down hard on that word. "When you reach my age, you have to pay for companionship." A bitter remark that bounced off Anne Falk as if unspoken. She was a beautiful blond woman, about twenty-nine, and appeared, Cassidy thought, to have been carved out of ice. She said only three words in his presence.

"You will ride with the child, Anne," commanded Amanda Shotover, "and show her the trails."

"Yes," said Anne Falk. "Excuse me." Her only three words. She left the table immediately and was now very properly dressed in jodhpurs and riding coat and riding hat—none of which Lucia would bother with.

The two females trotted off down the beautifully kept driveway in the direction of the mountain, neither speaking or looking at one another.

"Take her on the lake ride," Amanda called after them. "It's beautiful."

Anne Falk didn't even turn around, but she did nod a very small nod.

"Does she talk?" asked Cassidy. "Words?"

"Oh, she knows some words," said Amanda, dismissing the subject and Anne Falk curtly.

A strange companionship, both of them suffering the other. Anne Falk was now two hundred yards away, broadside to him in the saddle—slim, blue-eyed, beautiful, cold as marble. Cassidy wondered if Lucia could break into that silence.

"Come, I'll show you the stables."

"I know nothing about horses," said Cassidy.

"Then it's high time you learned."

Amanda Shotover introduced him to the six remaining horses in the stable, all big, strong Hanoverians who, the old lady said, could jump six-foot fences and run all day.

"Who rides all these horses?" asked Cassidy.

Amanda pursed her old lips and said nothing. Joseph was sweeping the floor and he didn't answer either, but he looked as if he knew.

The tack room was hung with enough saddles and bridles to outfit a cavalry platoon—all beautifully polished.

Next door to the tack room was the carriage room, which contained eight carriages of all sizes, these, too, highly polished and ready to go. One coach looked high as a train.

"This was the express coach that ran between London and Dover in the seventeen hundreds. My husband's grandfather brought it over from England and he used to drive it around the estate with six horses. Beautiful thing, isn't it?" It was indeed—lights dancing on its surfaces as if it were alive.

The next coach was much smaller. "This one was made for an English circus. See how small the interior is? They used to fill it with midgets, both inside and on the top seats, and the midgets would ride around the ring waving their hats at the crowd—back in the eighteen forties."

The past, always the past.

"When were these carriages last used?"

The old woman got very vague. "Oh, we used to take them out on Halloween every year. My oldest son, Francesco, used to drive the Dover coach with four horses. He was very strong. My second son, Dominick, drove the midget coach with two horses, and my third son, Averell, drove the Lancia brougham with two horses. I would drive the Irish gig—just one horse—oh, a long time ago."

It must have been. The oldest son (what peculiar names they all had!) had been killed almost forty years ago.

"What did Armand drive?"

Amanda acted as if she hadn't heard. She was showing Cassidy a glass case (so much of Shotover Hall was in glass cases. A museum!) full of harnesses for the coach horses, its brightwork gleaming as if polished that morning. "I used to

63

hitch the horses up myself. I knew every buckle and shank on all this harness. It's getting to be a lost art. When Joseph goes, I just don't know...."

Later, when they were driving from the stables down to the stud farm where the thoroughbreds were bred and raised, Amanda Shotover said absently, as if the question had been simmering in her all that time, "Armand never drove. I tried to teach him. Joseph tried. He had no gift for driving. It's a gift, you know." A moment later she added, a touch of acid in her voice, "Anne Falk has the gift. She's a very good driver."

Cassidy was driving the CIA Mercedes along miles of white fences, some of them double white fences to keep the stallions from getting close to the mares. They passed white stone houses where the groom, stable managers, and farm workers lived, dozens of them. The fields were dotted with thoroughbred mares with their foals, the stallions in separate pastures behind two rows of white fences.

Cassidy said: "How did Armand have the great good fortune to stay out of Vietnam, Mrs. Shotover?"

She took her time answering that. "He had a bad heart—his father's bad heart. It kept him out of many things his brothers were all very good at—football, skiing, tennis. Now the doctors say exercise is good for the heart, but when Armand was growing up they didn't think so. He was kept very quiet. He watched the others. He spent his life watching. He was a watcher. He watched a lot of television. All that rubbish!"

His father's bad heart. Almost the first mention of the father of these four boys. Grandfather. Great-grandfather, all that. Father and husband, no. Not even a picture of him anywhere.

They went through the stud farm, talked to the manager, a cryptic Welshman who didn't like to be disturbed, admired the yearlings who would be sold at Keeneland. After that Amanda Shotover directed him to the lake house. A man-made lake. The house was a huge modern structure, all planes and rectangles and picture windows, designed, Amanda Shotover said, for parties. The main room was enormous, thirty feet long and almost as wide, with a great piano in it, a huge stone fireplace, and lots of big wide sofas. There were six bedrooms, all small and elemental, containing only single beds and bureaus and mirrors. Several of the rooms looked occupied, with suitcases on the floor, hurriedly made beds that had been slept in. One had an ashtray with a cigarette butt in it. Cassidy waited to hear Amanda explain who was staying there. She didn't.

How many people to service this domain? They'd passed gardeners at work on flowerbeds, men on tractors taking manure to the fields, three men digging a drainage ditch. The house swarmed with maids, cooks, butler, companion, secretary. All evidence of much wealth. But if there was all that money, why had Armand borrowed a million and a half dollars?

"You don't talk much, Mr. Cassidy."

Cassidy grinned. "Sometimes you can't shut me up."

"Why are you so quiet around me?"

"I find you so interesting, Mrs. Shotover. I don't want to interrupt."

"I think I'm an old bore. I bore *me* anyway. Tell me something I don't know. What was my son doing in the CIA?"

"I don't know. I never met your son except once. He tried to hold me up and got shot by strangers."

"Mr. Alison told me."

"You don't like Alison, do you?"

"No, do you?"

"We've been through a lot together. It makes a bond."

Cassidy was driving the CIA car around the lake and into deep woods that climbed sharply up the mountain.

"I haven't been in these woods in years, now that I don't ride anymore. I've forgotten what's in here. I believe we had some cabins. The boys would sleep in them when they were young."

Also an airstrip, said Cassidy to himself. Is it possible to forget an airstrip? She didn't mention it.

The woods were crisscrossed by trails and a few dirt roads, all well kept. Cassidy headed in what he thought was the general direction of the airstrip. He never got there. The road ended in a high pile of brush which contained two large trees, a pine and a maple, with eight-inch trunks. Too big to move, completely obstructing the road right up to the trees at either side of the road. A car couldn't get through it or around it.

"What a shame!" sighed Amanda Shotover. "I was enjoying my ride. You'll have to turn around, Mr. Cassidy."

Cassidy didn't want to turn around. He wanted badly to get to the airstrip.

"Why would anyone block up the road that way?"

"I don't know."

"It's your place, Mrs. Shotover. Why don't you ask?"

"It's not my place. It's Armand's. Their father left it to the four boys equally. Now there's only one boy left."

"He's in a coma. You're in charge now, Mrs. Shotover."

"Oh, I wouldn't like to interfere with whatever Armand is up to. Armand never liked my interfering. . . ."

Lucia and Anne Falk rode their horses right up the front lawn where Joseph was waiting and dismounted, Cassidy watching from his room. Lucia's cheeks were glowing, her eyes sparkling. Anne Falk was smiling. Also talking. Cassidy could see her lips moving in speech, couldn't hear a word. The two chattering away as they disappeared into the house.

Cassidy went downstairs and found them in the sun room where he'd first met Amanda Shotover.

"Latin lesson," said Cassidy.

"Oh," said Lucia, piercing the air with sorrow. "Virgil! I hate Virgil. He has nothing to do with *me*."

"That's why we study him—to get out of our mingy selves and into something a bit larger."

"Good-bye, Anne. Thanks for the ride. See you later."

"Good-bye, Lucia." She bestowed another of those smiles on Lucia, not even glancing at Cassidy. Cassidy didn't like it much and liked even less Lucia chattering away about Anne Falk.

"She's a marvelous rider, Daddy, and she knows all about horses—their pedigrees, their capabilities, their peculiarities, everything. We talked and talked and rode and rode. There's miles of trails. We went right up the mountain. There's a log cabin up there that's supposed to be an authentic eighteenth-century mountain cabin, with all the original chairs and tables. There's someone living in it!"

And someone living at the lake house. All these people . . .

Cassidy asked, "Did you see anything resembling an airstrip?"

"Airstrip? No. We were in the woods all the time. I'll ask Anne tomorrow when we ride."

"No!" said Cassidy violently. "Don't! Don't mention the airstrip to Anne or to Mrs. Shotover. Mind, now."

"I'm going to get you on a horse, Daddy. Tomorrow. Or anyway, soon."

"Poor horse," said Cassidy, "Let's get on with Virgil." They were in book four, that bit where Jupiter sends his son Mercury to tell Aeneas he must leave Dido—all that frivolous love play—and get on with the serious business of founding Rome and changing the history of the world. Cassidy made Lucia read it aloud in Latin, not so much for her education as for his. Lucia read Latin as if she owned it, as if it were her native tongue.

In the middle of this, it happened. The machine went *blip*. They both heard it and looked up. The machine went on automatically to decoding and writing the message out, the keys chattering away.

Lucia read the message off the roll of paper: "JELLYROLL URGENT SENDING PEACHES IN PLACE OVERRIPE BANANAS ELEANOR TOO SICK TO TRAVEL WISH YOU WERE HERE HARBURG."

Cassidy took a deep breath, let it out slowly.

"What's the matter, Daddy? You look as if you've seen a ghost."

"Look, Lucia, I've got to make a phone call. Do you think Anne Falk might carry on with the Latin for ten minutes? . . ."

"Oooh, yeah!" Lucia was overjoyed. Much too overjoyed, thought Cassidy sourly. He felt a swift pang of jealousy sharp as a knife.

Eleven A.M. Where would Alison be at this hour? He doubted he'd be home, but nevertheless he tried the most secret number (Alison's numbers were all secret, but some were more secret than others) because if Alison weren't there no one would answer. . . .

Except someone did.

Grace, Alison's rich and frosty wife.

"Cassidy," she said in her High Anglican way, transfixing him with his own name as if it were an arrow. "You're the wrong man. I'm to wait here for a call from the *right* man, and it's not you."

"Who is it?"

"I'm not to tell, but I'll give you a hint. It's from Balisario. *Long* long-distance. Very, very important! Is there anything my goddamned husband does that is not *very*, very important? I would like to catch him at something trivial just once, like taking me to the theater. . . ."

Cassidy let her run down. "Are you telling me, Grace, that you have been dragooned into listening for a phone call for your lord and master, Hugh Alison? I don't believe it."

"I don't either. But there it is. Once in a blue moon I

allow myself to do one of these degrading little tasks just to reassure myself that everything he does is as despicable as I think it is."

"And is it?"

"Of course. My husband is consistent in nothing except that—being despicable. He puts Iago to shame. What the hell do you want, Cassidy? Why are you calling on this most secret phone, which is used only by prime ministers and other evil people? You're not evil enough to use this phone."

"Oh, yes, I am. Where is he, Grace? It's very, *very* important."

He could have bitten his tongue for saying that. It provoked from Grace a high yelp of laughter.

"There's that phrase again!" she yipped. "Very, *very* important! My goddamned husband! He hasn't got blood in his veins. He's got importance. He *bleeds* importance—all over the rug—and you can't get it out and it smells of old headlines. Ordure of importance. A real stink!"

Cassidy let her run down again. "Where is he, Grace?"

Grace spat the number out of her mouth—one of Alison's other secret numbers Cassidy had in his black book—as if she had bitten into a worm in an apple.

"Come see me, you silly bastard. We'll cuckold my rotten husband on the living room rug and laugh like lunatics. . . ."

Cassidy got away from her and called Alison, who was in a big, big meeting. He'd ring back soonest. He did too, almost at once. Cassidy read him the message and let it sink in. Not that that would take very much time. They both knew Harburg would never send his name in the clear that way, even encoded, would never preface the message with Jellyroll or the word *urgent* (they were all urgent, those messages, like Alison's very, *very* important phone calls). OVERRIPE BANANAS was a gag that didn't need to be topped. ELEANOR TOO SICK TO TRAVEL stopped them cold. It was black comedy. Too black.

"I told you *no action*," said Alison crisply. "Why did you send that crazy message?"

"Harburg and I are old buddies," said Cassidy. "I wanted to get a reply out of him. See if he's all right. He's *not* all right, Hugh. Something's very rotten in Balisario. Who else you got down there?"

But of course Alison wasn't answering. "You've got to go, Horatio. Find out what's up."

"I told you, I'm not leaving Lucia. I don't know what you and Armand were up to in these 27,642 acres—with its airstrip . . ."

"Not on the phone!" Alison's cry was an agonized whisper. Cassidy had hit pay dirt with that mention of airstrip.

"Send Keefe. He's unemployed and dying for a mission," said Cassidy.

"Keefe's not coherent."

Alison used a kind of double-talk that was like Orwell's doublethink, saying exactly the opposite of what the words meant. Coherence was Keefe's long suit. He'd gone to Trinity in Dublin and never stopped talking since. Very big words.

"He drinks," amended Alison.

"Well, don't send him alone."

"*You* go with him."

The argument was long and passionate. There was more than Lucia's welfare at stake. There was much to be explored at Shotover Hall, much to be learned. Cassidy wanted to stick around.

"How about Rattigan? You'll need two people, maybe three, if there's big trouble down there."

"I don't even know where either of those guys are." Alison making a last stab.

"I know where they are. You can't get that quality man overnight—not outside the Agency—and I know you want to stay out of the Agency."

Alison didn't like it, but he had no choice. He knew he couldn't whistle up trained manpower like Keefe and Rattigan, ex-agents both of them, at a moment's notice, men who knew language, procedures, the score.

"They'll have to come through Shotover Hall," said Alison reluctantly, hating to divulge that that was what Shotover Hall was for. "Just for one night, just a stopover, Horatio. Now, damn it, none of your smart-ass nonsense!"

"We'll sit around the fire and talk old times, don't worry."

"Not in the main house!" commanded Alison sharply. "They're to stay down in the lake house. They're not to see the old lady. Get that straight, Cassidy!"

"Okay! Okay!"

So that's what the lake house was for.

The CIA had the run of the place? And the airstrip? In exchange for a million and a half. Two hours' drive from Langley. How very convenient.

"How's Armand?" asked Cassidy.

"The same, neither better nor worse. Tell Amanda and give her my love. Behave yourself."

Alison hung up.

That night as Lucia prepared for bed, she was still chattering about Anne Falk. "Tomorrow, we're going to ride in a different direction—that way—which is mostly fields and pastures so we can have a good gallop. We'll wind up on top of the mountain. There's a big signal tower up there."

"Signaling what?"

"Who knows? There's someone up there running it—a man named Kaska. A Russian. You like Russians, don't you, Daddy? You always say they're much like Americans."

"Some of them are. Some of them aren't."

That night he woke up at 3 A.M. and heard automatic rifle fire in the woods above the house. It went on for quite a while.

71

8

Keefe and Rattigan arrived the next day in a CIA car that deposited Alison at the main house and then dropped the two ex-agents at the lake house, where Cassidy was waiting for them. Keefe was in full cry, like a pack of Irish hounds.

"Well, and what a grand arrangement for yourself, Cassidy! It'll ruin your character, all this conspicuous consumption. Already I see a grave weakening of resolve around the corner of the eyelids, which is the seat of resolution."

Rattigan said nothing, as was his wont, smiling his little clown smile. He was a great listener, Keefe an unstoppable talker. Cassidy sat them down before the great fireplace in the main hall, handed around the Wild Turkey, and told them a few things.

"They turned my apartment upside down looking for what—money? Just to stage that operation—twenty men flown in, equipped with rockets and machine guns—must have cost a couple hundred thousand dollars. They must be looking for millions. Nobody handles that kind of money except the cocaine crowd."

Keefe took a long slug of Wild Turkey, passed the bottle to Rattigan, and said, "I can't believe Alison is in the drug trade. He's got a rich wife. He doesn't need to take chances like that."

"That's a clue right there," said Cassidy. "Alison would never mix in this, and he wouldn't let the Agency mix in it either. Balisario is running the graft and the Agency is turning a blind eye in exchange for a free hand at whatever low business they're up to down there, and I don't know what that is."

Rattigan spoke up. "What's Armand's role in all this? I don't understand Armand at all."

"Nobody understands Armand, including his mother," said Cassidy. "He sidles into my apartment with a gun and says, 'This is a life-and-death matter.' He calls Victor, getting the number out of my black book, which has no Victors in it, and says, 'Surprise. It's me.' As if he were supposed to be dead. Then he says he's going to blow the whistle on Victor to the *New York Times* and he has the documentation to prove it. In come two thugs who try to put him in the clouds. Alison comes to town and puts a lid on the whole business—the Mayor, the Police Commissioner, the Drug Enforcement Agency—pretty high-level stuff. Also, I can't escape the feeling Alison doesn't know quite *why* he's shutting all these people up. He's taking orders and there are not many who can give Alison orders. You've got to get right up into the Oval Office before Alison says yes sir, no sir without at least an explanation."

Keefe said, "What was Harburg doing down there in Balisario?"

"The usual thing—a double role. He was supposed to be Roberto Garcia's liaison, arranging transport, all that, but also I think the CIA had him keeping an eye on Balisario itself. Harburg is a financial analyst, and they must have had him watching the cash flow for some reason or other. Maybe they caught him looking at what they didn't want looked at. That last message signed with his cryptonym is not from Harburg. He'd never send a message like that."

They'd brought two radios along and Cassidy showed them Armand's radio. "I'm going to leave it preset. Just to see what might come in from the character who sent that other message." He took one of the two other radios for himself. Keefe said, "Alison says to set it at 26.2. Ho ho."

Cassidy grinned and set both radios at 21.7. "We don't want Alison listening in on our private jokes, do we? They know my old cryptonym Jellyroll, so for this dance I'll be Asp, you'll be Beetle. Okay? You've been in Balisario before?"

Keefe nodded. "Running guns to keep down the Communists, 1974. I know it well and a sleazier town I have never set foot in. The corruption runs from El Presidente Hermanos Fuentes to the waitresses. A moral sinkhole, Cassidy. I'm glad you're not going down there with us. It's no place for a closet idealist like yourself."

Cassidy said, "Harburg is—or was—staying at a fleabag named Diablo's. You know it?"

"Dear boy, Balisario is about the size of Oconomowoc, Wisconsin. I know every fleabag in it. I was a great pal of Pedro, the bar boy at Diablo's. Taught him how to shoot a pistol, which I may live to regret because his ambition is to grow up to be a bully boy for El Presidente, and I gather we are in opposite corners from El Presidente."

"I wouldn't stay at Diablo's. Try some other fleabag. What's your cover?"

"Guns. We've got a nice line of Kalashnikovs we stole in Beirut from those murderin' Druse." Keefe took a huge draft of Wild Turkey. "El Presidente would like to have a few more Kalashnikovs. He only owns half the country. He would like to own all of it. But will owning all of Balisario bring El Presidente happiness? In a word, no. He'll be like Alexander—crying because he has no more victims to torture."

The telephone rang and Cassidy answered. It was Amanda Shotover. "We're waiting dinner for you, Professor. Mr. Alison and I." Bearing down heavily on the words *Mr. Alison* in her high-toned sarcasm, the dislike showing plainly.

"Start without me, Mrs. Shotover. I'll be along in a few minutes."

"I'm to cope with Mr. Alison by myself, Professor? How very unkind." She hung up on him.

Cassidy said, "I don't know why you're being kept out of sight like this. Alison is up to something, as always; there are steaks and beer in the icebox. You'll have to cook your own grub, which you've certainly done before. Tell me about Father Flaherty."

Keefe showed him Father Flaherty's photographs. "A clown but not bad with the lens. That's very good of Wolff." A good photo of Wolff on Cassidy's front steps. Wolff was one of the Agency's wire-and-film men. "I'm all wired, am I?" commented Cassidy sourly.

"You won't even be able to take a leak in your own apartment without being filmed in four colors with sound effects. Anyway, the Agency cleaned up the place for you. It looks neater than I've ever seen it, Cassidy. They even made the beds."

Cassidy was looking at another of Flaherty's photographs. "I don't know this lout, do you? But then I don't know a lot of people. He could be a guest of my landlord, who lives over me."

A square-cut man with a bulldog jaw. Also on Cassidy's front steps.

Both Keefe and Rattigan shook their heads. They didn't know the man.

Cassidy looked at his watch. "I've got to cut along. When are you leaving?"

Keefe said, "Midnight—Alison's best hour. It makes him feel conspiratorial, don't you know?"

"He's not going?"

"Never fear. Alison stays well away. He's seeing us off on the airplane, seeing that we don't get into mischief."

Cassidy told them he'd been trying to find his way to that airstrip ever since he'd got to Shotover Hall. "You can't get there from here," said Cassidy. "So if one of you boys has an idea, could you leave me a little trail?"

Rattigan spoke up then with his little clown smile. He had just the gadget, and he showed it to Cassidy.

"Does it work?"

"I hope so."

The phone rang again and Cassidy leaped up. "That'll be Mrs. Shotover telling me the roast is getting cold. Tell her I'm on my way." Keefe delivered that message on the telephone.

Cassidy was at the door when he remembered Armand. "How is he? What's the word?"

Keefe threw up his hands in an Irish gesture of despair. "The pulse is steady, the mind is absent, the eyes are closed."

Cassidy said, "He was born and grew up in this... prison. You have no idea of the deprivation suffered by a small, sensitive boy isolated in 27,642 acres with three big brothers who skied and played football and rode horses while he watched television and read books. Ah, the miseries of the very rich!"

"What were you doing down at the lake house?" asked Amanda Shotover.

"Playing three-cushion billiards with myself," said Cassidy.

"I don't recall a billiard table at the lake house."

"*Mental* three-cushion billiards," explained Cassidy. "It's all in the head."

"How entertaining! Who won?"

"I did. I also lost. I was elated by my victory, cast down by my defeat. Simultaneously."

"Very confusing, emotionally," observed Amanda Shotover.

"Emotional confusion is one of the hallmarks of the late twentieth century. Every defeat a victory. Our enemies are our friends."

And so on—Cassidy and Amanda Shotover cutting a conversational rug while the others listened—Alison, stony-faced, Anne Falk impassive, Lucia bright-eyed.

It got them through the salad course, when Alison flung himself headlong into the conversation like an Army tank with the observation that the dining room they sat in was an exact replica of the Adams dining room in Fenster Hall in Suffolk, which belonged to his great good friend Lord Inchkellen. "Jefferson, as we know, was intensely influenced by Adam, and imitation is the sincerest form of flatter, Mrs. Shotover. This is one of the finest Jefferson dining rooms I have ever sat in."

"I never discuss Jefferson's architecture at dinner, Mr. Alison," said Amanda Shotover. "It's too heavy for dinner. Too heavy for after dinner too. It's more a late afternoon subject."

Poor Alison, thought Cassidy. You should never try snobbery on true aristocrats. They'll shoot you down every time.

After dinner Amanda Shotover rose to her full four-foot-six-inch height and announced she was going to bed. Good night. Good night. Good night. Each good-night directed to a specific person, looking at each one full in the face and each good-night, Cassidy thought, with a different inflection—warmth to Lucia, total contempt to Alison, cold hauteur to Anne Falk (what on earth was going on between those two?), and to Cassidy a sort of conspiratorial wink, as if she was saying: We're all in this together.

Cassidy shepherded Lucia to bed immediately afterwards because it was 9:30 and she had a tough day with the books coming up. "I'm going to stuff a little learning in you very early tomorrow before you climb on that horse."

"Arrgh." Throaty and defiant but loving.

"I'm going riding with you," announced Cassidy.

"Daddy!" gasped Lucia. "Why?"

"I have my reasons. I thought you'd be pleased. You've been trying to get me on a horse ever since I've been here."

"Now that I have, I'm scared."

"We'll take it very easy. No galloping the first day."

"Anne will give you a lesson. She's very good."

"Oh," said Cassidy. "Anne." He hadn't counted on Anne. It changed the play. "Couldn't we leave her behind? Just have a ride by ourselves?"

"Oh, Daddy, no. I'd get lost."

"Mmm," said Cassidy. He kissed her on the forehead, felt the velvety cheek with his fingertips, and left her.

Outside, at the very end of one of Mr. Jefferson's cavernous corridors, Cassidy saw Alison and Anne Falk imbedded in discussion. He stood quietly watching, unnoticed. Alison was doing all the talking, Anne Falk looking angry. (But then she frequently looked angry.) Presently she gave a curt nod and walked away from Alison and directly at Cassidy. She passed him without a flicker of recognition or change of expression—the way that girl walked past Joseph Cotten in the last scene of *The Third Man*.

"Good night," said Cassidy softly.

No reply.

Cassidy strolled down the long corridor to Alison.

"A nightcap, old boy?" said Cassidy.

"You sound like a 1928 drawing room comedy," muttered Alison.

"I'm trying to live up to my surroundings," said Cassidy. "You never will."

They went downstairs to the drawing room where the drink table was and poured themselves brandy. "I didn't know you and Miss Falk were such friends."

"I've known her for years," said Alison. "She's one of the Boston Falks, you know. Shipping. Certainly you've heard of the Falk Lines—but the family is a bit down on its luck. So—uh . . ." He let it trail off.

"Aren't we all?" said Cassidy. "Including the Shotovers—another old shipping family. How much of Shotover Hall does the CIA own?"

Alison didn't dignify that with an answer. Instead he said, "I've got to get back."

"Tonight?"

"Early tomorrow morning. I won't see you again, Cassidy. Keep that radio on the old channel and tell me instantly if anything comes in. It's important."

Cassidy smiled his wolfish smile. "You're an important man, Hugh."

"Always the needle, eh, Horatio?"

"It's because I care. I really care." Cassidy didn't say for *what*.

Alison looked exasperated. "Anything at all to report before I go?"

"Gunfire in the night."

Alison sniffed. "Poachers shooting deer."

"With submachine guns? The CIA wouldn't be doing a little invasion training in these here twenty-seven thousand acres, would they?"

Alison drank his brandy. "Good night, Horatio."

"Sleep well, old chap. I hope the gunfire doesn't keep you awake."

Cassidy sat up in bed reading Emily Dickinson, whose poems he'd plucked from the library downstairs:

Remorse—is Memory—awoke—
Her Parties all astir—
A Presence of Departed Acts—
At window and at Door—
It's Past—set down with the Soul

And lighted with a Match—
Perusal to facilitate—
And help Belief to stretch—
Remorse is cureless—the Disease
Not even God—can heal—
For 'tis His institution—and
The adequate of Hell—

A little after midnight he heard the sound he was listening for—a jet engine making its special racket. Not a propeller, a jet engine. The Agency always traveled first class.

Cassidy turned out the light.

He dreamt of horses trampling him underfoot, masses of them.

It was very quiet in the little CIA jet and there were only two passengers, Keefe and Rattigan. Keefe had his long legs stretched out in front of him, a bottle of Wild Turkey in his hand, and was talking away with high glee.

"Ah, Balisario, Rattigan, what an experience you have ahead of you! It is a truly *evil* city, my boy, and there are not too many of those left anymore. In Balisario you have the very rich—thieving, murdering, torturing swine, every last one of them—and the very poor, who have their dreams of an afterlife provided for them by the Catholic Church who charge them for the privilege of hearing they will be roasted over the fire for all eternity in place of their present misery. In between the rich and the poor in Balisario are the middle classes, who are composed exclusively of smugglers, ex-Nazis, deserters, pimps, prostitutes, murderers, rapists, oh, *delightful* people! If we get caught, the *policía* will suspend us upside down and tickle our balls with electricity. Truly, Balisario is the garden spot of evil, my friend."

Rattigan had fallen asleep with a little smile on his face, as if he couldn't wait.

9

Roberto Garcia had been summoned from lunch, an indecency that had never before happened to him. As he hurried up the great square steps of the *palacio*, he was assailed by stomach cramps from all this rushing about on top of roast goat. An ill omen.

The *guardia* saluted and he answered absently, his mind on other things. Just inside was a long colonnaded interior court, with its high windows which cast dazzling light on the stone floor. Roberto walked unseeing past the Virgin and Child (which Hermanos Fuentes had stolen from Valerta after that brief disastrous war ten years earlier), past the El Greco of St. Sebastian and the arrows (almost certainly a fake), past four *guardia* standing at rigid attention in their ill-fitting uniforms.

El Presidente's office was enormous and square and heavy with its Spanish armor figures and Christ on the cross, all of it covered with dust which nothing could quite erase. The desk was vast, a sea of walnut, behind which sat El Presidente, a short, square, thuggish man with a thin Fu

Manchu mustache. Seated before the desk was another man Roberto instantly recognized.

"You know Señor Quarimiento," said El Presidente without any greeting at all. (He had no manners, El Presidente.) "He has just come from Bogotá."

Roberto inclined his head graciously. He despised the man, but one must perform the formalities. "With the merchandise?"

"No, without the merchandise," barked El Presidente.

Quarimiento, who had bad teeth and torpid, half-closed eyes, explained: "Valdez will not release the merchandise until he is paid for the last two shipments. Four million American dollars." The trade was always in American dollars. No other currency was trusted.

"There has been an unfortunate accident in New York."

"In Colombia we read the papers, *comendador*. Valdez has said . . ."

El Presidente, that boor, interrupted. "Señor Quarimiento, if you will step outside a moment. I must have a word in private with the *comendador*."

The tongue-lashing he got in private was one of the worst. Roberto stood at attention for it, his face blank; Roberto, the aristocrat, educated in Spain, listening to the illiterate ravings of this backcountry peasant. The essence of the tongue-lashing was to the effect that twenty-six million dollars had somehow vanished and now another shipment worth the same amount would not be forthcoming so that he, El Presidente, was out of pocket fifty-two million American dollars, which meant he could not pay the *soldados*.

Balisario, Roberto reflected, had managed for three hundred years to get along without these inflated cocaine profits but now was totally dependent on this money. Instead of rolling in wealth, their country was rolling in poverty worse than before. A rich paradox which warmed his Latin soul and also passed the time while El Presidente ran through his brief vocabulary of epithet.

"You will go to America, Roberto Garcia. You personally this time to recover the money. You understand?"

"Yes, *presidente*, I understand."

Keefe and Rattigan were walking around the great square which was the center of Balisario as it is the center of all South American towns of that size. The cathedral was immense, with two square towers which looked like battlements. "The Virgin inside is life-size and of solid gold," explained Keefe. "The peasants have nothing to eat, but the cathedral has a solid-gold Virgin. That tells more about South America than anything else."

They passed the *palacio* with its *guardia*, each with a submachine gun cradled in his arm, past *el comendador's* stone wall with its barbed-wire and broken-glass top, past the archbishop's house. "In most Spanish towns the biggest house is the *comendador's* and the second biggest is the archbishop's, sometimes right next door. At the moment the Catholics and the military don't see eye to eye. In fact, they shot the last archbishop trying to bring a little social conscience into his worship, a grave heresy."

Later the two men sat at Rodrigo's café on the square, drinking *cerveza*. Keefe called Rattigan's attention to the street lights, which were of wrought iron and very fancy. "Balisario has always had very fine street lights and very strong. They hang the outgoing politicians on them when they are defeated by gunfire."

Rattigan spoke up for the first time. "Arguello has just gone into the *comendador's* house."

"Aaah," said Keefe. "No rest for the weary. Come on, we'll go to Diablo's in Arguello's absence."

At Diablo's, Keefe was greeted with happy cries by Pedro, the bar boy. The place was empty and Pedro was glad to have company. He told them all the news—the *cerveza* was from Peru where they spiked the stuff with cyanide, just a tiny bit, very good for the digestion. Angelina, the whore most favored by the locals, had retired with her millions and bought a house on the coast where he heard she was into gunrunning and other profitable activities less taxing to the backbone. And so forth. They learned everything except news about Harburg, the one person they were interested in. They couldn't bring up the name, of course. Instead they played the match game, banging their fists on the table and shouting—with fierce expressions and eye-rolling—"Two" or perhaps "Three."

After a bit, Pedro responded to this play. "There was another man here played that game—man by the name of Harburg."

"Summon him, Pedro!" roared Keefe. "I will challenge him. I am the champion of the Western world at this game."

Pedro grew confidential. He approached the two match players and lowered his voice though there was no one in the bar. "They took him to the *sótano*. That's what the *soldados* say."

"Poor fellow," said Keefe without change of expression. Then to Rattigan, with a fierce glare: "Three." His heart heavy within him. Nobody got out of Roberto Garcia's *sótano*. Nobody ever had. It was terminal, the *sótano*.

They played on for half an hour because it would be unseemly to rush away on top of this bad news.

Later, walking back to Moldavia's, they passed a pile of bodies, stinking away under the bright afternoon sun at the corner of a little square. Some of the bodies were clothed, some naked—men, women, two children, all in a heap, the flies walking into the open mouths.

"Comunistas," explained Keefe. "You can tell by the horns on their heads and the tails growing out of their spines. They won't be permitted to fry for all eternity because they are *comunistas*. They are not entitled to eternity. What a shame!"

Back at Moldavia's, they stripped off their clothes and went to bed because they had much to do that night.

10

Cassidy was astride Sandpiper, the gentlest horse in the Shotover stable. Lucia was ahead of him on Ariel, half turned in the saddle to keep an eye on her father. Behind him was Anne Falk on Faun. She was beautifully turned out as always—the kind of girl who would dress for dinner in prison, thought Cassidy.

The sunlight filtered through the heavy leaf cover, dappling the trail with a mixture of fierce light and deep shade. They were following the lake trail, which crossed numerous other trails and an occasional dirt road in the huge woods. Cassidy had the electronic sensor in his coat pocket.

"You're doing very well, Daddy, but you can't spend your whole life at a walk. You must learn to trot."

"Why?" asked Cassidy.

"Because this is boring."

"I'm not bored. I'm petrified."

"You don't look petrified." This from Anne Falk. The very first words she had ever addressed to him. Cassidy was astonished. She looked as usual like cold marble, but she had actually spoken to him. Because I got on a horse, thought Cassidy. That puts me in the class of people to whom one speaks.

The trail crossed a dirt road and Cassidy took out his sensor and directed it at the base of the tree. About three feet from the ground, Rattigan had said. The sensor did nothing and Cassidy pointed it at some of the other trees. Nothing.

"Daddy, what *is* that thing?"

"This is a flugelkind. It distinguishes fact from fiction. Now, if that were a fake tree it would emit a bleep."

"*Daddy!* That's not even a good joke."

"You'll see," said Cassidy. "It's a very good joke—when it works."

If it worked. The next crossing of a road Cassidy tried again with the sensor and again got nothing at all. Had Rattigan forgotten? On the third try, crossing a dirt road that looked a little larger than the other two, Cassidy got a bleep out of the sensor and he immediately turned Sandpiper left up the road. "Let's try this road. I like this road."

"No! No! That's the wrong road!" cried Anne Falk.

"Wrong for what?" asked Cassidy. He dug his heels into Sandpiper's soft flanks and Sandpiper, who had been waiting for that, leaped forward, Cassidy hanging on, bent over the horse's neck.

"Daddy!" wailed Lucia. "You said no galloping the first day!"

Sandpiper was cantering easily down the broad dirt road in the bright sunshine, Cassidy holding the reins in one hand and the sensor in the other. This was fortunate because the road crossed another, and Cassidy had to decide which one to take. The sensor said: straight ahead, and he plunged on at a full gallop now, which was a bit more than he'd bargained for.

"Daddy!"

The cry was quite a ways behind him now; the other riders, having been caught by surprise, were far behind.

Another road and another shot with the sensor, which said: turn right. Cassidy barely made it around the turn at full gallop, losing a stirrup, hanging on.

Now he was passing what looked like a bivouac area, Sandpiper galloping right past men in Army fatigue uniforms, cutting brush, startled into immobility by the sight of a galloping horse. Dozens of tents in full camouflage, the sides rolled up revealing men inside lying on Army cots.

Cassidy turned in the saddle to get a fuller look at the bivouac area, and that led to disaster.

Sandpiper shot around a small bend. Ahead lay a sentry box with the sentry lolling outside in the sunshine. Across the road was a barrier pole that could be raised or lowered. It was lowered across the dirt road, but Cassidy, turned in the saddle, didn't see it. Sandpiper did and stopped dead in his tracks. Cassidy flew over the barricade, landing on the soft grass, rolling over and over, stunned but quite conscious, eyes closed. (What the hell! A little sympathy wouldn't do any harm.)

Lucia got to him first, having jumped the barrier on Ariel despite the shouted, "*No! No! Es prohibido!*" from the sentry.

"Daddy! Daddy!" She was right beside him now, feeling his face with her hands. Cassidy opened his eyes gravely. "Does this train stop at Weehawken?"

"Daddy, are you all right?"

"I won't live through the night."

He saw Anne Falk on foot standing three feet away and winked at her. She didn't wink back. She said, "You *can* ride a horse, can't you?"

"I haven't ridden since I was fifteen, and a lot of water has gone under the bridge since then." He sat up awkwardly, feeling for broken bones. "So this is the airstrip.

Why is it *prohibido*? If I had a nice airstrip like this, I'd tell all my friends."

Cassidy hunched himself off the grass and walked down the center of the airstrip, which was all in grass and looked three-quarters of a mile long. Some of the new small jets could land on grass and didn't need the long runways anymore. Where was the control tower, the hangars, all the detritus of airports? Under the trees probably. The strip looked as if it had been carved out of the oak and pine forest (at taxpayers' expense). Very straight rectangle and, for Virginia, very flat.

Anne Falk was trying to placate the sentry: *"El caballo desbocarsido."* The sentry was saying that *el caballo* didn't look to him like it was running away—yelling after Cassidy: *"Prohibido! Prohibido! Vuelve!"*

Cassidy ignored him until the man shot off his machine pistol in the air. That stopped Cassidy. "If you feel that strongly . . ." he said and strolled back.

Anne Falk was protesting to the sentry in Spanish that gunfire was not necessary, glaring at Cassidy, who now had his arm around Lucia's shoulder. He grinned at her.

His horse was grazing on the other side of the barricade.

Cassidy mounted it stiffly and walked the horse back in the direction from which they had come, feeling in his pocket to be sure the sensor was still there.

He heard the hoofbeats behind him coming fast and pulled Sandpiper in tight to prevent the horse from bolting. Anne Falk drew abreast of him on Faun. "You're not to tell Amanda Shotover any of this," she panted. "It would greatly upset her."

"Why shouldn't she know? It's her place."

"It's not. It's Armand's."

Armand's. Not Mrs. Shotover's. There was a familiarity there that changed all his assumptions.

Lucia galloped up on Ariel. "Daddy, you *can* ride a horse. Why didn't you say so?"

"I'm a lapsed horseman. I haven't been on a horse in thirty years." All three horses walking abreast now down the wide dirt road. "Miss Falk doesn't want us to mention the airstrip to Amanda Shotover. It would upset her." Trying to keep the irony out of his voice.

"Or the soldiers either," said Anne Falk stiffly. "If you would be so kind. She's an old lady. She wouldn't like it and she can't do anything about it—so why upset her?"

Nobody said anything.

They arrived at the junction of the lake trail and the road. Anne Falk turned her horse right and Lucia followed. Cassidy said: "I'll see you later," and dug into Sandpiper's soft flank with his heel. The horse galloped straight down the dirt road, Cassidy on his neck. He heard hoofbeats behind him.

The dirt road came out half a mile from the junction on the main highway, an obscure little entrance shaded by big trees without a sign, looking as if it had been newly made. Cassidy turned right and walked his horse down the macadam road toward the main entrance of Shotover Hall a mile away. Presently the others caught up with him and walked beside him.

"What are you going to do next, Daddy?" said Lucia. "Play polo?"

"I've shot my bolt. I have only two speeds on a horse—a walk and a gallop. Just like the cowboys in westerns. Have you ever noticed, Miss Falk, that nobody in a western ever trots? They always walk or they're all out, at full gallop. Have you ever noticed that?"

"I don't see many westerns," said Anne Falk.

"Pity," said Cassidy.

At ten o'clock that night, Cassidy was seated at Armand Shotover's desk, working over the notebook he'd dredged out of the bureau, when the door opened. Anne Falk came in wearing a floor-length red dressing gown. She closed the door behind her.

"I think we should have a talk."

"That would be nice," said Cassidy. "Sit down."

She sat on the bed, her hands in the pockets of her dressing gown, and looked at the floor.

"What would you like to talk about? I have a very sore bottom. Does that interest you?"

She dragged a toe around the carpet, not looking at him. "How did you know about the airstrip? It's a very big secret."

Cassidy used one of Alison's tricks, answering a question with one of his own. "You're working for Alison, are you?"

She ignored that, pursuing her own line. "The other thing you know that you shouldn't know is the code Armand was using, because you used that code."

She looked up from the floor now, the look boring right into him. "The only way you could know that code is because you have the deed of trust which, I suspect, you got out of Armand's pocket when he was shot. You must give it back."

Cassidy said: "I think you're operating out of CT under PP. That right? I think Alison detached Armand from paramilitary so that nosy Senators wouldn't find out what was going on at Shotover Hall. I'm just woolgathering here, Miss Falk, but it occurred to me that Armand was a lonely little boy playing in these big 27,642 acres. Forty years old but still a little boy who had big dreams. Covert operations seemed just the answer to those dreams."

Trying to needle her into saying a few things. Instead she laughed. "Look who's talking? What got *you* into covert operations, Professor? Were you a lonely little boy too?"

"That was a long time ago," said Cassidy harshly. "I'm a professor of medieval history now. I've grown up."

"Then what are you doing galloping around the country-side on a horse, doing pratfalls?"

"I was dispatched down here, kicking and screaming, by your boss, Hugh Alison. Maybe you could tell me what I'm supposed to be doing here. You're one of Alison's tame pigeons."

That got under her skin. "I'm *not* one of Alison's tame pigeons! I'm Armand's fiancée!"

That changed the play altogether.

Cassidy got out of his chair, walked to the window, and stared out into the velvety night, trying to reassemble his speculations into something that would fit this new fact. That explained Amanda's hostility; Anne Falk was absconding with her last surviving son.

Anne Falk bit her lip and stared at the floor. For the first time she looked defenseless.

"I see," said Cassidy.

"I doubt it," said Anne Falk.

Cassidy favored her with one of his wolfish smiles. "It's beginning to sound like something written by Emily Brontë. You were the old lady's companion and you fell in love with the master. . . ."

"I was *not* the old lady's companion. I *run* this place. I pay the grooms and fire the gardeners and fix the roof because Armand can't and the old lady won't! I do it because nobody else does it. The place was running out of money. . . ."

"So you invited the CIA in?"

"I didn't! Armand did! He was in over his head. He couldn't handle the codes and I . . . ." She trailed off here because she was getting into areas she shouldn't reveal.

Cassidy tried to fill in a few crevices: "Alison applied a little pressure, which is his specialty, and persuaded you to join the club to save the old manse, that right?"

She looked at her fingernails, bit her lip, and frowned.

"One of the Boston Falks of the Falk Lines," Cassidy said ironically. "Alison always loved to have the upper classes in the outfit. It gave the Agency tone."

She said wearily, "I'm a working girl. The Falks haven't owned the Falk Lines for decades. The Falk Lines are owned by Gulf and Western, like everything else. I came down here to ride the horses. That was my first job here. I acquired all the others because no one else *did* them and they had to be done."

She stood up, hands in the pockets of her long red dressing gown, and faced him. "It's much more serious than that."

Cassidy said, "Armand was in over his head. Now you're in over yours."

She smiled a sad smile. "Alison is in over his."

"Does he knows it?"

"He doesn't admit it. I think he knows it."

Complicity started right at that moment. They had been antagonists. Now they shared concern. The emotional climate of the room changed from hostility to anxiety. Shared anxiety. Cassidy sat on the bed and Anne Falk stood at the window, looking out at the great trees moon-brushed with silver.

Staring out, she told him a few things. It started with the radio station on the hill. Communications with the operatives in Central America. Then came the airstrip built to fly the paramilitary to wherever they wanted to go in Central and South America. Two hours from Washington, very secret, very convenient.

"The next step was . . . bad. They started flying in Hispanic guerrillas to give them advanced training on modern weapons and communications. Armand didn't like it and said so."

"But there was money in it?"

"Yes."

"When did the nose candy start to arrive?"

Anne Falk turned away from the window. "We don't know. How could we? The soldiers brought it in in their knapsacks on the planes, and God knows how they got it to New York. But they did. And the money started pouring in from New York."

"Money?"

"They took the money back on the planes when the soldiers went back. We didn't find out about *that* until two weeks ago. Tons of money! Millions! The money is worse than the cocaine. It's corrupting everyone! I don't trust a soul anymore!"

"Including Armand?"

She turned fiercely protective. "Armand would never, never get mixed up in cocaine."

"They tore my place apart looking for something. What? Money?"

"Maybe. I don't know."

"Armand came to my place in pursuit of a telephone number of somebody named Victor. There are no Victors in my phone book so it must be a cryptonym. He called Victor and said he was going to the *New York Times* and spill his guts. Then the hoods came in and shot him. Who's Victor?"

Anne Falk didn't have a chance to answer that. The radio on Armand's desk went *blip*, noisily, followed by a pregnant pause while it marshaled its decoding wits. After that the keys rattled at high speed, printing the message:

JELLYROLL URGENT COCONUTS ARRIVE WISHBONE THREE-PENNY DIX EXPEDITE PERSONALLY HARBURG.

Anne Falk tore the message off the spindle and passed it on to Cassidy. "Harburg would never send a message like that."

"I know," said Cassidy.

"He would never sign his own name or say *urgent*. He'd never, never say *expedite personally* to whoever Jellyroll is."

Cassidy said, "What is Wishbone—Shotover Hall?"

"Yes."

"And what are coconuts?"

"Soldiers. Threepenny is Thursday and dix is ten o'clock at night, because they never arrived in daylight."

"Did they always radio ahead?"

95

"Always. We had to light the landing strip and have trucks ready to take them to the bivouac area."

"Would Armand be on hand for each landing?"

"Not always. Sometimes we'd send . . . someone else."

"Kaska?"

She looked unhappy, as if she was afraid she was revealing too much, but finally nodded, frowning. "Why would they want Jellyroll to expedite personally?"

Cassidy was working on that question in the privacy of his own mind. He lay on his back on the bed and stared at the ceiling a long time, working it out.

"I think they know who Jellyroll is."

"And who is he?"

"Me." He sighed. "They want me personally to be there to ask some rude questions."

"What about?"

"Whatever they were looking for in my apartment. Money, I guess. We'll have to plan a little welcoming committee."

"It had better be a fairly big welcoming committee. There are usually twenty-four soldiers in each plane, all heavily armed."

"Lovely," said Cassidy, and yawned—a huge yawn.

"In that case, we'd better get some sleep."

He smiled at her. She didn't smile back. She moved toward the door, hands in the pockets of her long red dressing gown.

"They killed eleven cops in New York," she said flatly. "Looking for whatever they're looking for. We can't handle this by ourselves, Cassidy. I'm going to call Alison."

Cassidy snorted derisively. "If you depend on Alison to get you out of things, you're insane. Alison doesn't get people out of things. He gets people into things. Getting out is your own concern."

That made her laugh, showing her white teeth, crinkling

her eyes. It made her human, laughter. Cassidy decided he liked her laugh.

"Thanks," she said and opened the door.

Cassidy threw a high hard one right at her head. "Who is Victor—Alison?"

"No. Alison is many things, few of which I like, but he's not Victor."

"Who *is* Victor?"

"Armand knows. I don't."

Cassidy raised himself on his elbow and stared hard at her. "Why would Armand know something Alison doesn't? That's not the way the Agency works."

Anne was fiercely protective as always where Armand was concerned. "Armand is an innocent," she said. "You can put things over on Armand that Alison would spot instantly."

"Armand was not being fooled by the time he got to my apartment. He called Victor on my phone and told him he was going to tell all to the *New York Times*. He must have known Victor's real name or how would he get the telephone number from my book?"

Anne Falk was halfway out the door. She stopped and made a little grimace and ran her fingers through her hair. "Good night, Professor."

She closed the door after her.

Cassidy got off the bed, took off his clothes, and put on his pajamas. He picked up the black book, intending to go through it one more time, then decided the hell with it. Tomorrow, he thought. Just like Scarlett O'Hara, I'll think about all that tomorrow. He picked up Emily Dickinson and plunged into the nineteenth century, where the problems were more abstract though no less difficult.

> *It dropped so low—in my Regard*
> *I heard it hit the Ground*
> *And go to pieces on the Stones*
> *At bottom of my Mind— ...*

Cassidy turned off the light and went to sleep. At 5 A.M. the automatic radio, the one tuned to 21.7, went *blip* and then rattled off its message, signed Beetle. Cassidy was sound asleep and didn't hear any of that.

11

In Balisario the street lights went out at 10 P.M. when they turned off the generator to save electricity. The drinkers who had tarried too long in the bars ran home down the center of the dark streets fast as they could because the soldiers would shoot at them for violating the curfew, almost always missing but sometimes not. Ten minutes after ten the town was silent as an empty grave.

Rattigan and Keefe waited until 2 A.M. before setting forth from their stinking room, Keefe carrying the stainless-steel ladder that folded into a two-foot rectangle. Rattigan led, wearing the special glasses that saw through darkness. They encountered no *guardia*, who were all asleep in their posts as was customary at 2 A.M. in that town. The spot Keefe had selected was not on the avenida but at the side street farthest away from the main entrance where the *guardia* was snoring away. Rattigan scrambled up the ladder, cut the wires, and put thick styrofoam pads on the broken glass. He pulled the ladder up after him, put it down the other side, and made his way to the big house, carrying

99

the ladder in one hand, the gun with the tranquilizer in the other. There would be a dog. Harburg had reported a dog, a big mastiff. Rattigan's little clown face was set in stern lines as he made his way through the maze of flowers and ferns on the gravel path with the special glasses, waiting for the dog. Rounding the corner, the dog jumped on him silently . . .

And licked his ear. A big dog with big paws reaching up to well beyond his waist, wagging his tail, licking his face, absolutely delighted in his company. Rattigan laughed silently and rubbed the dog's belly with his fingers. Very comical, this little country. In some ways. In others, not.

Harburg had sent detailed sketches which Rattigan had memorized. He placed the stainless-steel ladder in the gravel underneath the tall window of Roberto's study and climbed to its highest point, where he worked with the steel tool. Snap! He hadn't meant to do *that*. The big window opened easily now, but the latch was broken. Too bad, but there it was.

Inside, Rattigan risked his little pencil flash to get his bearings. Great big desk—the Hispanics always liked big desks as a symbol of power—in a big square room littered with documents, ledgers, memoranda, account books. Rattigan went to work with the minicam, snapping page after page—memos, letters, account pages; some of the figures in the account pages made his eyes bug out—putting each item back in its place after it was photographed, his hands in the silk gloves. One sheaf of memoranda was all in gibberish. Clearly coded messages.

In three-quarters of an hour he was done and out of the place. Before he went down the ladder, he restored the clipped wires as best he could, carefully picked up the styrofoam, and blew a kiss to the big mastiff wagging his tail in the garden.

Back in the stinking room, Rattigan ran the negatives through the developer under the red light while Keefe slept. At 4 A.M. Rattigan was done. He woke Keefe, who yawned and moaned and stretched and then set about reading the still-wet negatives under the enlarger, swearing softly to himself. Rattigan slept while Keefe wrote out a long dispatch with all the news, most of it bad.

Double coding the long message was a bit much, so Keefe depended on the machine's automatic single coding. Some of the figures opened his eyes, as they had Rattigan's. Only at the end did he insert a bit of the private code Cassidy and Keefe had used between themselves for years.

BEWARE THE IDES OF MARCH BEETLE.

The ides of March were Russians. Or in this case, one Russian. Cassidy would figure out who it was.

Cassidy was only half awake, yawning, stretching, bleary-eyed when he saw the message on the second of the two automatic radios. He read the long message carefully, put it away in the drawer of Armand's desk, showered, shaved, and dressed, his mind snapping.

In the corridor he passed one of the two black maids that patrolled that wing of the house. "Good morning, Ada," he said.

"Pretty morning, Professor," said Ada and showed her white teeth.

In the long drawing room were two downstairs maids, one putting fresh flowers in the big cut-glass vases, the other vacuuming a room that had hardly been entered since the last time it was vacuumed. Big bosomy, motherly blacks and they, too, smiled their big smiles and said, "Mawnin', Professor."

"The money is worse than the cocaine. It's corrupting everyone."

These bosomy, motherly ladies?

In the dining room Amanda Shotover was reading the *Washington Post*. Geoffrey, the black butler with the white hair, was putting a silver toast rack with fresh toast on it at her elbow with hands as delicate as a brain surgeon's. Had that nice old man been got to? Cassidy hated to think so.

"Good mawnin', Professor," said Geoffrey and pulled out a chair and put Cassidy into it as if he were the Prince of Wales.

Amanda Shotover put down her newspaper and looked at him critically. "You look terrible," she said.

"Bad dreams."

She poured him a cup of coffee from the Georgian pot with the claw feet and the spout carved into the shape of a lion's head. "Tell me about your dreams," she said.

"Nobody's interested in someone else's dreams."

"I am. I can tell a lot about a man from his dreams. Frequently I tell a man more about himself than he wants to know."

Cassidy grinned and sipped the coffee. "Well, I'll tell you this much. There was a big black snake in this dream."

"You fear betrayal," said the old lady calmly.

Cassidy was stunned. That's exactly what he feared.

He chewed a slice of toast and said, "Where are the others?"

"Anne and Lucia have gone riding. Lucia said you were not to worry about her French lesson. She said she and Anne were going to conjugate irregular French verbs on horseback. If you believe that, you'll believe anything."

Sunshine streamed into the vast dining room, big enough to dine two score rich men and rich women, crying out for more diners to fill its big spaces, the two of them dwarfed by the dimensions. Cassidy had dimensions on the brain. All those wild figures in Keefe's message setting fire to his brain. A hundred million! Corrupting cops, district attorneys, judges, and—well, how far up the ladder did it go? How about this place? They were running out of money. Yet Shotover Hall ran effortlessly with its platoons of maids and chauffeurs and stable boys and butler.

"Will you take me for another drive on this place? I enjoyed our last drive."

With all her money, Amanda Shotover seemed to have little to do. The servants did it all, even planning the meals. Cassidy was reminded of a passage in Vladimir Nabokov's *Speak, Memory* in which the author wrote that his mother not only had never set foot in the kitchen of their vast St. Petersburg palace but didn't even know where it was.

Cassidy drove the old lady down the mile-and-a-half-long drive under the towering cedars to the main highway. Two miles down the highway was a little gas station which also sold soft drinks and candy. Cassidy got a pocketful of quarters and dimes from the ancient who ran the place and called Lieutenant Fletcher at the precinct station in New York, praying that he was in. He was.

"Have you solved the crime of the century yet, Lieutenant?"

Fletcher uttered a short, sharp obscenity. "Where the hell are you, Cassidy. You're not supposed to have left town."

"I was kidnapped. I'm living in a sea of luxury, all paid for by the CIA. Come on down. I have a lead for you. Very hot stuff."

"I got to have more than that, Cassidy."

"I can't tell you over the phone. These guys got informers in the police department. I don't trust your phone."

Fletcher uttered another obscenity, this one longer and more foul. "The Captain hates detached service. It costs the department money. He won't let me go unless you got something."

"Does the Captain want revenge for the murder of eleven New York cops?" A rhetorical question. The Captain as well as all seventeen thousand other New York cops thirsted for revenge.

"It's an hour by air from La Guardia. There's a ten P.M. plane gets into Marietta Municipal Airport at eleven. Be on it. I'll be waiting for you."

Back in the car, Amanda Shotover said frostily, "We have telephones in Shotover Hall, Professor."

"I fear betrayal," said Cassidy.

Amanda Shotover was indignant. "At Shotover Hall! You mean my telephones are . . . what's that word?"

"Bugged."

He drove back to the little half-concealed entrance to the estate he'd found on horseback and turned into it.

"I didn't know about this road," said Amanda, bewildered and hurt by the discovery, as if someone had defaced her parlor. "Where are we going?"

"Up the mountain," said Cassidy.

The mountain loomed in front of them, not much of a mountain, a tamed, rounded, smoothed-out eastern mountain. The road was narrow and dusty, but it had been used recently. After twenty minutes Cassidy came out on a grassy plateau with a splendid view of the countryside including Shotover Hall.

Ahead of them was a large log cabin, which looked early nineteenth century, with a modern extension of whitewashed brick. Next to it was a finger of steel perhaps two hundred feet high, anchored by steel cable, and next to that was a twelve-foot dish antenna pointed skyward.

Amanda said, "That's old Barker's cabin. He took care of the horses for my husband's father. He built that extension himself. Been dead for years. I'd forgotten it was here."

"Armand remembered," said Cassidy.

They got out of the car. "After Barker died no one would live here. It was too far from the rest of the houses on the estate. What's that big round thing?"

"An antenna," said Cassidy.

Next to the antenna was a smallish rectangle that was a far older instrumentality than the dish antenna—a hive of bees. Bees were flying in and out of the small slit at the bottom of the brood chamber.

Even as they watched, a man came from around the

corner of the house, his face covered by the beekeeper's veil, dressed all in white like an astronaut, his hands in long elbow-length white gloves. At the rear of the cabin were two more beehives the man had been tending to. He watched Amanda and Cassidy as they approached and then spoke in a musical foreign accent. "You were not supposed to come up here, Cassidy. But then, I knew you would. You never obey orders, do you?"

He took off the hat with the beekeeper's veil on it, revealing a square-cut face with piercing blue eyes surmounted by iron-gray hair.

"Yuli," said Cassidy quietly.

"We don't use that name here," said the man.

Cassidy smiled a thin smile. "Kaska then. How are you?"

The two men shook hands warily, like two boxers about to try and knock each other's brains over. "This is Amanda Shotover, Kaska. It's her place."

"Armand's," corrected Amanda.

Kaska bowed from the waist, a little European bow. "You're Armand's mother. I'm Kaska. He must have told you of me."

"No," said the old lady. "He didn't."

"A nice boy," said Kaska.

Cassidy was thinking: Armand is forty years old and still called a boy. Even his mother still spoke of him as if he were six. Aloud he said, "Bees, Kaska? One of your newer enthusiasms?"

"Not at all. I always kept bees in the old country. I like bees very much. Highly disciplined, the bees."

"And hierarchical—just like the old country," Cassidy showed his teeth in one of his ferocious grins. To Armanda he said, "Kaska is a Russian peasant who has not spent much time in Russia in the last thirty years. Aren't you going to ask us in for a cup of tea, Kaska?"

The last thing in the world Kaska wanted. He gave Cassidy a reproachful look, but nevertheless he extended one hand in that infinitely European gesture which means: Won't you step into my parlor. "I'm afraid you'll find it a bit messy."

The cottage was truly a mess. Strewn around the room on tabletops, chairs, the floor, everywhere were cables, dials, printouts, sensors, graphs, electronic junk of all description. On a table at the center of the room, Cassidy recognized an RD-11, the latest of the CIA wonder toys, which could almost read your mind.

Kaska cleared the rest of that table by lifting up piles of printouts and depositing them somewhere else, and seated Amanda at the table with a flourish.

Cassidy cleared off a chair for himself. One of the objects he picked up was a copy of Dostoevsky's *The Possessed* in Russian. Cassidy put the book on top of others in Kaska's arms.

"In his lecture on Russian writers," said Cassidy, "Nabokov said again and again that Dostoevsky was a very poor Russian writer."

"Nabokov," said Kaska quietly, "was a depraved idiot. Not one of ours either. Nabokov himself said he was not a Russian but an American writer who was born in Russia. He had the worst vices of both our countries."

The Russian put the kettle on, talking away in his musical way. "Dostoevsky is the first modern writer. He invented all the others—Faulkner, Sartre, Camus, Joyce, the whole lot."

The tea was delicious. "Literature," said Kaska, "is suffering from obscurantism. Writers are difficult to comprehend for no reason except to be difficult. Why is this? Russian writers have always been accessible in all languages and to all levels of intelligence. Chekhov can be understood by children—and by everyone else—even as complicated an intelligence as yourself, Cassidy."

"Am I complicated?" asked Cassidy mildly.

"Obsessively so. You can look at a piece of pure blue sky and see dragons that are altogether in your mind."

"You should have been a poet, Kaska," said Cassidy. "It would have been more fulfilling than—" he waved his arms, taking in all the electronic junk—"this."

Later going on down the mountain, Amanda said, "He seems a very nice man."

Cassidy chuckled, "He's killed at least thirteen people that I know of. He shot at me twice but missed. Though *why* he missed . . ." Cassidy had never made up his mind about that. Yuli was a marvelous shot. He wouldn't miss. Certainly not twice.

"Oh," said Amanda, the old face crinkled. "I thought you were old friends."

"Well, in a way," said Cassidy and let it go at that.

Kaska had been one of the brightest and most effective KGB agents in Europe until the CIA turned him years earlier.

Cassidy had never believed in the turning. It was one of the many things that had got him into trouble at the CIA, his insistence that Yuli—or Kaska as he now was known— had not been turned, that he was too Russian ever to be turned.

Now the CIA had him on a mountaintop with all that electronic gadgetry—doing what?

Keeping bees.

Cassidy picked up Lieutenant Fletcher at the Marietta Airport at eleven that night and drove him back to Shotover Hall, the atmosphere between them thunderous. "Look," protested Cassidy, "*I* didn't kill those eleven cops."

"You're with the spooks," snarled Fletcher. He was huddled against the door as far away from Cassidy as he could get. "The spooks have throttled us. We can't talk to the press. We can't push our noses anywhere in spic country."

Cassidy spoke soothingly. "It's not the CIA. It's the State Department. These clowns are our allies, God forgive us. The whole country—all of Balisario—is into cocaine. It supports the place, runs the Army, pays the President, everyone. And we're using their soldiers for our cannon fodder to keep nice young American boys from being shot at. Now do you understand?"

"No," said Fletcher, the fury in him boiling away.

Cassidy let him simmer because he hoped the fury would be useful. He drove the CIA car straight to the lake house, mixed the New York detective Wild Turkey and water and sat him down before the huge unlit fireplace.

"Nice setup you got here," said Fletcher bitterly. "You spooks live it up."

Cassidy didn't think of himself as a spook anymore but he didn't want to get into that. "This is a sort of guest house. The main house is up there." He pointed. "I put you down here because I don't want the old lady or anyone else to know you're here. Or why you're here."

"*I* don't know why I'm here."

Cassidy took it slow. "The killers aren't in this country, Lieutenant. They're in Balisario. They went back that night."

"You think I don't know that, spook? You think we're idiots in the New York Police Department?"

"You'll never extradite 'em in a million years," said Cassidy calmly. "Balisario has no laws against drugs, no conspiracy law at all."

"How about murder? They got no laws against that?"

"Come off it, Lieutenant. You people can't make a murder conviction stick in our courts, even when you catch 'em with a smoking gun. Against these guys you got nothing. These soldiers—that's what they were, soldiers obeying orders—these soldiers were never in this country officially at all. They were sneaked in and sneaked out."

"Who sneaked 'em in and out? Your goddamned agency. That's who.

Cassidy took the glass out of Fletcher's hand and filled it again. "We're on the same side of this thing, Lieutenant."

He handed Fletcher the glass and let him drink a mouthful. Then another.

"Good whiskey, Horatio," said Fletcher, the first time he'd used the first name. "What the hell am I doing down here, man? You got something in mind?"

"Yeah," said Cassidy. He outlined it, keeping it simple.

Fletcher sipped his whiskey and listened and sipped some more.

When it was over, he said, "You're insane, Cassidy."

But he was smiling.

Cassidy said, "A little insanity freshens the blood, stimulates the mind, blows away the cobwebs."

"We're likely to get blown away with it."

Cassidy said, "Nobody else is interested in, shall we say, vengeance? The cover-up goes very high. The Agency doesn't want this setup exposed. It isn't even on the books."

"What about the narcs? They got money and manpower. This should be their shtick."

Cassidy explained the politics of drugs control. "It's an alphabetical nightmare. You got the DEA and the ONNI— the Office of National Narcotic Intelligence, a real laugh— and EPIC and IDIG-M—all of them at each other's throats. The first thing they'd do if we invited them in would be to order us off their turf and then botch the job. All these groups are fighting each other so hard they have no energy left to fight the drug problem. This is organized bureaucracy at work, man."

Fletcher kept snapping away, loving the plan and hating it. He was an organization man. "Why not a task force? I could get that approved, if the Commissioner thought there was any chance of nabbing these guys who killed eleven New York cops. . . ."

"We got to keep it under the table. They got informers in your police department. Look." Cassidy hated to part with the information but he did. He showed Fletcher part of Keefe's radio message. Not all of it but some of it.

"Twenty-six million dollars!" exploded Fletcher. "What is this, Cassidy?"

"That's what they're coming back to find. That's what they were looking for in my apartment."

"Jesus!"

"With that kind of money you can corrupt anyone—cops, district attorneys, judges."

"How about you, Cassidy? Are you incorruptible?"

Cassidy laughed. "The devil might manage it. If he promised me I'd know everything—in all languages."

"A real spook. You want all the gossip."

They got down to specifics. When and how much and where. "They're coming back here Thursday at ten P.M. Can you swing it? It doesn't give you much time."

"There are a lot of angry cops in New York. I can try."

Midnight. Even the night frogs had given up and stopped their outcries. Cassidy showed Fletcher his room, the bathroom, the refrigerator, both men groggy with plans. Cassidy was at the door.

Fletcher said; "You think that twenty-six million is here? On this place?"

"There are a lot of hiding places in twenty-seven thousand acres." Cassidy said. "Good night, Lieutenant."

Back in the main house, he climbed the wide, curving stairs built for big nineteenth-century parties where the girls sat in their hoop skirts and spooned with the boys. He was dead on his feet when he entered his room. In the blackness he was feeling for the light switch when the first punch caught him in the stomach, doubling him over. The second blow was at the base of the neck, and Cassidy went out like a candle.

12

Roberto Garcia was eating a melon and reading Jorge Luis Borges at breakfast in his vast dining room when his wife, Maria, pattered in. She looked like three circles—head, bust, the rest of her—placed on top of one another. She had never had breakfast with her husband in her whole life. She stood there—it would never have occurred to her to sit down—while her husband read and munched. Finally he noticed her. "My dear," he said politely. He was always polite to her.

"I was watching over Consuelo as she cleaned your study. A window has been forced."

Without a word Roberto Garcia put down Jorge Luis Borges (a marvelous writer, though politically unreliable) and followed his wife down the long corridor with its murmurous fountain, its massed greenery, the high Spanish windows, to the study with its account books, its neat piles of ledgers (if he didn't keep meticulous accounts, El Presidente would accuse him of stealing), its accounts receivable, all in orderly piles.

Maria showed him the broken sash. "Aah," said the *comendador* "Maria, have you or Consuelo opened any of the ledgers?"

"Of course not."

"I had to be sure, my dear."

He opened the ledger with the principal account—and yes, the hair he'd placed on the edge had fallen into the center fold. Something he'd long feared.

"Thank you, my dear," said Roberto and sent for Arguello.

While he waited, he thought about it. None of the locals would dare. They might shoot at him, blow up his car with himself in it, assassinate his whole family. Enter his study, never.

When Arguello arrived, the *comendador* said: "What foreigners have entered the city in the last forty-eight hours?"

. . . the black snake slithered out of the grapefruit just as he was poised to eat it, a very superior black snake with a demonic face which recalled another demonic face. . . .

Cassidy opened his eyes and found himself staring directly into those of Alison, who was leaning over the bed. From a black snake to Alison. On the other side of the bed was Anne Falk.

"Comment ça va?" said Cassidy. "I love French irregular verbs, especially before breakfast."

"He's delirious," said Alison.

Perhaps. He certainly felt peculiar. Everything was wavy lines—Alison and Anne Falk—coming into focus and going out of focus. "Did someone stick a needle in me? I'm floating in a sea of anomie. What time is it?"

It was 10 A.M. Anne Falk brought him coffee and presently the waviness receded, though he still felt vaguely hilarious, as if everything was very funny.

"We found you on the floor. Anne and I put you on the bed."

"I got punched." Cassidy lurched off the bed across the room to Armand's desk, opened the drawer where he'd put Keefe's decoded message. It was gone. So was the notebook with its record of Armand's coded messages. So was the deed of trust. Cassidy whistled two sharp notes—one high, one low.

One of the radios was gone too—Armand's radio. The other one, set at 21.7, was still there. Cassidy sat down at the desk and turned the machine on. He typed: "Far Bombay," and transmitted it, *blip*, like that.

Alison was looking over his shoulder. "What are you saying?"

"Get out. Fast." The old Keefe-Cassidy code could never be broken because it had never been written down. It was little bits of common experience boiled down to its essence. "It's from an old Frank Sinatra song," said Cassidy. He sang a bit of it:

"Come fly with me, come fly, come fly away.

"If you could use some exotic booze

"There's a bar in far Bombay."

Alison was not entertained. "They can't get out now. They have a mission—to find Harburg."

"Harburg's dead."

Anne Falk standing there, frozen, silent as a stone.

"They got the radio, the code, Armand's messages, the whole bit. They can put it together. I want Keefe and Rattigan to get out of the building wherever they are, take to the woods, anywhere before they're grabbed. Keefe will catch on."

Alison was white. He said, "Anne, leave us, please."

Anne Falk left without a word.

"You're holding out again, Cassidy. Why wasn't I told?"

"The message come in late last night." A lie, but what the hell. Cassidy took the offensive. "Harburg was tortured to death in *el comendador's* private torture chamber. And the same thing is going to happen to Rattigan and Keefe unless we get them out of there fast. You've got to get a plane down there today, this minute. . . ."

"I can't order planes that fast. You know that."

The argument raged, Alison accusing Cassidy of playing his private game, exceeding his instructions. Cassidy hammered away.

"I'll go down there myself. We can't leave them in that hellhole. You do that and no one will ever play games with you again, Alison. By God, I'll go to Philip Hinds myself and spill the whole thing."

"You do that and you're dead, Cassidy. Dead in the water. You won't even have that lousy history post."

They both came up short then, not because of the other's threats but because each of them was horrified at his own intemperance. Their relationship was one of restrained hostility; short, sharp jabs, never the knockout punch. They fed on one another, and they both knew it.

Silence fell. Cassidy looked out at the sunshine on the lawn and got hold of himself. Alison played with his knuckles, standing there in his new beautifully pressed sharkskin suit.

"Perhaps you'd better tell me the rest of that message."

Cassidy told him as much as he could remember, leaving out the numbers and the fact that the soldiers were going to return. He was going to deal with the soldiers privately. He didn't want Alison messing around in it.

"Perhaps I can get a plane today. I'll call now. Will you really go down there, Horatio?"

"Yes."

"It might be dangerous."

"They could use another *pistolero.*"

Alison went to the phone and telephoned Operations. It took a bit of argument, Cassidy staring out the window, feeling the lump at the base of his neck. A professional blow.

114

Why hadn't he been killed? The sensible thing to do. Outside, one of the farm's new thirty-five-thousand-dollar tractors carried a large round bale on its forks to the stud farm below.

"The plane should get here at ten tonight. That's seven in Balisario. You should arrive about eleven-thirty their time."

Cassidy sat down at the machine and typed out: TWENTYTHREEE SKIDOO LEONARDO ASP. The machine digested this gibberish and turned it into even greater gibberish at high speed and then set it out at even higher speed, *blip*.

Alison was saying, "There's only one airport in the whole country, largely unpoliced. We can just get the jets into it. The airport manager, Hans Raddermacher, a German, is in our pocket—most of the time."

Cassidy was shaving and he grunted. "What do you mean—most of the time?"

"When El Presidente gets in a temper about something, Raddermacher has to pay attention, or he'd lose his job— and maybe his life. It could get nasty."

Already Cassidy was regretting having volunteered. He hated leaving Lucia, but he couldn't run out on Keefe and Rattigan.

He looked into the mirror and bared his yellow teeth in a snarl. "What brings you down here, Hugh? Besides social climbing?"

Alison looked at him, not rising to the needle, the knuckles white.

"Armand has disappeared."

"Jupiter!" Cassidy's strongest cuss word.

"He came out of the coma yesterday. Snap! Like that. The doctors say that sometimes happens. They just wake up. Even his shoulder wound has pretty well healed. I was going down there today to debrief him myself when they called."

"You think he was grabbed?"

"Nobody knew he was in that safe house. Nobody, I swear. Nobody at the Agency."

Cassidy was thinking about the case of a young cocaine courier in Florida. They'd taken him into the Everglades and cut his ears off, then they shot him. The police found him and took him to the hospital where the doctors patched him up. When he came to, he went out the window, terrified they'd come back and cut something else off—his balls, his feet, his head. They were a tough bunch.

Alison was saying, "That's why I came here. I thought he might have come here."

"Have you talked to the old lady about her son?"

"I thought you might do that. You have such a way with old ladies, Horatio." A bit of a snarl in that last sentence.

Cassidy said, "Did you take his money away? He had quite a lot of cash in a briefcase when he was in my apartment."

"Just some of the loot, not all of it. You can't carry twenty-six million dollars around in a briefcase."

Cassidy kept his face on straight. A bit of an effort. Twenty-six million dollars. He hadn't told Alison that number, hadn't mentioned that number at all. A fellow could go through life and never mention twenty-six million, not once.

"What makes you think he'd come here, Hugh? Last I saw him he was on his way to the *New York Times* to spill his guts."

"I think he's changed his mind about that."

"Now, Hugh, what did you do to the poor innocent to change his mind?"

"It wasn't me changed his mind. I haven't seen him. Anyway I'm only guessing."

Cassidy doubted that.

Cassidy changed his shirt and combed his hair.

"Shall we join the ladies?"

In Balisario it was 7 A.M. when the *blip* on the machine woke Rattigan. He crawled out of bed and read the message aloud: "FAR BOMBAY."

Keefe was barely awake, shaking the sleep out of his skull.

Far below them, on the first floor, came the tramp of feet, many feet.

"Far Bombay?" Keefe blinking. It struck home. That and the marching feet.

"Holy Mother of God!" He was out of the bed, reaching for his trousers. "Into your clothes, man. They're coming after us."

Rattigan was already pulling on his shirt.

They'd rehearsed the exit, picked the top floor for this very emergency. Rattigan slung the radio around his neck, stuffed the silenced .25 into one back pocket, his big .44 magnum in the other, coiled the rope around his stomach. Keefe was unfolding the steel ladder, then held it out the window, holding it tight against the building with his massive arms. Rattigan, agile as a monkey, shinnied up the ladder from Keefe's shoulders, leaped over the parapet onto the flat roof, took the steel ladder away from Keefe, and laid in on the roof.

He was uncoiling the knotted rope, which he was to steady around the drainpipe for Keefe to climb up, when he heard Keefe's agonized whisper: "Bust it, lad. They're at the door."

Keefe had his magnum in hand, but the odds were too great. He was facing three soldiers with carbines in their hands.

Keefe dropped the magnum and turned on his big Irish smile. "Aah, *guardia*! How was I to know? I was afraid you were *pistoleros*! Welcome, *amigos*! Let me pour you a little something to cement our relationship!" And other Irish malarkey, none of which did any good.

Rattigan huddled under the parapet on the roof, listening.

They trussed Keefe up under the direction of a demon-faced leader called Arguello, and when they'd finished, the demon-faced one barked out a single word: "*Sótano!*"

Rattigan on the roof formed an O with his lips. *Sótano.* Roberto Garcia's private torture chamber.

A few minutes later—the soldiers had tramped off down the stairs—the radio cradled in Rattigan's arms gave a *blip*. Rattigan laid it flat on the roof. As always, the machine took its time digesting the message, then rattled it off at high speed.

TWENTYTHREE SKIDOO LEONARDO ASP.

Rattigan smiled a little sad clown's smile. Cassidy would be at the airport at 11:30 that night. Keefe would be in the *sótano*, that bourne from which no traveler returns, sixteen and a half hours. . . .

Roberto Garcia had a full morning. It started badly at the *palacio* with a shouting affray in which El Presidente did all the shouting and Roberto all the listening, followed by a disheartening inspection of the M-12 tanks the Americans had unloaded on them. (The gringos were sticking them with all the outworn, unworkable junk every other country had refused.)

There were some bright moments—a review of the cavalry honor guard at the *palacio*, the guard wearing the new uniforms, all blue and gold and resplendent, that Roberto had himself designed; a very fine luncheon in his own dining room with three of his officers, the few intelligent ones on his staff, and after that a long siesta with his mistress, Ramona, a passionate girl of eighteen, in the hacienda he'd bought her on the outskirts of town.

It was well past five before he got to the *sótano*. Keefe was lying on the iron bed, manacled to it by arm and foot, exuding Irish charm. "Roberto Garcia," he boomed. "How nice of you to drop in! The very man I came to Balisario to see. I have some very nice Kalashnikovs for your *soldados*—barely used, very low priced. . . ."

"Have you, indeed?" Roberto sat on the camp stool, full of his own Hispanic bonhomie. "I hope you've been quite comfortable."

"The stink, your worship, is very bad. I have known sewers that smelled better than this cell, your honor, not meaning any offense. Now, if you'd just explain to this nice fellow that there has been a ghastly mistake. I am a respectable arms merchant. It was I, your reverence, who sold you those magnificent German machine guns three years ago. . . ."

"You broke into my study," said Roberto pleasantly.

Juan was already fixing the electrodes on Keefe's ankles.

"Señor, why would I do such a thing? Dear boy—" this to Juan—"let's have none of that! *Comendador*, what is it you wish to know? I will tell you every . . . eeeeeYOW . . ."

Roberto had the rheostat in his hand and he was smiling. "Just a test, señor, to see how well the connection is working. Shall we begin? What is your name, señor—your real name, please?"

"Clancy, your worship. Jasper Clancy, at your service. EeeeeYIIII . . ." The current coursing up his legs straight into his vocal cords, Irish tenor and very strong.

Roberto was feeling a sexual pleasure almost exactly equal to the voltage—surely there was a physiological equation there that bore looking into. . . . "I don't entirely trust that name Jasper Clancy. Entirely too euphonic. Try again."

Another squirt of electricity, Keefe howling like a wolf, which was the right way to handle electricity. Let it all hang out, if only to make the torturer think it's worse than it is and delay, delay, delay. . . .

"Your reverence, you are interfering with my thought processes. How can a man concentrate on the questions with this electricity pulsing through his very soul? What sort of

name would you like? A Spanish name? How about
Valdez . . . iiiiiIIIIyYEEEE."

A high-pitched scream, Roberto listening as if to a violin
sonata.

"I think the electricity is getting to the bottom of your
black heart, where resides no thought processes at all."
Roberto turned up the rheostat, recalling through Keefe's
howls that one of the many things he'd been upbraided for
by El Presidente that morning was his extravagant use of
expensive electricity when there were so many cheaper
instrumentalities—knives, whips, thumbscrews, spikes—
that could accomplish the same results at so much less cost.

Keefe had collapsed into himself, his eyes closed, his
mouth open, head hanging over the side of the bed. Roberto
was skeptical. He inflicted a shot of juice on the recumbent
Irishman. The body twitched galvanically, but there was no
sound.

"A little water," said Roberto to Juan, who drenched
Keefe with a pail of cold water. Keefe shuddered and
moaned and presently opened his eyes.

"How are your thought processes, señor?" asked Roberto
solicitously.

Keefe took a long time replying (delay, delay, delay!)
going into the second part of his act. Where before he was
nimble witted, now he was slow, contrite, humble. "My
name is . . . O'Malley. Sean O'Malley . . . one of the Cork
O'Malleys, your worship. . . . You must surely have heard of
the Cork O'Malleys? . . . ."

All this coming out of Keefe's mouth so slowly, so faintly
that Roberto laid aside the rheostat for the moment and
engaged in conversation.

"What a big fellow you are! The biggest, I believe, we
have ever entertained here, eh, Juan?" He did not want to
lose this fine fellow just yet. He didn't get a literate fellow
like this very often, and Roberto relished the dialogue of
torment. Many of his torturees could barely talk at all

beyond curses, and even the curses were of low imagination. Whereas this delightful Irish could speak whole balanced sentences and when the time for cursing came—as it would—the oaths should be truly monumental. But there was no hurry.

Roberto gave Keefe a glass of water before resuming and when he got back to the questions—who sent you and why—he kept the voltage low. In gratitude Keefe kept his fainting spells at the minimum and unloosed a flood of information, all of it false as a crooked judge. Roberto deeply distrusted this information, but there was plenty of time, when he'd turn up the juice to get some real answers. . . .

After an hour and a half he took off the electrodes with his own hands and bathed Keefe's burned ankles with soda water and cold cream.

13

Before the others were awake, Cassidy drove Lieutenant Fletcher to the airport, down the long driveway under the big cedars past the blooded Jersey cows, the thoroughbred horses, the whitewashed cottages of the farm workers, Fletcher taking it all in with his twisted Brooklyn smile.

"Ever been to Matteawan?" said the Lieutenant. "Big place for criminally insane up the Hudson. Looks just like this."

"I'll tell Amanda Shotover. She'll be amused."

"I'll bet."

"You've got two and a half days, Lieutenant. Can you do it?"

"Eleven dead cops is strong incentive."

Cassidy was counting on that.

"Highest secrecy. If it gets around, we're dead."

As if Fletcher didn't know.

Alison left next. Alison in his knife-crease sharkskin suit, his stick (with the single-shot .38 in the handle), his specially built calfskin briefcase (with the built-in radio). Also the blow drier for his hair, which he was never without. Alison was combed, shaved, washed, blow-dried, pressed, shined, polished, perfumed—and Cassidy admired him perhaps a little too extravagantly. "You look," said Cassidy, "the way I wish I'd look when I'm in my cóffin. The way a man should look when he goes into the great beyond."

"You don't believe in the great beyond," said Alison. "Mind, you call the moment you're back. I want to know everything."

"Even at four in the morning?"

Alison winced and stepped into the long black limousine (bulletproof, souped up to go 140 miles an hour if necessary) with its black chauffeur. Alison sat in the back with the glass partition between chauffeur and passenger closed. The last of him Cassidy saw as the car went down the long driveway, Alison was taking out the speaker of his radio and was talking to Langley, to the President, to God, anyway to someone important because he had his important look—respectful but authoritative—telling the important one half a secret. Alison never told a whole secret to anyone, not even God.

After lunch Cassidy and Amanda Shotover sat down to a game of cribbage. He let the old lady win one and then broke the news.

"Armand!" she said, taut as a spring. It was hard to tell if she was pleased. She stood up, all four feet six of her. The cribbage game was definitely over. "You think he's here?"

Cassidy was adding up the score, not looking at her. "Do *you* think he's here? You're his mother."

"You think I know his mind because I'm his mother? Don't be silly. The delivery boys know more about Armand than I do. If he's here, why hasn't he presented himself?"

Presented himself. As if at court.

Cassidy put the cribbage set in its little Chinese lacquered box. "Because he's afraid of Alison, I think. Maybe of Anne . . . his fiancée."

Dropping the other shoe.

"Fiancée! Fiddlesticks."

Not many used fiddlesticks anymore. The contemporary term was bullshit. . . .

"Didn't you know?" asked Cassidy.

"I don't believe it. He wouldn't. He couldn't."

"Why not?"

"Because I won't allow it!"

As if he were six years old. It was his place, not hers. Still: "I won't allow it."

Cassidy shifted his ground. "Armand spent his whole life here. Where was his favorite hideout? He must have had one."

A crafty look appeared in the old woman's eyes. Pure malice.

"Barker's place. Atop the mountain. He loved to get as far away from me as possible."

The rest of the afternoon Cassidy spent with Lucia riding in the woods, letting her show him her treasure spots, Cassidy telling her nothing because she'd want to come along.

They were walking the horses through the thick woods, brushing the branches away from their faces, Lucia very much at ease on the big horse, Cassidy tense and tight, the worst way to be.

"You sure we're not lost?"

"I know these woods—every foot. Just follow along."

They found it half a mile further along.

"My witch's cottage!" said Lucia blissfully. "Look how the roof slants. It's like a child's drawing! The whole house leans over like a drunken sailor. I love it. I want it for my very own!"

The porch, which ran clear around the house, was crumbling away and it, too, leaned drunkenly. The long walls, however, were still firmly in place, but chinks showed where the plaster had fallen away. Cassidy got off his horse and walked inside, looking for footprints. There were lots of those—too many.

"Anne and I have been here several times," Lucia said.

Anne Falk had not been seen all morning.

"Shall we go upstairs?" said Cassidy.

"I wouldn't dare. Look at the staircase."

It leaned like the rest of the house. "I think it's all right," said Cassidy. He walked up slowly, looking for prints in the dust, but the stairs were too rough to tell much.

Lucia on his heels.

"Anne says it's an old slave cabin. There were a whole nest of them out here, but the others have crumbled away because they were thin clapboard while this one is log. . . ." Lucia chattering away.

There were four rooms on top, the doors hanging open on three of them. Bedsprings rusting away. A tall cupboard with its door hanging askew. A broken chair in one. In another a marble-topped washbasin once elegant, cast off from the big house when they put in running water.

"You didn't come up here before?"

"No."

Somebody had. The wood floor was full of prints. One door was locked. Cassidy put his back to it, the whole house shaking. But the door remained tightly shut.

"Perhaps it's rusted shut. Or something is leaning against it inside," said Lucia.

"Yeah," said Cassidy.

They went down the leaning stairs, out into the mottled forest sunshine, mounted their horses. Could he find the place again? Well, Lucia could. Anne Falk could.

It was a big place, 27,642 acres. Plenty of room to hide twenty-six million dollars.

"He loves to get as far away from me as possible."

Why had he never left Shotover Hall? The other brothers all had.

The little CIA jet came in at 10 P.M. right on the button. Cassidy's luggage consisted entirely of his little pencil flashlight in an inside pocket, his .357 magnum in his armpit, his switchblade in his side pocket. The pilot was Herman Deidrich, a silent stateless fellow sucked up out of one of the wastelands long ago. The co-pilot was Jorge Mendoza, an Hispanic from New York who spoke the language.

Cassidy slept all the way to Balisario.

Mendoza woke him with bad news. "We've been warned off."

Cassidy shaking the sleep out of his head. "Warned off?"

Mendoza pointed out the window. An orange glow in the black night, thirty thousand feet straight down.

"Signal fire. Stay away. That's the message."

Cassidy fully awake, raging, "We can't stay away! Two of our men down there in bad trouble."

Mendoza stared out at the orange glow. "Those are the orders. Signal fire. No dice. You want to join your friends, you hit the silk. We can't take the plane in."

Cassidy hated all of it. He'd only jumped once—and been scared out of his skull. This would be worse. Jumping into a strange country, not knowing who was down there.

"How do I make contact?"

"Head for the fire. Should be friends set that fire—unless. . . ."

Unless the signal had been tortured out of his friends, in which case. . . .

Cassidy went forward and talked to the pilot—codes, radio channels, time, procedures.

Crazy, all of it.

He hadn't even said good-bye to Lucia or told her he was going away.

The plane circled back toward the fire, thirty thousand feet down, Cassidy in the jump suit. Where do my loyalties lie? To my adopted daughter? To my friends below? Everyone gets what he richly deserves—so says the philosopher Tzung Te, a very great man. . . .

Cassidy jumped into the icy blackness, arms spread outward as if praying. To whom—Jupiter? Jesus was a minor deity who didn't play at thirty thousand feet, a ground-level earthling god not negotiable in the upper air.

The black cold taking his breath away, counting one, two, pick up your shoe, three, four, open the door, five, six, pick up sticks. Groucho Marx had once found himself suspended upside down from thirty feet up, and he said to himself he said: "What am I doing at my age, sixty, hanging upside down in this ridiculous caper?" and straightaway quit moviemaking forever. Here am I tumbling through this black hole at my advanced age. Why didn't I quit when I was ahead—if I was ever ahead? Arms outstretched as if begging forgiveness. From Lucia. So irrevocable (that unforgiving word), jumping out of airplanes. Or buildings. Hurtling, outstretched, to an unknown destiny through the black night and who knows what lurks near that orange glow below, hello, hello. We have been betrayed. Nobody knew I was coming, so why is the plane warned off? Something rotten in Balisario. Or Virginia. Or both.

The chute opened automatically at ten thousand feet, pulling Cassidy seatwise, slowing the stream of consciousness, slowing everything. I wish I were on Thirteenth Street asleep, back in Virginia, anywhere. The fire drifting off to the right. The night chute black as ink, billowing overhead.

Cassidy pulled the cords and sideslipped the chute back to a spot over the fire on the ground, falling fast. He felt for the .357 magnum in the jump suit. He would have trouble grabbing it if those were unfriendlies, but he didn't dare pull it out for fear of losing it. The ground coming up fast. Were those trees? Yes, they were. He didn't want anything to do with trees, pulling the cord again, slipping out of reach of the branches in the nick of time, his bent legs touching down, tumbling him over and over, fighting the cords. . . .

He was on his feet, unsnapping the harness, when a pair of arms encircled his shoulders.

"Buenas noches, señor!"

Right in his ear.

Rattigan with his little clown smile, holding him upright against the pulling chute.

"Thought you'd never get here!"

"Suavamente, señor."

Rattigan pointed to his ears. After that, everything in whispers, the two of them gathering up the chute.

"Where's Keefe?"

Rattigan told him.

All the news, very bad. Rattigan had been in the brush beside the runway, staying out of sight, waiting for Cassidy's plane when the *guardia* arrived, two jeeploads, eight in all. Very sinister. The airport was never patrolled by *guardia*. Customs and Immigration had their own guards and they were in the pockets of the Agency, some of them actually agents. *Guardia* represented Hermanos Fuentes, El Presidente, a nasty fellow.

"You would have walked off the plane right into their arms," whispered Rattigan. He pointed to the airfield two hundred yards off, two *guardia* marching along the near perimeter.

Cassidy mussed his hair, thanking him.

"We had Fuentes bought," whispered Rattigan, "but he didn't stay bought. They never stay bought. Who said that—Napoleon?"

Everyone said that. It was one of the great universal truths. Betrayal went to the highest bidder and the bidders changed daily.

They bundled up the chute and walked in the darkness, Rattigan leading him by hand away from the airfield to the road, where Cassidy walked right into the car, banging his knees.

Even in the blackness he could make out that it was very

old. Running boards. When did cars last have running boards—in the thirties?

Rattigan talking in ordinary tones now. "A long walk to Balisario from the airport. Ten miles. I didn't want to do it again, so I liberated this antique from the *colono*. . . ."

"You took care of the *colono*?"

"He sleeps, not quite forever. I jabbed a little needle into him. Perhaps twenty-four hours. If we're not out by then, we're in big trouble."

Rattigan showed Cassidy where to set the spark, and what to do if the ancient Ford caught hold. Rattigan spun the crank again and again and yet again before it shook itself awake, coughing and spitting. . . .

"Dare we risk a light?"

"No."

Rattigan drove, face uplifted as if to God, guiding the car through the trees at about ten miles an hour. Cassidy watched the road for sleeping oxen while Rattigan told him all about Roberto Garcia and his *sótano* and his nasty habits. "A very polite torturer. Always asks if you are quite comfortable before turning on the juice. Always bathes the wounds afterwards."

"If there are no survivors, who tells these tales?"

Rattigan smiled his sad clown's smile. "Common knowledge. Perhaps he tells on himself. It's a comical country—if you like black comedy."

Folklore, Cassidy was thinking. There are some things the people know without being told—like Roberto's asking if you're comfortable before applying the torment. The dead cry out—and these things pass into tribal memory along with all the other enormities. . . .

The ancient Ford with its brass square-cut radiator drifting through the black night, spluttering and coughing. The noise was not a healthy thing in the curfew but better than lights, which gave away too much, said Rattigan.

They were in the town now, feeling their way at five miles

an hour, when the shot whistled over their heads, the report distant. Cassidy ducked instinctively. Rattigan smiled his clown smile. "They always miss. Well, almost always."

"Perhaps they don't want to hit."

"No, it's naked incompetence, of which there is an enormous amount in Balisario. The trains do not run on time here. In fact, they don't run at all. Nothing works here except the torture chambers—and the Church."

Rattigan pulled the old car to the curb and turned off the engine. He was back to whispering again. "We'll have to walk from here. We'd better send an ETA."

He got out the radio. The two men looked at their watches—1 A.M.—and made their calculations. Rescue Keefe. Get back to the airport. Take out eight *guardia*. Dance a hornpipe. Kiss a few girls. Sing a song of sixpence—all in one hour. Well, perhaps an hour and fifteen minutes. And if they didn't do all those things in one hour and fifteen minutes, the plane and the pilot and co-pilot — that stateless German and that New York Hispanic with the contemptuous sneer—were for it up to their assholes. Cassidy coded the bit and sent it out, *blip*, like that. To the CIA plane which was on its way to Texas for more fuel.

They were on their feet now, Cassidy carrying the aluminum ladder, down the avenida to the little side street, the farthest away from the guard tower, the air smelling of hibiscus and jacaranda, languorous, voluptuous smells, all wrong for the task at hand.

Rattigan was first up the ladder, snipping the wires and pulling them apart. Cassidy climbed the ladder and stood precariously on the broken bottles while Rattigan pulled up the ladder and put it down the other side. Far away the tree frogs sounded their love song, sharp and querulous.

The big house dark and silent.

Cassidy went down the ladder first and held the ladder for Rattigan. They were folding up the ladder when the beast struck, straight at Cassidy's throat, and only the fact that he had the ladder before his face kept the snapping jaws away. The dog bounced off the ladder and made for Rattigan. Rattigan shot him through the mouth with the silenced .25—and still he came on—tumbling Rattigan over backward. When Cassidy pulled the dog away, it was dead.

Rattigan astonished. His comical friendly dog! But it wasn't. Another dog altogether. There had been a changing of the guard, a tightening of security. Bad news. The two men stood stock-still, getting breath back to normal, listening hard.

It had been a piece of cake. So Rattigan had told Cassidy. A piece of cake. The first time.

Footfalls now near the house. Unhurried, unalarmed footsteps. A man making a routine patrol. A soft, wheedling call: "Pelo! Pelo!" Calling the dog.

Rattigan tapped Cassidy on the shoulder and waggled the silenced .25 under his nose. He crept away. Cassidy put his hands in front of his face to diminish the whiteness, wishing they'd blacked up. No time! No time! Peeking out behind fingers.

"Pelo! Pelo!"

The call much closer. Cassidy could see the man now between his outstretched fingers. In another moment the man would see him. Cassidy had the .357 in his hand.

Shusss! The silenced .25 sounded its sibilants like a steam pipe.

The man fell forward at Cassidy's feet, blood pouring from his ear. Not quite dead. The body convulsed and rolled over, eyes staring at Cassidy, accusing, the mouth open. But no sound came. The accusing eyes dimmed and the mouth went slack. A brown face, quite young, the character still unformed on young cheeks, young brow, young mouth.

Rattigan led Cassidy away by the hand. The two saying nothing because there might be others, treading silently on the hard earth, listening for footsteps, for breathing, for anything.

At the study window, Rattigan went up the aluminum ladder, the steel in his hand. Again things had changed. The window was bolted shut, solid as a bank vault. Rattigan had to use the cutters and then his little saw, making a hell of a noise, taking too much time. Cassidy looking at his watch ticking away. They'd now chewed up twelve minutes of their hour and a quarter.

Rattigan was inside the house now, beckoning. Cassidy followed him in, the two men inside Roberto Garcia's study. There was no time to be lost but still Cassidy tarried in the study while Rattigan went searching for the right door to the *sótano*.

Cassidy risked a light, the little hooded pencil light which shot out its private ray discreet as a bank teller, Cassidy searching for he knew not what. The ledgers they already had. It would be elsewhere. Cassidy went through the drawers looking for a name, an identity.

Victor.

Bank statements. Correspondence with banks all in Spanish. He flipped through the letters, looking for names. Bahamian banks. Swiss banks. Roberto had other weaknesses besides torture. Money.

Rattigan at his side now, whispering: "I've got it!"

Cassidy sighed. He could have spent an hour with these papers. He stuffed a wad of bank letters into the pocket of his jump suit and followed along through the darkened house, down the long gallery, past the murmurous fountain under the high windows, past the foliage and into the kitchen.

The door to the *sótano* stood open. Cassidy went down first with his pencil light darting about—the .357 in the other hand, himself jumpy as a cat. Rattigan followed with the silenced .25 in hand. The long corridor smelling of earth and country vegetables. At the end of it they found the steel door under which shone a sliver of light. Rattigan saw the light first and called Cassidy's attention to it. Cassidy thought it over, the pencil light exploring the steel door. At eye level was the square eyehole of the sort used the world over in prisons and whorehouses to check who's trying to get in.

Cassidy lifted the iron latch gently and pushed. Locked. He turned off the pencil flash and in the blackness opened the little eyehole. The guard Juan was asleep on a chair, his upper half sprawled across a table.

Cassidy let Rattigan have a look.

The two men tried the door again, pushing hard with their shoulders. It didn't budge. The door felt solid as cement; Cassidy was sure there was a crossbar, probably of oak, holding it closed. They couldn't shoot it out or smash it open with their shoulders.

Cassidy made a mouth with fingers and thumb—flapping it up and down and pointing to Rattigan's mouth. Rattigan was better with the Spanish.

Rattigan scowled his clown's scowl. He didn't like it. He shut his eyes, took a deep breath, thought about it.

Then he put his mouth to the eyehole and bawled—very loud: "Juan! Juan!"

He'd got the name from the bar boy at Diablo's. Juan loomed large in Balisario demonology.

"Pronto! Pronto! Juan!"

The figure sprawled on the table stirred and the head came up.

Rattigan threw his high hard one: *"El comendador es asesinado! Socorro! Socorro!"*

It had to be shocking to inhibit thought. To get him to open the door without thinking. Juan and *el comendador* had shared many delightful murders and nothing brings men closer than that. Rattigan kept bawling out the shocking news: *"Es asesinado, el comendador! Juan! Prisa! Prisa!"*

Juan was awake now, stumbling toward the door, eyes

wide with the shocking news. He pulled the crossbar up and opened the door.

Rattigan shot him between the eyes with the silenced .25.

Cassidy caught the body as it fell forward and pulled it back into the corridor. Rattigan went through the pockets for keys.

The door to the torture chamber was unlocked. Keefe lay on the cot, manacled hand and foot to the springs, grinning hugely.

"Bejesus and bejabbers!" Keefe claimed to be the only living Irishman who still used that antique expression. "Welcome to Balisario, Professor! You should feel right at home, you slimy medievalist, in this citadel of culture. Mankind's oldest traditions are preserved here—torture, starvation, poverty—with the reverence they deserve."

Cassidy was examining the wounds on the ankles. Rattigan was opening the locks on the manacles.

"You might say hello, greetings, and all that, you two, instead of looking so glum."

"We couldn't get a word in edgewise," said Cassidy. "Can you travel on those ankles?"

"I shouldn't be surprised. The feet are okay. They didn't use the bastinado, don't you know. These modern torturers have turned their backs on the bastinado in their enchantment with electricity, thinking this is an improvement over the old methods, which it isn't. Now where's the whiskey? Don't tell me you two fellows haven't brought a drop of cheer for the victim? What kind of angel of mercy is it that would be so neglectful?"

Cassidy pulled a pint of Wild Turkey from the pocket of his jump suit and handed it to Keefe. "Two big swigs and that is all," he said. "We have many miles before we sleep, ye drunken sot. Sssh. . . ."

They listened hard. A rattle of small sounds as if the house was shuddering under its accumulation of horrors.

Keefe took two deep swallows of the whiskey, stood up,

and pitched forward. "Jesus, Mother and Mary!" he gasped, the face white. "They've done something to the muscles."

Cassidy and Rattigan pulled him off the floor and he tried again, his face contorted. "Better!" gasped Keefe. "Better than the first time! Let's have a go!"

He had an arm around the shoulders of Cassidy and Rattigan. They had their arms around his waist. It was slow work but they got him down the corridor, which smelled like a sewer, and into the other corridor, which smelled of fresh vegetables and earth, Rattigan closing the door with the dead Juan on the far side.

Keefe's legs couldn't manage the stairs, so they had to carry him up.

"We'll never get him out the window," whispered Cassidy. "It's the front door." Down the murmurous gallery with its fountain and flowers, they went to the huge main door imbedded in a gray stone which was pierced with small windows in colored glass. Cassidy doused the pencil light when he saw the windows.

The big door was locked with an immense brass key sticking out from the iron lock. Cassidy unlocked it, and the two men supporting Keefe between them went down the stone steps into the dark garden.

Out of the blackness, like a blow in the face, came the searchlight, the blinding white light missing them by two feet. The three men had been making their way, slowly because of Keefe's great weight, along the edge of the house, which was bordered by masses of elegant bushes with shiny green leaves. The three men dove into the shiny green leaves and hunkered down, waiting for the shots.

No shots. Instead there were voices. Two voices talking in Spanish argot, low, indistinct. The voices came from the guard tower where the searchlight was; there appeared to be an argument. The men under the cover of the shiny leaves could see the light probing here and there.

Cassidy could hear the men clumping down their wooden

ladder from the guard tower. The garden was still lit by the searchlight, but now the beam lay still. Cassidy groped for his switchblade in the upper pocket of his jump suit. Rattigan was next to him, the two men face to face. Cassidy opened the switchblade in Rattigan's face. The little man nodded and drew out his ice pick from his boot.

The grumbling voices getting closer now, the argot a little clearer. The guards had a flashlight, which they were shooting this way and that.

Cassidy hunched forward on his knees. The flashlight swung suddenly straight into Cassidy's face and at that moment he sprang, so swiftly he bumped into the man's Kalashnikov and turned it sidewise with his left hand. With his right, he slashed the man's throat. One slash, one push. The man went backward, the blood gushing like a fountain. The Kalashnikov was in Cassidy's left hand, jerked loose by the man's fall.

All this in the bright glare of the searchlight.

Two feet away, Rattigan sat astride the other guard, wrenching his ice pick from the man's ear.

All of it very well lit by the searchlight, both men breathless with anticipation of bullets. No shot came from either watchtower. The two dead ones were the whole watch team.

With Rattigan's help, Cassidy pulled Keefe out of the bushes and onto his feet. The three men, Keefe's arms around the shoulders of the other two, hobbled slowly down the main path to the steel main gate. There Rattigan clambered up into the watchtower and turned off the searchlight but not before Cassidy looked at his watch. Twenty-one more minutes had elapsed since he'd last looked. Forty-two minutes before the CIA jet came back.

Seven minutes of this was spent getting Keefe to the ancient Ford; the big Irishman was suspended between Rattigan and Cassidy, his legs slowly pumping back to life. "I'm getting the hang of the thing," he whispered. "Another hundred yards and I'll be pole vaulting."

"Ssh," said Cassidy.

Rattigan set the spark and spun the crank—and spun it and spun it. It was Keefe who spotted the trouble. In his preoccupation with the spark, Rattigan had forgotten to turn the key to the *on* position. The car chuffed off without lights at five miles an hour. Rattigan at the wheel, Keefe next to him on the front seat, Cassidy in the back with magnum in hand. Making too much noise. When they had left the town, Rattigan accelerated to ten, sometimes fifteen miles an hour.

It still took nineteen of their precious minutes to get to the little dirt road adjoining the airport where there was much to be done. First they had to set two fires, fifty yards apart. That was the agreed signal. Otherwise the CIA pilot wouldn't come in. The old fire Rattigan had set was still glowing faintly in thick brush, screened from the airport by a line of tall trees. With a pair of pliers he found in the Ford toolbox, Rattigan pulled out a couple of embers from the old fire and set a new one while Cassidy revived the old fire with pine boughs and dead wood.

Keefe was left on guard with the Kalashnikov Cassidy had taken off the dead man in Garcia's garden. He had a good view of the airfield a hundred yards away. The *guardia* were patrolling the perimeters, two of them at the head of the runway three-quarters of a mile from the airport building, itself a modest tin structure with a big plate-glass window overlooking the field. Two others patrolled the east perimeter and the other two the west perimeter. One *soldado* would march along his particular edge of the airfield as his colleague marched toward him. They'd meet in the middle, about-face, and march back.

The two *cabos* were acting like noncoms everywhere. They were taking their ease in the airport lounge, seated in wicker armchairs, drinking coffee, plainly visible through the plate-glass window.

The two jeeps sat unattended on the tarmac.

When Cassidy and Rattigan finished with their fires and came back to the Ford, there were four minutes left to take out eight guards. Far away, very high, they could hear the approaching jet. Cassidy's plan was wild and vicious. No one had a better one.

They waited until the four guards on the east and west perimeters had their backs to the airport building and were marching to the center. Cassidy and Rattigan broke into a dead run toward the two jeeps.

Keefe stood up in the front seat of the Ford and leveled the Kalashnikov along the edge of the windshield.

If the keys were not in the ignition, Cassidy and Rattigan would have had to deal with the two *cabos* on the spot, but the keys *were* in the ignition. The two men flung themselves into the two jeeps, started the cars, and raced off on divergent paths—Cassidy to the east perimeter, Rattigan to the west.

The two *cabos* dropped their coffee cups and came racing out of the airport terminal firing their handguns wildly after the jeeps.

Fifty yards away Keefe sighted down the barrel of the Kalashnikov and squeezed off a shot that caught the lead *cabo* in the chest and sent him sprawling head over heels. The other *cabo* reversed himself and ran back toward the building. He was only a step away when Keefe's second shot caught him in the back, folding him up like an accordion, Keefe wincing. He didn't like shooting men in the back, not even noncoms.

Cassidy had turned on his headlights, the better to confuse the *soldados*, who were already very confused by the shooting and the sight of their jeeps pelting at them. They were too far away to see what the shooting was all about, and Cassidy was counting on their assumption that the *cabos* were driving the jeeps.

With the windshield down flat in front of him, Cassidy drove at fifty miles an hour toward the nearest *soldado*, who stood waiting for him with his rifle hanging from his hand. When he was twenty feet away, Cassidy swerved the jeep and accelerated right into him, hitting him with a sickening crunch. Hating himself for it.

The left wheel passed directly over the *soldado*, sending the jeep into a wild skid which turned it over, Cassidy flying through the air into the brush where he rolled twice, the breath clean out of him. The .357 had been on the seat next to him and that flew off into the darkness.

Cassidy on his back fighting for his breath. Where the hell was the other *soldado*, the man's partner? Then he saw him twenty feet away, calmly aiming his rifle at him, Cassidy, with no breath in him to move a muscle, seeing only that long black barrel aimed right at his chest from so short a distance even a Balisario *soldado* could hardly miss, though he seemed to be taking a bloody long time about it.

The man's mouth flew open and he crumpled his arms outward, the rifle falling away. Only later did Cassidy hear the report. A very long shot, but Keefe was an expert.

Cassidy rolled the body over to make sure. Another young face, a boy scarcely in his teens. Cassidy picked up the boy's Kalashnikov, wishing he were back in Virginia.

I shouldn't be doing this. This is none of my affair.

The CIA jet was closer, much closer. Cassidy could hear the roar and even see the blinking lights. Maybe five miles away. In jet time, that was no distance at all and much still to be done.

The other jeep was zigzagging crazily across the airport straight at Cassidy. Cassidy could hear the shots and see the flashes from the other side of the field.

Rattigan pulled up next to him, shouting, "Get in!" Cassidy jumped aboard and the jeep roared off on its zigzag path toward the airport building.

"What's up?"

"Got one. Had trouble with the other."

Cassidy hanging on. "Where we going?"

"Got to collect Keefe. We're running out of time."

Keefe was on foot, hobbling toward them, the Kalashnikov in hand. He hopped aboard and Rattigan sent the jeep off, swerving right and left, toward the north perimeter.

"Two guards still up there, probably radioing for assistance," shouted Rattigan.

Behind them the roar of the jet was very clear and much lower. Cassidy turned for a look. The jet seemed to hang in the air at about, he guessed, five thousand feet. Even as he looked, the plane's landing lights went on, one on each wing. The craft would be landing without any assistance from field lights, a risky business.

Rattigan was zigzagging the jeep, slowing down. "I'm trying to draw a little fire to see where they are."

That did it. The flashes from automatic weapons came from the dead center of the field about a hundred yards in front of them.

"They're together," yelled Cassidy.

"Covering fire!"

Keefe and Cassidy were already standing up, blazing away over the windshield, keeping the *soldados* pinned to the ground.

The jet behind them was no longer screaming. The pilot had cut his engines and was coming in at 150 miles an hour.

Now it was a test of nerves. Rattigan aimed straight at the two men on the ground, giving them the choice of being run over or getting out of there. They chose to get out. When they rose and stumbled toward the woods, Cassidy took out the right one and Keefe the one on the left. Sitting ducks. Easy shots.

"I'm sick of this," snarled Cassidy. "Killing teenagers. This is not my war. What am I doing here?"

"There's still one left," said Keefe. "Over there. What do we do about him?"

"Ignore him," said Cassidy. "He wouldn't dare."

The little jet was braking hard, slowing itself, cutting its speed to ninety, eighty, seventy. Now it was almost on them—Cassidy standing, waving them down in the full glare of the plane's landing lights.

The little jet made a graceful turn just in front of their jeep and stopped altogether.

That's when the last shot came from the west perimeter. They saw the flash and a round hole appeared in the windscreen.

"Let's go get him," said Rattigan.

Cassidy leaped out. "I'm going to talk to the pilot, keep him from flying away."

The jeep roared off and Cassidy ran toward the jet, now motionless on the runway. The door opened and the ladder came out, automatically unfolding. Cassidy ran up and inside, keeping his head down.

"A spot of trouble," he said. "Keefe and Rattigan are taking care of it."

Deidrich stared back at him unsympathetically. "I thought we had agreed the trouble would be taken care of before we landed."

Cassidy was slumped in a seat, exhausted. "These things don't always go according to plan. You should know that by now, Deidrich. All the years you have been on the run."

A nasty crack.

Deidrich glared. Cassidy glared back. He was in a rotten mood.

Outside came the crackle of automatic fire. Deidrich didn't like it. He started back toward the flight deck. "I'm getting out of here."

"No, you're not," snarled Cassidy. "We're here to get these men out. Sit down."

Deidrich paused at the door. "You're not giving me orders in my airplane, Professor." He went inside, Cassidy lunging after him.

The co-pilot was seated at the controls, looking out the

window. "They're coming back, Captain. They'll be here in about a minute."

Deidrich muttered something unintelligible and hunched himself into his seat, taking up his earphones, busying himself with the controls.

A minute later Keefe and Rattigan were scrambling up the ladder. The co-pilot punched the button that brought the ladder up, folding itself away. Two minutes later they were racing down the runway—the wrong way—for takeoff, the twin jets thundering. By the time they reached the airport building, they were at fifteen hundred feet, climbing almost vertically.

Cassidy, who hadn't even put his seat belt on, grumbled, "What's the hurry."

Rattigan pointed down, and Cassidy saw out the window the red, white, and blue tracer flashes. "Machine gun fire!" he said.

"He was using his radio when we got to him, babbling away. They'd called for help long before, I guess, and it just arrived."

Keefe was in the lavatory throwing up. He came out looking white as paper and slumped into a chair saying nothing. Very unusual for Keefe, saying nothing. Soon he was asleep.

"Something bothering him?" asked Cassidy.

"Killing teenagers. The last one didn't even have a weapon in his hand."

"Yeah," said Cassidy.

Mission accomplished. He'd sky-dived into a strange country, rescued two men against impossible odds. He should feel wonderful. He felt rotten clean through.

14

Cassidy opened his eyes reluctantly, himself still full of sleep and old despair. A splash of sunlight on the faded Turkish carpet at a westward slant. The sun didn't assume that angle until . . . Cassidy looked at his watch. Four-ten. He rolled over and only then saw Amanda Shotover standing next to his bed, very straight, very silent, holding a silver tray. On the tray a Georgian silver coffeepot. Brioche and butter on the red Minton china. Very Continental.

"I thought you'd better wake up," said the old lady. "It's almost teatime." Tea was still observed like a religious rite every day at Shotover Hall.

Cassidy hunched himself up to a sitting position. "Very kind," he mumbled. Actually, Cassidy considered breakfast in bed immoral, indecent, and probably unhealthful, but he was not about to say such a thing to Amanda Shotover, who had placed the tray on his lap and poured him his coffee. "I'm honored by this unaccustomed luxury—but why?"

The old lady sat on the edge of the bed. "I wanted to talk

to you. I came to your room last night. You weren't here. Where were you?"

Cassidy buttered a bit of brioche. "Out dancing."

"Until 8 A.M.? In *Virginia*?"

They both laughed.

"I don't think you can dance a step," said the old lady.

"Madam, you wrong me. I know all the lastest dances—the two-step, the Charleston, the shimmy. What did you want to talk about?"

"Armand."

Cassidy bit into the brioche. "Delicious. What about Armand?"

"I think he's here, somewhere on the estate. Someone got into the gun cases last night and took Armand's favorite gun—a Hosford .307. The case was locked when I came down, but the gun was gone. Armand has a key to the case. I have the only other one."

Cassidy sipped his coffee, took another bite of brioche, and thought about it. "A Hosford .307? Never heard of it."

"It's a very expensive gun. It belonged to his father and was always one of Armand's great treasures."

Cassidy remembered Armand and the 9mm Frank which seemed to clash so sharply with his personality—as if he'd never had a gun in his life. "I didn't know Armand liked guns."

"He liked that gun and he was a very good shot."

"What did he shoot?"

"Only at targets. Never at animals. He didn't like to kill anything—unlike his brothers who liked to kill everything. He shot from horseback and was very good at that."

It was the first time Amanda Shotover had had a good word for her son that Cassidy could remember.

"Are any horses missing?"

"It's unkind of you to be flippant," said the old lady reproachfully.

"I wasn't being flippant. There are a great many bits of

the estate that are only approachable by horseback. Or foot. If Armand's hiding out here. . . ." The whole thing seemed terribly unlikely, but then everything about Armand seemed unlikely. Shooting at targets from horseback. How many people did that?

Cassidy finished the brioche, sipped some more coffee, and didn't say anything for a long time. Amanda Shotover sat with her hands folded in her lap like Whistler's mother. Cassidy looking at the faded but elegant tea roses on the fabric of the curtains, the faded but elegant carpet, the room's magnificent symmetry. The contrast with Balisario and its primitivism smote him.

"You're not being very helpful."

Cassidy sighed. He would almost rather cut out his tongue than ask the question on the tip of it. "Who paid the bills when Armand was here?"

A flicker of distaste crossed the old lady's face. She stood up. "Armand. It's his place."

She moved to the door.

"And who pays them now?"

"They're unpaid."

The face clearly registering that that was none of Cassidy's business. Amanda Shotover left, closing the door after her. Cassidy grimaced. He hated any estrangement from the old lady. He needed her friendship. Besides, he liked her. But he needed to know. Money was the root of all evil, and twenty-six million dollars was a powerful lot of evil.

"Money, money, money, money," he said aloud.

Lucia walked in. "Daddy! Breakfast in bed! How shameful!" She kissed him on the cheek, soft as a whisper. "What are you doing in bed at this hour? You're not sick?"

"I had a late night," said Cassidy. "And you, my precious. Have you done your French lessons? Your Latin?"

"I've done the lessons, but there's no one to do them *with*. I can't *find* anyone."

Sulkily. She didn't like being abandoned.

"Where is Anne Falk?"

"I don't know. Washington, I think."

Cassidy caressed her cheek lightly, feeling the youthfulness of her. "Will you do me a favor? Slip down to the stables and count the horses—including the ones in the field."

"Daddy!"

"You've always wanted to help when I'm doing a bit of spookery. Now go do it. And don't tell anyone—including Joseph—what you're doing." When she was halfway to the door—eyes shining—Cassidy added: "If a horse is missing, I want to know which one and anything you know about it."

Lucia left. Cassidy got out of the bed and picked up his jump suit. He'd remembered that packet of letters he'd filched from Roberto Garcia's study. He was fumbling with the jump suit when he heard the knock. A sharp, peremptory knock. Alison's voice. "Cassidy!"

Cassidy shoved the jump suit in his closet and closed the door.

"Come in! come in! All of you out there—and bring your friends and relatives. We are open for inspection at all hours of the day. Oh, it's you, Hugh, in your new gray flannel suit. You are a credit to your agency, your country, and your mother in that suit. . . ."

Alison was in no mood for badinage. He walked to the only upholstered chair in the room and sat on its edge stiffly, both hands on his stick.

Furious.

"I thought you were going to call me the minute you got back."

"For God's sake, Hugh, I was dead on my feet. I flew forty-five hundred miles, rescued Keefe and Rattigan. . . ."

"And left a trail of dead bodies all over Balisario. The cables have been pouring in all morning from our Embassy and their Ministry. They're our *allies*, you idiot!"

"Some allies! Murderers, torturers, dope smugglers, thieves, assassins. . . ."

"Are you making policy now, schoolteacher? Grow up!" Cassidy had never seen Alison so angry.

"How did you expect me to get Keefe and Rattigan out of there alive? It's the seventeenth century down there. You shoot your way out or you don't get out."

Both of them shouting now. Alison rapped on the floor with his stick. Blap! Blap! A sharp, authoritative noise to shut Cassidy up.

"You're off the case. I'm taking over as of right now."

That silenced Cassidy. He sat on the edge of the bed and stared at the floor. Alison was pulling three envelopes out of his inner breast pocket. "Here's your money, Horatio. Also Keefe's and Rattigan's." Alison put the envelopes on the bed next to Cassidy. His voice had changed tone altogether. Mollifying. Almost apologetic.

Cassidy said nothing. He was thinking of Fletcher. Fletcher would be turning up with forty off-duty cops tomorrow afternoon, all of them thirsting for blood.

Alison was saying apologetically: "It's not my doing, Horatio. It's the Director himself. His orders."

Cassidy was stunned. "The Director? I thought this was your private show."

"Not anymore. It's very high policy, Horatio." Alison almost pleading now. "The highest."

"The Oval Office?"

"Horatio, these troops are being specially trained here for a very big mission that is very close to the heart of the Great White Face himself. I can't tell you more."

"They better be a little more skillful than those children we massacred at the airport," snarled Cassidy.

Alison went on (as was his habit) as if he'd not heard. "Fortunately, we have complete deniability about what happened at the airport and at Roberto Garcia's house. You killed all the witnesses. We have assumed a posture of outraged innocence in which I insist you cooperate."

Deniability. One of those words invented for twentieth-century diplomacy that matched the fourteenth century Venetians in mendacity, deviousness, and skulduggery. *Posture of outraged innocence* was a new phrase to Cassidy. Trust Alison to be first to employ the very newest in Doublespeak.

Alison was still talking: ". . . well aware of your moral scruples, but in this case you must think of the good name not only of the Agency but of your country. We cannot *officially* have taken part in an armed intervention in their country. . . ."

"Even though they did one in ours—killing eleven cops."

"For that very reason. For God's sake, Horatio, this looks like retaliation for that unfortunate business in New York, which it wasn't at all. As you know I was very reluctant to let you go down there. Now our story is, we had nothing to do with it. Roberto Garcia and Hermanos Fuentes both know no one else has the jets to fly in and out of Balisario, kill twelve people, and escape without a scratch, but we must never, never admit it. It never happened. But we have to take you out to atone for . . ."

"What never happened. Very Orwellian," grunted Cassidy. He was counting the money. My God, the full twelve thousand in his envelope. Alison must truly be ashamed of himself to come up with the full amount. Cassidy would have settled for half.

Alison's voice was tight. "The Director insists you get out of here today. I'll be wanting this room and the CIA car and all your notes and memoranda, of course."

Cassidy smiled bleakly. "I'm going to take a shower. Can I take it alone or do you want to come in and watch to be sure I'm not stealing the soap."

Alison grimaced and fiddled with his stick, throwing it up in the air, catching it, twirling it, his face thunderous.

Cassidy went into the bathroom and closed the door. He felt lightheaded. Absolved. This was now Alison's party. Except that it wasn't. Fletcher would be arriving—unless he stopped him—with forty angry cops, and what to do about *that*? Cassidy showered noisily and long, shaved, washed his hair, brushed his teeth, took his time.

When he came out of the bathroom, Alison was gone and Lucia was sitting there blazing with excitement. "There are two horses missing, Daddy! Leatherstocking and Faun. Joseph calls Leatherstocking Leadbelly because he's so calm. He's Armand Shotover's favorite horse. Armand used to shoot from his back. How clever of you to think of counting the horses, Daddy! You know a lot of those horses are never ridden; they're out in the field night and day in the spring and summer. You could run off with half dozen and nobody'd notice."

Cassidy smiled and kissed her on the top of the head. "Very clever of *you*, Princess, to spot the missing horses with identifying characteristics. I have a bit of bad news. I've been taken off the case. We're to be out of here today."

Lucia's face went from high ecstasy to high tragedy in a quarter of a second. "Oh, *Daddy*! Back to *school*!"

"Maybe not. I got to get dressed. Go find Amanda Shotover, and if she's talking to Alison just sit there and listen. Unless Amanda orders you out of the room—and she won't; she can't stand Alison—just sit there. You understand?"

"No."

"Well, do it anyway or it's back to school with you."

Lucia dragged herself to the door, face full of misery. Everything showed on that plain Italianate face—joy, misery, pain—as explicit as a sunset.

"We're going to find Thirteenth Street very tiny after this house," she said.

"But cozy," said Cassidy. "Run along. I've got to get dressed and packed."

He packed slowly and carefully. Much was missing. The deed of trust was missing, as was Armand's message diary and one radio. The other belonged to the CIA. He put in his good suit and dressed in a sweater and his old country tweed trousers because, if things worked out. . . .

He called Fletcher at the station house. "Fletcher's not here. He's taken special leave for a couple days. Can I help? I'm his partner."

Cassidy said no, it was a personal matter and rang Fletcher's home. His wife answered, sounding peeved. "He's off with the boys—his poker-playing pals. I don't know where they are." She sounded deeply aggrieved. I'm probably breaking up the marriage, Cassidy thought.

Next he called Grace Alison at home. "Cassidy, you Irish soak, how are you? If you're looking for Alison, I thought he was with you. He's left a number here. . . ."

"Grace, if you still harbor a bit of fondness for this old Irish soak, I need a favor."

"You bastard, I knew you weren't calling because you loved me. What is it?"

He told her.

Cassidy left his bag and his jacket in the outer hall and walked through the huge sitting room, the music room, the library, the gun room to the sun room, where he knew Amanda would be serving tea.

She was not only serving tea, she was instructing Lucia in how to serve it, even how to drink it. ". . . you hold the tea in the teacup in the left hand *comme ça*, and the ladyfinger in the right hand *comme ça*, the eyes alert, following the conversation, you must leap in and leap out, take another tiny bite *comme ça*, because the conversation is even more important than the tea. You do realize that, don't you? Ah, Mr. Cassidy. Do you wish tea on top of breakfast?"

Alison was sitting in the corner, being pointedly ignored and hating it.

"No, please go on with the lesson. I'm all ears."

152

Amanda Shotover said, "She's a good pupil, your daughter. A marvelous listener, and if there's anything an old lady needs it's a listener. We have all this bottled-up wisdom—years and years of experience—and no one wants to hear it."

Geoffrey, the white-haired butler, entered the room on his noiseless feet: "Mr. Alison, your wife is on the phone. You can take it in the sitting room."

Alison looked dumbfounded. He got all kinds of calls—from Shanghai, Budapest, Madagascar—but hardly ever one from his wife. "You'll excuse me," he said to Amanda Shotover, who looked clear through him and said, "Of course."

The moment Alison left the room, Cassidy sat down next to Amanda Shotover. "Amanda," he said.

The first time he'd ever called her by her first name.

"I've been ordered off the case. . . ."

"Oh, dear!"

"Alison is taking over. He'll be moving into your son's room immediately."

"I'll hate that."

But she couldn't do much about it. The Agency had a handle on the estate that went very deep.

Cassidy said, "My work here isn't finished and I need your help. Here's my plan. Please don't interrupt because Alison will be back and I don't want him to know anything about it. Or Anne Falk either. . . ."

15

Deep in the high woods on the eastern slope of the mountain, Armand sat motionless on the horse called Leatherstocking, leveling the Hosford .307, holding it steady by holding his left elbow in tight against his ribs. He squeezed off the shot and the tin can flew off the branch a hundred yards away, a hole in its very middle.

Anne Falk, astride Faun just behind him, said unhappily, "Now, what does that prove?"

"That I can still do it."

"Roberto Garcia is coming here with forty men, Armand."

"I know every foot of these woods. He doesn't."

"He's the most dangerous man in the hemisphere, and he's got forty trained guerrilla fighters with him. You're insane, Armand."

Armand had opened the Hosford and now he blew smoke out of the barrel, lovingly, caressing the gun as if it were a puppy. "He tried to have me killed. He'll try again. What have I got to lose?"

"You need help, Armand."

"Where am I going to get it—the Agency? They didn't help much the first time, did they?"

"Armand, you brought that on yourself. You didn't tell anyone anything. Twenty-six million dollars, my God!"

Armand laughed mischievously. "I think I belong in the Guinness Book of Records."

"Where is it, Armand?"

"That would be telling." He was reloading the rifle. "Anyway, it's not as if I stole the money. *They* stole the money from a lot of wretched addicts who got the money stealing it from their bosses or their children's lunch money or somewhere. It's thieves' money and it belongs to whoever has possession."

"Oh, Armand!" Tears glittered in her eyes. She was determined not to shed them. "Why did you go to Cassidy? What on earth possessed you?"

He had that faraway look in his golden eyes. "Cassidy's the only one who can get us out of this mess, Anne. You don't know how bad it is—the corruption. The horror in high places! What they're doing is worse than criminal, it's treason!"

Armand's face and, yes, his voice both shining with an idealism that approached—Anne couldn't avoid thinking—idiocy. There was a point where purity and insanity were the same thing.

She said, "Armand, you overestimate—you have always overestimated—Cassidy. He's not Superman. . . ."

"Oh, but he is! If you knew what he did in Guatemala! In China! Single-handed in China! He's the only one I could turn to, because they were trying to kill me, Anne. And they almost did."

"If you wanted his help, why did you go after him with a gun, for God's sake?"

"I wanted to capture his attention. He would never have stopped to talk otherwise." Armand laughed a little wildly.

"Actually, the gun was not for Cassidy. They were right behind me, Anne. I had the gun out to protect myself. Cassidy walked right into it, and I used the gun to get him back into his apartment. Anyway, I wanted to have a look at his black book and see if Victor's name was in it—and it is."

"Cassidy says it isn't."

"It's there, all right. If we all get out of this alive, I'll show it to him. Anyway, you have no right to reproach me. Who recruited me in the first place?"

"Oh, God, I wish I hadn't."

He smiled at her—a boyish smile, dreamy and loving. "You are always using God's name, Anne, but do you believe in Him? I do."

"I know."

"I think someday I'll meet him and I keep wondering how to address him. You can't say, 'How are you?' God doesn't have colds. 'Your Excellency, I'm happy to meet you.' No, that's hardly the right note. I suppose I should cast myself at his feet, but I can't see myself doing that. It's not my style."

Anne smiled sadly. "You have great charm, Armand. Charm perched on the edge of a volcano. I don't know how much more of it I can take. I have to get back. She's already begun to notice my absence."

"How is the old battle-ax?"

"She'll outlive us both—and dance on our graves." She turned Faun down the mountain. "I'll try to come this evening. Can I bring you something?"

"Bacon and a couple tomatoes. I want to make bacon, lettuce, and tomato sandwiches. I love bacon, lettuce, and tomato sandwiches."

"I know," said Anne and walked the horse away through the thick woods without turning around so he couldn't see the tears.

"Oh, Anne!" He called after her as she and Faun were fifty feet from him. "Where's Cassidy?"

"He's been taken off the case. He's on his way back to New York by now."

He wasn't.

In another part of the forest, Lucia was on the lead horse, Ariel. Behind her came Cassidy on Sandpiper, Keefe on a big black horse named Black Prince, and Rattigan on a medium-sized buckskin pony named Peppermint. It was a particularly dense bit of woods, with huge loops of very tough vine hanging from the tallest trees, making the place look like a setting for Tarzan. Keefe was pushing the vine out of his hair, muttering, "I had no idea Virginia was jungle. I thought they'd civilized the place."

Cassidy was thinking: This is where it all started—America the beautiful, for amber waves of grain. Virginia had retained in its woods and fields some of the original innocence. At least in places like Shotover Hall. He ran his hands over the Winchester he'd taken from the gun case. A pump gun. 30.37. The ammunition thirty years old. He hoped it would work. The .357 had been lost in Balisario.

"You were in the DEA for a while, Keefe," said Cassidy. "Tell me, what does a fellow do with twenty-six million dollars? Where does a man put that kind of cash?"

"Car washes, check-cashing outfits, fast-food chains—anything that has a big flow in cold cash. For the long-term stuff they wash the money in the Bahamas—or Switzerland—and put it in real estate. Four billion of cocaine money is supposed to be in real estate alone in this country. They buy banks with it, condominiums, shopping centers, Congressmen, judges. They get expensive lawyers who ask for and get one adjournment after another until everyone forgets the original charge. The evidence disappears. The judicial system in this country is a joke."

"Hark," said Cassidy.

They all stopped their horses and listened. They'd all heard the same thing—a shot. Distant, far up the mountain, to the north.

Now there was no sound at all except the wind in the stands of white oak, the soughing of the pines.

"How much farther, Lucia?" asked Cassidy.

"Just up here, maybe another three hundred yards."

Shining eyes. Loving every minute.

Adventures in the cocaine trade with Daddy. What a lark! Cassidy thinking: Why in hell did I bring her? But I didn't know it was going to take a turn like this. How could I?

The horses were laden down with blanket rolls and leather saddlebags bulging with food and a few pots and pans. Cassidy carried the water in leather jugs, one on each side of the saddle.

The log cabin was on a ridge with a bit of clearing on all sides. A porch ran around three sides of it. The back side had neither porch nor windows. "This is not my favorite, Daddy, because it's out in the open. I love the ones that are shrouded by woods. Real witches' cabins. This is . . . a people's cabin."

It had been built in the early eighteenth century by the mountain men. One large room with a big stone chimney in the center of its east wall. In the center of the back wall was a small iron stove that had been added a century or so later. This room had served the mountain men as living room, kitchen, dining room, workroom, where the pots and pans, the looms, the grindstones had been kept but were there no more. There was only a sturdy table with a kerosene lamp on it and four homemade chairs around it.

In the center of the room, hanging from the beams, was a kind of huge shelf which roofed over half the room. A ladder led up to it. Here is where the mountain men slept, up under the eaves where the fire kept them warmest.

The three men unloaded the horses. Lucia took off the saddles and led the horses to the mule stables fifty feet from the house. These were rickety affairs, two of them, made of saplings lashed together with wire. Lucia put two horses in each stall—one placid horse with one fire-eater—Sandpiper with Ariel, Black Prince, a gelding, with Peppermint.

Cassidy collected twigs and small sticks of wood to start a fire in the iron stove while Keefe and Rattigan foraged for bigger hunks of wood in the fast-falling twilight. Lucia made them supper—beans and bacon with lots of coffee and bread, topped off by a cheesecake she'd begged off one of the cooks at Shotover Hall.

Directly after supper, she climbed the ladder and crawled into her sleeping bag stretched out on the upper deck. Cassidy kissed her on the cheek. "This is the most fun I ever had in my life," she whispered. "I wish I knew what it was about."

"We all wish that, Princess. Sleep tight."

The three men sat around the candlelit table, keeping their voices low until she fell asleep, which was almost instantly. Then Keefe: "What'll we do with her when the action starts?"

"Take her back to the big house."

"She won't like that."

"In Central America we talk of land reform," Rattigan said. "Spread the stuff around a little more equally. This place is twenty-seven thousand acres. Me, I don't own ten square feet of land anywhere. America is owned by Malcolm Forbes and six other guys."

Cassidy was rummaging through his saddlebag, bringing out the swatch of letters he'd filched from Roberto Garcia's study and spreading them around the table. "Let's see how good your Spanish is. Letters from banks and letters *to* banks. For a military man, Roberto seemed too much preoccupied with banks—and money."

"We're all interested in money, Cassidy—all of us except medieval historians," grumbled Keefe. "The bastard lived very well. That house!"

Rattigan said, "He had an expensive girl friend crosstown

in her own house he bought her. And a house in Spain he went to in the summer."

Silence fell as the men rooted in the bank statements like pigs snorting for truffles. Many of the statements were simple acknowledgments of the receipt of cash—hair-raising amounts.

"Oho," said Keefe. "I've struck pay dirt." He showed Cassidy an acknowledgment of bank transfer for 165,000 escuderos from the Banco de Amazonas. "Banco de Amazonas is a CIA cover bank. They own it. When I was down there for the Agency, that's where the money came from. Money for pay. Subversion. Bribery. All the pretty things we did."

There were other drafts on the Banco de Amazonas but none after November 1981. "He was our man in Balisario—but is no longer ours. He didn't stay bought because we stopped buying."

Silence while they read through more bank paper. Drafts from the Banco de España in the Bahamas, Credit Suisse in Zurich, to numbered accounts. Cassidy was thinking: The Agency does this all the time. Instill in a man a love of cash that hadn't bothered him before, then take away the cash flow so he has to get the stuff somewhere else. "Cocaine money. He's stealing from his own country."

"Why was Harburg killed? If they were both CIA?"

"Harburg was a trained accountant," said Cassidy. "That's what he was doing down there—keeping track of the cash flow into Balisario, trying to figure out how much was coming from Soviet and Cuban sources—and who it was flowing to."

The same thought struck all three of them simultaneously. Was any Soviet cash flowing to Roberto Garcia? Had he ceased being an American agent and become a Soviet agent? Or perhaps always been both?

Rattigan spoke up. "How did Roberto Garcia tumble to the fact that Harburg was wise to him?"

"Betrayal," said Cassidy. "From the Latin *tradere*. To place in the power of the enemy by treachery."

Keefe said, "In this business you learn something new every day."

Alison drove the CIA car up the mountainside to the cabin with the huge antenna. He switched off the lights and walked into the cabin without knocking. Kaska was at his apparatus with a screwdriver, coils of wire on the floor. He looked up when Alison walked in and then rose to his feet, impassive as always. "If I'd known you were coming, I'd have brewed a little something. As it is, I have some nice Irish whiskey."

Alison sat in the most comfortable chair, as was his custom, fiddling with his stick. He accepted the whiskey without comment and took a very small sip.

"We're closing down this station next week, Kaska." He took another small sip. "It's fulfilled its purpose." Another small sip. "And it's getting hot."

"Aah," said Kaska. "That happens to all of them."

"You'll be reassigned, of course."

"You don't know where?"

"It's not up to me. It's up to the Director."

"The Director sometimes does what you recommend."

"What should I recommend?"

Kaska was putting away his tools in the toolbox—the screwdriver, the wrenches, the pliers. Very carefully, "I'd like to disappear. I've had enough."

It took the breath out of Alison. "*You*, Kaska! Had enough?" He could not conceive anyone having enough. Like having enough money. It was not possible to have enough.

Kaska smiled his faint European smile. "Look at this place. Feast your eyes. Is this a life? I've spent my life in situations like this. I'd like something else." He put the toolbox away underneath a table that was crammed with electronic equipment. "Perhaps a little cowardice, Mr. Alison. I've made enemies. They want to close me down. If I just . . . close myself down. . . ." He waved his hand in an expressive European gesture. "Would you be so kind as to put in a word with the Director?"

Alison nodded, a brief, curt nod. He was opening the beautiful dispatch case with the gold locks. He brought out three sheets of single-spaced disinformation. "This will be the last of it. It should be on its way by tomorrow afternoon. Did the other stuff get through?"

Kaska was looking through the sheets, which were in Russian. "It all went out . . . to someone. I get acknowledgment, but whether it's KGB—who knows? If it's not KGB, they certainly intercept—but of course, that takes much longer to get a response. It has to go through the bureaucracy—analysis, operations, interpretation—well, you know. You've got all that nonsense too."

Alison's mind was elsewhere. "What's the word from Balisario?"

"They'll be here tomorrow night. Eleven-thirty. Forty soldiers. Roberto Garcia commanding."

"Roberto himself? Why?"

Kaska smiled his European smile. "Analysis is your department, not mine. However, if you'd like an educated guess, I think he was ordered to come. I have an idea Roberto doesn't like field operations very much."

"A training mission! He'd hate it."

"Are you sure it's a training mission?"

Alison stood up. The whole thing was getting out of hand; he'd lost control. Even the Agency had lost control. The whole thing was in the hands of those maniacs in the White House. "I'll talk to the Director about . . . that other matter. I wouldn't get too optimistic."

Again that European smile. "Optimism is not one of my vices, Mr. Alison." Kaska picked up his flashlight and escorted Alison, leading him down the path past the huge dishlike antenna. A few moments after they passed the antenna and approached the CIA car, a figure darted out from behind the antenna and into the house. Neither of the men noticed.

The two men chatted for a moment and then Alison drove away. Kaska returned to the house. He picked up the disinformation and read it, rubbing his ear, expressionless. He smoked a cigarette and sighed. After a bit, he set the channel to 122.11, inserted a roll of paper in the machine, and started typing in Russian, the machine automatically encoding the material and sending the information 22,335 miles above the equator where the Russian satellite in geosynchronous orbit transmitted it to Moscow.

He was still working on the first page, working slowly, getting it right (because, of course, they would be monitoring him at Fort Meade), when Armand walked out of the bedroom door directly behind Kaska. Armand had a 9mm Walther in his right hand and he trod softly, so softly Kaska wasn't aware of his presence until Armand was three feet away. Then he caught the reflection in the chrome on the machine. His move was lightning fast. He fell sidewise, turning as he went, and his right hand went into the drawer where the gun was and out faster than the eye could follow. A much practiced defense.

All for nothing.

Armand held up the 9mm in his right hand. "I have the gun here, Kaska. I took the precaution of removing it. I know how fast you are and what a good shot."

Kaska lying on the floor, staring up at Armand. "Oh, it's just you, Armand. You frightened me." Kaska got up, brushing off his trousers.

"Sit on the chair, Kaska, facing away from me, please. I have some things to say and I don't want you mesmerizing me with those Slavic eyes. I know that's rude, Kaska, and I'm sorry, but you can't expect me to be polite after what you did."

Kaska was sitting on the chair now, his head drooping, his body drooping, his arms hanging low at his side. "And what is it that I did, exactly?"

"Betrayed me. Oh, I know betrayal is your business. It's what you do for a living. You've betrayed your country, my country, Balisario. But *me*, Kaska? The one who set you up here, sat at your feet, absorbed your Slavic charm, and loved you."

"Armand, Armand"—the voice was low, seductive—"what are you saying? Betray you! What nonsense is this?"

The head, the body drooping lower. Also the long arms, the hands getting microscopically closer to the boot where the stiletto was.

"You sent those killers to Cassidy's apartment. You, Kaska, you! Nobody else knew I was going there. Only you. No, don't turn around. I don't want to look at you. I know what you can do with those eyes."

"Armand, Armand." The voice low, throbbing with sincerity. "You are my friend, my protector! Would I betray my protector? Why should I? . . ."

The move came in the middle of the sentence, blurring time. Kaska whirled, the stiletto in his hand, and came out of the chair with tremendous force, the stiletto outthrust right into Armand's chest. Armand flew backward like a rocket from the force of it. At the same moment the gun in Armand's hand went off—blam!—like that. Armand hadn't pulled the trigger consciously. The force of Kaska's thrust had triggered the gun.

Armand stumbled backward, clear to the wall, where he steadied himself, hand on his chest.

Kaska's mouth flew open, the stiletto dropping at his feet. The eyes shocked and, after a tiny moment, sad. He fell in a heap like a disintegrating scarecrow, blood oozing from the little round hole in the very center of the chest, and died without saying any last words.

Armand, limp as a towel, closed his eyes, his breath

coming rapidly as if he'd been running a race. He opened a few buttons of his shirt, revealing underneath the khaki-colored vest with the steel strips that had saved his life, and rubbed the bruised flesh. "I'm sorry," he said to the corpse, apologizing as always. "It was an accident." With a low, mirthless laugh. "You *should* have won, Kaska. You are a much better man at close combat than I am. What a *move*! So *fast*! It would have worked except that I put on your bulletproof vest while you were typing."

Still rubbing his bruised chest underneath the khaki vest, Armand sat on the chair that Kaska had been on, contemplating the dead face.

"You made a monkey out of all of us, didn't you, Kaska? You masterminded the theft of twenty-six million dollars and got me to do all the dirty work, even killing a man—on your instructions. Very clever instructions, killing the man with his own gun. You outwitted Roberto, which took some doing, and then me—which didn't take much doing because I am one of nature's born suckers—and you outwitted Alison and finally—this is the great irony, Kaska, and I wish you were alive to appreciate it—you outwitted yourself. If you hadn't pulled that magnificently expert move, stabbing me so hard that you made the gun go off, if you hadn't been so farsighted as to have this beautiful bulletproof vest—which I plan to wear tomorrow—I would be lying on the floor dead instead of you. I'm not capable of shooting anyone as expert as you, Kaska. My brothers, possibly. Not me. You had to engineer your own undoing with your own cleverness. Very Chekhovian. It's too bad you're not alive to . . . savor it."

Armand sat a long while rubbing his chest, looking at Kaska, his surrogate brother whom he had loved. Finally he tore his eyes away and turned to the three pages of disinformation, all in Russian. He took the paper out of the roller and inserted a fresh sheet. He went through the desk looking for the codes and the channel number. They weren't there. He searched the bedroom slowly, because he had lots of time. Finally he found what he was looking for on the body itself, in the breast pocket of the shirt.

Code and channel number.

He set the machine to its proper channel and coding instructions and typed in the clear.

URGENT TO ROBERTO GARCIA AFTER SOLDIERS BIVOUACKED SHOTOVER MEET ME KASKAS 0030 HOURS REPEAT 0030 HOURS.

He signed it Victor.

16

In the Situation Room, the Great White Face sat at the oak table, his famous crooked smile slightly awry because he hated listening. Harriet Van Fleet stood over him (it was always best to stand when talking to him) speaking in what William Safire called her ironclad soprano about the absolute necessity of secrecy.

"The Director will be here in a minute and he'll urge you to give him at least a memorandum. Don't do it. You must give verbal but not written direction. This thing must never be traced back here."

"Have you heard the one about the three Poles and the Jew?" asked the President.

"Yes," said Harriet Van Fleet. She went on quickly before his attention wandered. "Their mission is . . ."

"I know their mission," said the Great White Face engagingly. "You've explained it to me twice. They're to disrupt communications in Nicaragua. Very advanced electronics training from our best electronics experts on our latest equipment. You think I don't listen, but I do."

Harriet Van Fleet turned on her smile, which looked as if it hurt. (Grits her teeth when she smiles, the reporters said.)

"It's more complicated than that. They have a secondary mission to recover money stolen from them on their last training trip. A great deal of money—twenty-six million dollars."

"Holy Jehoshaphat!" exclaimed the President, the last man on earth to use that expression, which dated from his youth in Nebraska. "Twenty-six million! In *cash*!"

"It was to pay for very expensive equipment. Cash so it couldn't be traced. Soldiers' pay. Expenses. If it's lost for good, we would have to make it up to them out of CIA contingency funds, and those come under scrutiny of the Watch Committee of Congress. We don't want *that*, do we?"

"We should help. Call Pete Ross at the FBI. . . ."

"No! no!" said Harriet Van Fleet, putting her hand protectively on the telephone. The man was a menace with a telephone. "The most useful service we can perform in this business is to stay out of it. These people know who stole the money and they think they know where it is. We are requested to do nothing, which you must admit is in the great tradition of Republican government. It's what we do best, what we've always done best—nothing—with great panache. You yourself have always said that the art of government is in refraining."

"Very well put, if I do say so. It reminds me of the one about the Hungarian, the Indian, and the Jew. They were flying at thirty-thousand feet and. . . ."

This time there was no stopping him.

The site was deserted. The soldiers had been very neat. The tent flaps were rolled down. The wooden floors had been swept and the stoves had been swept clean of ash. The twin mattresses were rolled up and tied to the ends of the iron cots.

"I'm to find this in the dark, old hoss?" said Keefe. "There had better be a light in the sky."

"There'll be lots of light in the sky. Forty soldiers making camp, for heaven's sake. There's electricity in every tent. You just have to follow that trail, which is very broad. . . ."

"Without lights."

"There'll be starlight. That'll be enough. Make sure you don't miss the turnoff." Cassidy had cut a great white slash in the tree to mark the ninety-degree turn where the trails crossed. "Then follow your nose."

"And when I get here?"

"Just point it out to Lieutenant Fletcher and tiptoe away."

"Leaving the little brown men to the mercy of forty New York cops who will sit down for a quiet chat with them, telling them how very wrong it is to kill eleven New York cops, after first reading them their rights."

Cassidy scowled. He didn't like it much either. "I don't know that it's going to be all that cut and dried. These are trained guerrilla fighters with machine guns, bazookas, rockets, and God knows what else. I may be leading the lambs to slaughter. There'll be guards to take out. It won't be easy. Also Roberto Garcia may be fourteen different kinds of a son of a bitch, but he isn't a fool."

"How am I going to transport forty men from the main road to here in the dark?"

Cassidy's face wrinkled into an evil grin. "That's the best part of all. You'll love that part . . ."

Roberto Garcia was in his study, wrapping the thick cables with the clamps around the rheostat with its guages which showed just how much juice was flowing. He placed the apparatus carefully in the wooden box and tried to snap the locks, but they wouldn't shut.

Arguello came in then with the message in his hand. "*Urgente*," he said.

Roberto said, "Help me with this, Arguello. It won't shut."

Arguello snapped the locks and lifted the heavy case to

the study door where the gardener waited for it. "Put it in the car and be careful. It's quite delicate," said Roberto, who fussed over his torture equipment like a surgeon over his scalpels.

"Are you taking it along?" said Arguello, surprised.

Roberto didn't answer. He took the message out of Arguello's hand and read it: URGENT TO ROBERTO GARCIA AFTER SOLDIERS BIVOUACKED SHOTOVER MEET ME KASKAS 0030 HOURS REPEAT 0030 HOURS VICTOR.

Roberto smiled skeptically. "I want the men well rested—and you too, Arguello. Go back to quarters and order the men to their bunks. They can sleep on the plane also because they'll get no sleep in Virginia. It'll be a long night."

After Arguello left, Roberto settled down with *One Hundred Years of Solitude,* which he'd read many times, turning to the very end where the prophecy culminated in its final irony. He loved the ending. Death and dissolution. So beautiful! Nothing else stirred the blood so richly as death and dissolution.

Late morning now and the four horses were going through the woods again, this time upward, Cassidy getting the lay of the land. In the dark it would be something else. Lucia in the lead on Ariel, the fiery little bay pony; Cassidy next on Sandpiper, Keefe on the placid Black Prince, Rattigan on Peppermint. The sun glinting down through the leaves. Eden full of its original innocence.

Not enough time, Cassidy was thinking. Never enough time.

"What's the plan, Captain?" asked Keefe.

"Tie him to a tree," growled Cassidy. "Put him out of action. He'll get himself killed."

They dismounted a hundred yards from the witch's cabin and left the horses in Lucia's charge. The three men approached, tree by tree from three different sides, Cassidy assigning himself to the front door, which hung open crazily.

He tried to be quiet but it was no use. The leaning staircase creaked horribly—enough to alert a dead man. There was no advantage in pretense so Cassidy ran up the stairs and threw himself against the door. It opened easily and Cassidy almost fell in.

A large empty room with low windows through which Cassidy could see Keefe creeping from tree to tree. A cot in the corner with army blankets hanging from it. At one corner of the room an iron bar was affixed from which hung clothes—old clothes, a new suit, shirts, all on hangers. Cassidy waved to Keefe to come up and searched the suit. Inside was Armand's wallet stuffed with hundred-dollar bills.

Keefe walked in as Cassidy was counting the money. "Twelve hundred dollars in cash. They took all the money from him at the CIA hospital. He's got another source."

Keefe said. "Where's everyone?"

"Everyone's not here," said Cassidy. He was looking at the low windowsill. On it was a small frying pan with the remains of bacon still in it, which had been cooked over a small spirit burner. On the ledge were remains of tomatoes and a head of lettuce with a jar of mayonnaise. A jug of water stood on the floor.

Cassidy picked up the spirit burner. Boy Scouts of America it said on the can. "This looks like the sort of thing they had in the Boy Scouts thirty years ago. The Scouts have much better equipment now. I think he's had this stuff here for years."

"This his favorite hideaway, you think?"

"I think he has a lot of favorites. That's our problem. Twenty-seven thousand acres is a very big sandbox for a little boy to play in."

At the stables Joseph flashed his toothless grin, clearly delighted. "Miz Shotover tell me give you anythin' you want. I be happy to do that."

"Forty-two men," said Cassidy. "Can you manage that?"

Joseph's smile vanished. "Woo Woo! Forty-two! I dunno 'bout *that*!"

"They don't have to be comfortable. They can hang out the window for all I care. Let's do a count."

They went into the carriage house and took it one at a time. The Dover coach was biggest, with three sets of seats including the driver's on the roof. The two rear roof seats would hold six, the driver's seat three, and the interior of the coach six, for a total of fifteen. The circus coach would hold seven and they'd be a tight fit. On the Lancia brougham, Cassidy hoped the coachman's seat would hold three, the footman's seat at the rear another three, if they clung to each other for support, and the interior of the coach another six. That all added up to thirty-four, which meant that eight would have to be squashed into the Irish jaunting car, many of them standing up and holding on for dear life.

Joseph was exceedingly dubious. "Be hell on the horses. Worse on the drivers, drivin' without lights through these woods."

"Better than trying to drive a car through these wood without lights," said Cassidy.

"Who gone drive?"

"You, for one, Joseph. The Dover coach—okay?"

Joseph grinned. "I better lead, I know these woods pretty good. Who gone drive the others?"

"I'll drive the Lancia and Keefe can drive the circus coach. He drove pairs in Ireland."

Joseph shook his head. "You ever drive four horses, Professor?"

"I drove two as a kid. Farm team. I think it's high time I moved up to four."

Joseph woo-wooed some more. "These very old, experienced, calm horses we got here. Still, ain't gone be easy. You make a mistake with four horses, you git in awful tangle. Who gone drive the jaunting car?"

"I got an idea. Tell you later. We got enough horses for all this?"

"We got horses runnin' out our ears."

"You'll have to harness the whole lot."

Joseph chuckled. "Be mah pleasure, Professor. I been keepin' that harness in good shape for forty years. I like to see it git a little use."

Cassidy approached the house from the rear carefully. He didn't want to run into Alison. At the northeast corner, on the footpath through the hydrangeas, the library window stopped him in his tracks. Alison and Anne Falk were framed in the window, engaged in what looked like a hot dispute. Tears glittered on Anne Falk's cheeks, but they were angry tears; Alison's lips were twisted in a knot that Cassidy knew well. He'd loved to have heard what it was about, but he hadn't his listening device. He bent double and crept past the window through the hydrangeas and ran as fast as he could to the end of the house where the sun porch was.

The sun porch had its own entrance from outside. Inside, Amanda Shotover was watching "The Way of the World" on television, derisive, but not missing a syllable. Cassidy lifted Amanda Shotover peremptorily out of her chair, turned off the television, and hustled her out of the room and down the steps.

She didn't like it. "Professor Cassidy!" she said, outraged.

"I'm sorry, Amanda. I need your help and I couldn't risk being caught by Alison."

In the library Alison was saying, "You're not to make these judgments, Anne. You don't know what's at issue here and I'm not going to tell you and, as a matter of fact, there's much I don't know. This is high policy, all the way to the Oval Office."

Anne Falk said fiercely, "Well, I'm not going to help you *or* the Oval Office again. I helped last time very much against my better judgment and I'll never forgive myself. He's a child, Hugh! You entangled him in this lunacy and now you're astonished that he's playing his own role."

"I'm trying to save his life. You don't know how deadly Roberto Garcia is. . . ."

"Oh, I know all right. And Armand knows. He's scared to death of Roberto *and of you*. That's why he's running loose. He's terrified of *both* of you, and I'm not going to betray him again."

"You think you're going to marry him, but you won't have much to marry if he's dead. If he'd tell us where the money is . . ."

"I asked him where the money was. He just laughed. He won't tell me and he won't tell you."

"We can find out. We were on the verge of finding out when he went out the window."

"I know, you were using drugs on him. That's why he's in the state he's in—the drugs. He's on a twelve o'clock high! He's flying! And I think he's got a lot more drugs he took from the hospital."

The tears flowed again, Anne hating herself for the tears, unable to stop. "First you got him playing soldier. Now you've made him a drug addict."

Alison was appalled. "Anne! Anne! Stop it! You make monsters of us."

"You *are* monsters!" Dabbing at her face with her handkerchief. "If you must know, I don't know where he is. I took him some food last night, and I went back this morning and he wasn't there. I don't think he came back last night. He's somewhere else—somewhere in the twenty-seven thousand acres. I can't find him."

"Well, if you can't find him, neither can Roberto."

"Don't count on *that*," Anne said fiercely. "Armand's going after Roberto and kill him. He told me so. And in that twelve o'clock high of his he might just try it."

"Oh, my God . . ."

Cassidy entered the bus station at the Water Street entrance, walked straight to the newsstand without looking either right or left (though catching a glimpse of Fletcher out of the corner of his eye, drinking a Coke at the lunch counter), bought the *Washington Post*, taking a lot of time about it to give the men a chance to pick up their bundles, and walked out the Main Street entrance, not looking back.

Peripherally, he did a head count, not very accurate. Certainly not forty. Men in jeans and plaid shirts. In khaki trousers, work shirts, picking up their papers, their luggage, shambling after him without appearing to be connected in any way to his movements.

Two blacks caught in the reflection in the glass door and, by Jupiter, a woman! Two *women*!

Drifting out of the bus station through both doors—the Main Street entrance, the Water Street entrance, in twos and threes.

Cassidy was marching down Main Street now, breathing hard for no reason. Why did I start this? When they told Einstein about Hiroshima, the old man wailed to the heavens, "One should never do anything!" A man's actions twist in his hands, become something else, cold, evil. Inaction is the thing. Someday when I have time. . . .

Walking down Main Street now, past Shotover Hall's Toyota pickup, past the Bronco, the Chevy half-ton. The men had been given license numbers and keys were on the floor. Cassidy walked two blocks to the Ford pickup, climbed in, and waited. In the side mirror he could watch the men peeling off, piling into the other cars, some in the cabs, some in the open back ends of the truck. The two women were sitting on the floor of the Chevy pickup, leaning their backs against the cab.

Cassidy could hear the men climbing into the back end of his own pickup now and thumping down on the floor of the truck. Presently Fletcher climbed into the cab next to him and said: "Go."

"You sure they all in?"

"Yup."

Cassidy pulled out on Main Street, driving slowly past Rexall Drugs, Elmer's Pipe Shoppe (which sold newspapers, T-shirts, canned goods, bread, cold meats, and about everything except pipes), and Telford's Garage, looking in the side mirror at the other cars straggling along after.

"Didn't look like forty men to me."

"Thirty-one's best I could do. Men gave up their days off, used their own money."

"Two women!"

"We got women in the police force now. One's a widow of one of the murdered cops. Other's her friend. They want a chance to kill a spic. . . ."

What have I done? What's done cannot be undone. Lady Macbeth. Very pithy character, Lady Macbeth. Also a woman.

Cassidy remembered the dead, unformed face in Roberto Garcia's garden. Very young. Very dead.

"Both those girls can shoot the ears off you, Cassidy."

Fletcher full of blood lust. We've changed roles, Cassidy was thinking sadly. He was the reluctant one. I was the activist.

The light turning from mauve to purple. The sidewalks dwindled and they were out of Marietta now, into the open country, night falling fast. Behind the Ford the headlights winked on one after another. Cassidy swung through the new unmarked entrance in the vast acreage of Shotover Hall he'd found that day with Anne Falk and drove slowly for about half a mile up the dirt road. There he pulled off into the trees, the trucks following him closely now, into a small clearing where he switched off his engine.

"From here on, it gets harder," said Cassidy.

17

"Just call me Pasionara." She snorted with laughter. A thick-waisted black-haired woman with a face like a boot and merry eyes.

"She been tryin' to get someone to call her Pasionara since she was seventeen. She reads too much." This from her female companion, who was slight and wiry and Italianate.

Pasionara was the widow of the helicopter cop killed in the New York massacre. "We didn't git along all that good, him and me," she told Cassidy frankly.

"Still, he was my husband, and these bastids killed him. I'm here to commit a little vengeance. Least I can do for the poor slob."

"I see," said Cassidy. Vengeance is mine, saith the Lord, thought Cassidy, who didn't believe in the Lord. Take it away, Lord. I don't want it.

"Just call me Anna, which ain't my name," said the Italianate woman.

None of them wanted their real names bandied about.

"We are here *ex officio*," said one of the black men. He

was swishing a little bamboo cane through the underbrush, making a vicious whistling noise.

His black friend said, "He can do some real nasty tricks with that cane. Show him, Snoops."

Snoops made a pass at a thick-stemmed bush, cutting it clean off near the ground.

"Mmmm," said Cassidy and exhaled a breath.

Snoops showed him the razor imbedded in the cane, the firelight flickering on his black face lighting up the hollows, making the white teeth shine.

Cassidy called the meeting to order, rapping on the front of the Ford truck, and this is where he could have said: Go home. This is foolishness. Murder. Insanity.

Instead he said, "How many here had combat experience, or if not experience combat training in the Army? Show of hands."

He got three ex-corporals and an ex-sergeant, and turned them over to Fletcher. Fletcher divided the group into five squads, put each of his noncoms in charge of a squad and himself in charge of another. "There'll be guards. We got to take them out first. Won't be easy in the blackness. Cassidy, you promised me starlight. Where's the starlight?"

Cassidy grunted. A bad omen, the blackness. It would make everything that much harder.

Fletcher was separating the squads now physically, so they'd get to know each other. The two women insisted on being in the same squad, as did the two blacks. The others all had nicknames—Scipio, Peanut, Pool Hall, Dugan. Taunts and wisecracks filled the air. There was a jollity about the group that chilled Cassidy to the bone.

"Weapons," he said to Fletcher quietly. "What you got?"

"Everyone got their service pistols," said Fletcher. "Most also got switchblades for the close stuff."

"They'll have bazookas, mortars, automatic weapons."

"We'll try and see they don't get to use 'em."

"Uh huh," said Cassidy. "You do that."

"Are we taking prisoners?" said Pasionara.

"No," said Fletcher.

That sent the crowd into a hoot of laughter. "He say a real sharp no, that man," said Snoops. "He is the Abominable No Man, that lieutenant."

"A little less noise," said Fletcher, pale in the firelight.

Keefe rode into the clearing on Black Prince, followed by Rattigan on Peppermint. "You can see that fire a mile and a half away. Is that a good idea?"

"We're getting organized. We'll put it out when the time comes. Where's Lucia?"

"Back at the cabin. That's what you wanted."

That's not what Cassidy wanted. That's what he got stuck with. He couldn't take Lucia back to the main house, not with Amanda Shotover now part of the operation. There was no one to leave her with at the main house. Alison thought she was back in New York and Anne Falk was Alison's point man in this operation.

Fletcher was drawing a map of the encampment in the dust on the rear window of the Ford truck. "The tents are lined up here to here." Slashing at the dust with his finger. "Twenty-two of them but they'll only be using maybe six, probably this six . . ." Pointing. "And the guards ought to be here, here, here, and there. We'll be approaching from the south—like this. . . ."

Cassidy said, low to Keefe, "We're not to get within half a mile of this. We drive the carriages, dump 'em."

"We got to drive them back," said Keefe.

"I suppose so," said Cassidy. He looked at his watch. Nine-twelve. "We'd better get going." He climbed up on Black Prince behind Keefe, which brought howls from the cops.

"Bad Day at Black Rock," hooted someone out of the darkness. "We're in a western." That brought down the house, hysteria just beneath the surface. Perhaps a little fear.

Several of the men around the fire were pulling at the whiskey bottle, passing it around. "That's enough of that," rapped Fletcher sharply. "We'll need clear heads. You can drink after."

There were angry mumbles. Fletcher was spoiling the party. Because that's what it was. A party. A murder party.

In the stable courtyard Amanda Shotover, her tiny body encased in black woolen trousers topped by a black sweater, was fastening the buckles on the Dover coach while Joseph held the horses in the stays. "You too old for this kind thing," scolded Joseph.

"So are you," snapped Amanda Shotover. "Hold that horse still."

The carriage gleaming green and gold in the lamplight, its brass lanterns glowing.

"Have you seen Armand, Joseph?"

"He come git his hoss, Leadbelly. Two days ago. Ain't seen him since. Don't know what he's feeding that hoss. Course they's plenty grass, but that hoss like a little grain at night."

"Why didn't you tell me you saw him, Joseph?"

"He tell me not to, Miz Shotover. Not tell anybody."

It was Armand who paid the bills and commanded the loyalty.

"Where do you think he is, Joseph?"

"Somewhere out there, Miz Shotover. You know Armand. He likely be anywhere. One of those cabin he loves so much. The more tumbledown dey be the better he like 'em. He never quite grow up, Miz Shotover."

"Is that an accusation, Joseph?"

"No m'aam. Ain't you fault. Others all grow up. Not him."

By the time Keefe and Cassidy came out of the blackness on Black Prince, the Dover coach was harnessed to the four

Morgans standing quietly as Morgans will. Joseph was finishing up with the pair of bays on the Irish jaunting car.

"We're a little behind schedule," said Cassidy. "Let's get on with it."

Amanda Shotover spoke up harshly. "I'll drive the Lancia, Professor. I've driven four horses before and you haven't. You drive the jaunting car. Joseph, you lead. I'll follow. You come next, Professor, and Mr. Keefe can drive the circus coach last."

Taking charge.

"Yes, m'aam," said Cassidy and climbed up to the driver's seat on the Irish jaunting car.

Lucia was stretched out in her sleeping bag on the floor next to the wood stove, reading by candlelight *The Black Stallion Returns* (soon to be a major motion picture) with intense absorption, living it. "The horses shot forward as one. Alec heard the shouts of the Bedouins as the Black bolted. Then he could hear nothing but the pounding of the hoofs; feel nothing but the surge of great muscles between his legs; see nothing but the ground slipping away in long rolling waves beneath him. . . ."

The Black would win because he always won, which was comforting to the thirteen-year-old-girl. She wasn't ready yet for defeat. Books were for victory.

The knocking at the door was at first soft, almost apologetic, but it grew bolder, and when it finally penetrated Lucia's stallion-drugged mind, it scared the wits out of her. She lay very quiet, eyes like moons. Until she heard the voice.

"Armand!"

She knew that voice. Lucia scrambled out of the sleeping bag and opened the door. Anne Falk stood there in the dim light, meticulously dressed in jodhpurs and boots and riding coat and hat, as if she'd come from a hunt meet.

Lucia emitted a nervous giggle. "Anne!" she said, and

gave her a big hug. "I'm not supposed to tell you anything. I'm not supposed to even talk to you, but I can give you a hug." And gave her another.

Anne disentangled herself from the girl's arms. "I thought you were back in New York."

"I'm not back in New York. I'm right here. Come in! Come in! Would you like some tea? Or coffee? We make it on the wood stove and it's *very* romantic. Don't ask me what we're doing here because I'm not supposed to tell you and anyway I don't *know* what we're doing here. I've been left behind while the men are off doing whatever they're doing, and I'm here alone and very lonely and I'm scared and I'm very happy to see you and I hope you'll stay and keep me company. What are *you* doing here?"

All in a mouthful.

Anne Falk took off her hat and sat down in one of the four chairs round the table, counting the cups. Four. She ran her fingers through her hair and finally smiled at Lucia, who was hovering anxiously.

"I'm looking for Armand," she said. "But I don't know what I'd do with him if I found him." She looked around her, at the saddlebags, the pile of luggage, not missing anything. "This is one of his favorite hideouts. Have you seen him?"

"I wouldn't know Armand if I saw him. I've never laid eyes on him. I've just heard tell of him, and not much of that. Daddy doesn't consider him a fit subject for me."

Anne said, "Oh, I should think he'd be a very fit subject for you. He's about your age emotionally. Maybe a little younger. He adored your father."

"Daddy says he doesn't know him. Never met him until he blew into the flat with a gun."

"He knew your father without ever having met him. He'd read the files, you see. Your father's file is very long and very . . . heartwarming. At least to Armand. A bit of hero worship ensued."

"Does Daddy know this?"

"If he doesn't, he ought to. It explains many things."

A soft whinny interjected itself.

"Faun," guessed Lucia.

"How do you think I got here? On foot? It's black as the inside of a bear outside. I would never have found this place if it weren't for the candlelight. I could see light for three hundred yards."

Another whinny, this time from a different horse.

"Ariel," guessed Anne Falk. "You've got Ariel here."

Then they heard the jet. Actually, the noise had been building for some time, but it had not yet commanded their attention, which was fixed on each other. Now the roar of the jet overrode all other thoughts. It was low, close.

"Golly, it sounds like it's going to land!" shouted Lucia.

The jet passed directly overhead going west, and the noise faded.

"Cassidy is out of his mind, leaving you here alone," said Anne angrily. "He doesn't know how dangerous Roberto is."

"Who's Roberto?"

"Never mind. Come on. I'm going up to Kaska's cabin. Armand might be there."

"Oooh, marvie!" yipped Lucia. "A ride in the woods at night! Daddy will be furious, but then he doesn't have to find out, does he?"

Fletcher had laid down the law. No cigarettes. No light of any kind. No booze. And very little talk. Joseph had greased the wheels so the carriages moved almost without sound except for the soft clop of the horses on the dirt road, the horses feeling their way in the blackness with Joseph's soft urgings from the driver's seat of the Dover coach.

Inside the Dover coach, the black man named Snoops was saying to his friend, who called himself Elf, "Don't see the sense of this vehicle, when we had all those nice trucks."

"You evah try drive a truck four miles a hour without lights through the woods?" Elf said. "Can't be done."

Pasionara was sitting sideways on the Irish jaunting car, holding tight her Italianate friend's hand in her own hand, feeling shivery in the warm night, and thinking about her dead husband. I'm closer to the guinea bastid in death than I was in life. He seemed to be hovering right over her now, spurring her on. First time he ever approved anything I did.

Four winding miles through the black woods at four miles an hour seemed forever. During the last fifteen minutes Fletcher commanded silence. "We gettin' close. No more talk."

In silence they heard the jet scream miles away, coming from the opposite direction. Even from inside the carriage he could see the lights.

Joseph pulled up and the others jolted to a halt behind, the horses' noses all but touching the carriage ahead.

"All out," whispered Fletcher. "Scipio, take your squad and fan out to the left. Dugan you to the right. Georgio, you follow Dugan. My squad follow me, straight ahead. All of you about fifty yards forward and then hit the dirt until I give the signal, and that'll be a long wait until they in their beds and lights out."

Armand was letting Leatherstocking graze in back of old Welch's cabin, holding the leash because Leatherstocking had been known to run away. In these backwoods Armand would never find him. Not that night anyway. Armand was talking away soothingly. "I know! I know! You've been gypped out of your supper once again, but it'll all be over tomorrow. I promise you not only supper but breakfast. Four cans of sweet feed and a box of Calf Manna. You'll like that, won't you?"

He tethered the horse close to keep Leatherstocking from tangling himself in the rope and went into the cabin.

He had pulled Kaska off the floor and propped him in an

armchair facing the door. There the body had stiffened and sat, eyes open, arms resting on the armrest, staring like an accusation at whoever entered.

"Did you ever talk to horses, Kaska? Or dogs? Or dead bodies? No, you didn't because you would be afraid someone was recording, and they would have been. Being a Communist you didn't talk to God either. So who did you talk to? You, the ultimate loner. The lonest man I ever knew. Loner even than me, and that's going some."

Armand sat on the desk facing Kaska's profile, cradling the Hosford in his arms.

"I've always talked to myself, Kaska, because I was the only person I could tell the truth to. Everyone else I tell what they want to hear or they get angry and shout at me. How about you, Kaska? You told everyone lies—me, Alison, Mother Russia, Roberto—but who did you tell the truth to? Anyone? Not even your horse? If you ever had one. Or a dog? How did you keep all those lies straight? You led a double life, triple life, quadruple life. My goodness, I can't even lead one life without getting all torn up inside. I don't understand how anyone could lead three or four lives—or would want to."

He heard the plane's high scream. "There comes Roberto, Kaska. I hope you give him a real turn. If I don't kill him first."

Armand worked the action on the Hosford, checked the sight at a hundred yards, inserted the clip, pulled the lever to get a round in the barrel, and clicked on the safety.

He looked around at all the communications equipment with his wide boyish smile. "All this lovely communications equipment, the very latest in communications technology, for the sole purpose of telling lies. What a joke!"

He was full of gaiety now, the voice light and high like a child's. "Have you ever told the truth on this machine, Kaska? Ever? Have you ever let one single tiny spark of honesty creep into all that prevarication? I bet you didn't.

187

Probably fearful it would blow out the works. Let us leave a little joker in the works, shall we, Kaska? In case I don't survive this evening, which is highly possible."

He was bubbling over with words now, eyes full of mischief, words pouring out of him like water over a spillway. He began typing on the switchboard, crooning away as he did so. "The whole truth and nothing but the truth, your honor. Are you ready, machine, for the whole truth and nothing but the truth? Are you sure you can handle it without blowing your ectoplasm or whatever it is that you blow? You want to know who Victor is, where the twenty-six million is? Well, listen, my children, and you shall hear . . ."

Typing away.

On his belly, chin in the dirt, Fletcher lay closest to the airfield, watching the jet after it came directly over him, going away, landing far down the three-quarter runway, braking to a halt, and cutting its engines.

All wrong, according to their calculations. The plane, they had figured, would taxi back to the end of the airstrip and disgorge the troops there where the encampment was.

Instead, from the three-quarters of a mile away, Fletcher could dimly hear the shouted Spanish commands after the men were marched off the plane.

Now what? Will they march them down here?

Instead the plane's engines started again and the plane taxied slowly down the field right toward the spot where Fletcher lay hidden. At the south end of the airstrip, the jet swung slowly in a curve, headed down the field, and with a great roar, hurtled back into the air again.

When the noise subsided, Fletcher waited, listening for the sound of approaching troops, the tramp of feet. Dead silence. He listened for fifteen minutes, twenty minutes. He rose to his feet, peering into the blackness. No sound.

He began searching through the underbrush for the others, kicking them to their feet, swearing. "Back to the carriages! We've been swindled! We've been outguessed! We've been anticipated! We've been betrayed!"

"Easy, Lieutenant," said Pasionara.

18

Arguello, he of the demonic face, led because he knew the way. Also because he operated in total darkness like the fer-de-lance, his country's most poisonous and dangerous snake. Behind him, the other soldiers stumbled and fell and straggled and got lost because they had not Arguello's magical night sight. Time and again the procession had to halt while Arguello rounded up the strays and Roberto counted heads. The others would fall to the ground breathing heavily, some of them going to sleep, and had to be kicked awake.

A slow business.

Next to Balisario's dank and steaming jungle, the Virginia woodland was open country, but the woods were cut with deep ravines, some of them with streams flowing at the bottom that had to be forded and steep banks that had to be climbed. The timber was oak and pine that had not been cut in two hundred years, some of the trees ten feet around, and the men would walk straight into them in the dark, crying out with fear and pain. Each of these soldiers brought his myths and superstitions with him into this new and fearsome country, and in the darkness these flourished and grew to mountainous size, peopling the Virginia woods with Hispanic demons and monsters that lurked behind every bush.

Roberto brought up the rear, kicking the stragglers back into place, keeping an eye on the four who carried his torture equipment. A bad bump could upset the oscilloscopes and then how could one assess the precise volume of agony? Besides that worry, Roberto was uncomfortable, and he loathed discomfort. He was a good and brave soldier and in several of the endless wars with Honduras Roberto had acquitted himself under fire with both valor and élan (such a lovely word)! But how could one demonstrate élan on a mission like this? Pillage and plunder were part of the soldier's trade, but recovering stolen money was quite definitely not. That was for policemen, and Roberto despised policemen. The mission was humiliating. As well as uncomfortable.

Anyway, the whole thing reeked of implausibility. Who had sent that message? Victor? Not a chance. Kaska? Never. Who then? Cassidy? Roberto smiled in the blackness. The medieval scholar. Perhaps we shall catch the medieval scholar and make him scream. Scream, perhaps, in thirteenth-century medieval French, which I understand he knows very well. That would be interesting.

It was five miles between the airstrip and Kaska's cabin.

In another part of the forest, to the south of the Hispanics, Faun with Anne Falk on her back picked her way delicately through the big trees, following an old familiar trail. Lucia on Ariel was following Faun so closely she could reach out and touch Faun's rump. The girl was crouched low, her head and neck next to Faun's neck to avoid the branches she couldn't see. Even then she got a mouthful of twigs from time to time.

"Blast!" said Anne. "This can't be right."

"Trust the horse," said Lucia. "She knows."

"It never took this long. I've done it a dozen times."

"Never at night. It's different at night."

Much different. She couldn't judge anything—distance, height, depth, sounds. Even the smells seemed more sinister at night.

"What time is it?"

Anne looked at the luminous face of her watch. "Almost midnight."

They were still on the flat, which meant the mountain lay ahead. Once they got to the mountain the land was more open and they could move faster.

"Where's Mr. Alison?" asked Lucia.

"I don't know. Why do you ask?"

"Daddy doesn't trust Mr. Alison." Even when she said it she knew she shouldn't.

"Mr. Alison doesn't trust your daddy. He says Cassidy is a romantic living in the past."

"If he doesn't trust him, why does he always hire him to do his dirty work?"

Anne laughed. "Good question. I think Cassidy is the person Alison wishes he were. Since he can't be him, he hires him, trying to acquire a little of the Cassidy magic secondhand."

Magic. The word struck fire in the darkness. Lucia smiled impishly and grew bolder.

"Are you going to marry Armand?" she asked.

Long pause as the horses threaded their slow way through the blackness.

"I don't know that Armand will ever concentrate long enough to marry me."

In Kaska's cabin Armand had finished the truth-telling lark and turned off the machine, looking at his watch. "He'll be coming soon, Kaska. We must make him welcome, mustn't we?" Good manners were of the highest importance.

193

Armand tried with his fingers to bend Kaska's dead face into a welcoming smile, to pull the lips open, to crinkle the eyes—but it was no use. The flesh had stiffened into a last sad look of deep skepticism which, Armand had to admit, was much more characteristic of Kaska than a welcoming smile.

Armand abandoned the smile and wrote in red chalk across Kaska's forehead: *Bienvenido!*

"Marvelous word!" said Armand. "It says everything."

He switched on the floodlight just outside the front door that Kaska had put there to help him when he had to go out to fix the big dish antenna at night.

Armand closed the door behind him, the lights still on in the cabin, and went to Leatherstocking. He saddled the horse and rode him up the steep slope, well out of the circle of bright light to the highest point of the hill, the Hosford .307 in his arms. Under his shirt the bulletproof vest felt clammy and heavy in the warm night.

Alison was seated at Armand's desk, using Armand's telephone to call the summer White House in Colorado. All these western hayseeds. First Nixon, who had boasted to Khrushchev how he had shoveled as much horseshit as Khrushchev, then Reagan, then this clown who floated like a gas bag with his great immovable grin over the realities of politics, economics, and diplomacy further and further into never-never land.

"You can't talk to him," said Harriet Van Fleet. (The damned woman never left his side.) "He's doing his push-ups."

"What?"

"Forty of them, Mr. Alison. Can you do forty push-ups? No, you can't."

Forty push-ups followed by twenty chin-ups—many of them photographed and appearing on the front pages. Carter had been a jogger (running into that wall on one occasion), followed by Reagan, with long horseback rides and his woodchopping, followed by this idiot with his push-ups and chin-ups and iron pumping. Roosevelt and Kennedy had filled the White House with intellectuals, Reagan with entertainers, and this mountebank with quarterbacks.

"I just wanted to keep him up to date. The operation has begun."

"He doesn't want to know," said Harriet Van Fleet and banged down the phone.

Alison flushed and hung up. The new diplomacy. The right to know had been highest privilege. Under Reagan there had appeared the even higher privilege of *not* knowing. (The U.S. had under Reagan actually initiated talks with the PLO without telling the President. If they'd come off, the President would have taken the credit. Otherwise, he never knew. Even better, it never happened.)

Alison went downstairs in the silent house, looking for a drink. Geoffrey always kept drink on the sideboard in the immense living room. Alison mixed himself whiskey and water and went into the gun room for another look at that antique Winchester which had caught his eye. It was missing.

Inside the coaches, something like mutiny was developing. Cassidy, third in the slow procession, could hear the roar of it back in the Irish jaunting car where he was. He couldn't understand what it was about but he could guess, because he'd heard a bit of it in the jaunting car. There were the ideologues who wanted to press forward with the operation. There were the others—the party gang—who had been gung ho for slitting a few throats as long as the slittees were sound asleep. Now that the victims were awake, afoot, and heavily armed, they were full of second thoughts. Whiskey was being passed around and the second thoughts were getting louder and louder.

Cassidy in the Irish jaunting car said to Fletcher next to

him, "This can't go on. You can hear these guys for miles. We'll be ambushed."

Fletcher jumped off the jaunting car and ran to the head of the procession, past the slow-moving coaches, urging the drivers to pull up. He went from coach to coach, demanding discipline and silence, reminding the cops they were putting their lives at risk with loud talk. The idea of dropping the operation altogether was not mentioned by Fletcher and no one else brought it up because Fletcher ranked them all.

Fletcher, pale and resolute, climbed back onto the driver's seat next to Cassidy and the coaches resumed their slow march through the dark woods. In a low voice Cassidy suggested that it might be wise to drop the whole thing and go back to New York.

"Are you insane?" snarled Fletcher.

Insanity was calling the thing off. Sanity was pushing on to attack heavily armed, well-trained soldiers in the dark. Why don't I just walk away? thought Cassidy. But he wouldn't. He couldn't. So that was just bloody-well that. Wars, thought Cassidy sadly, had their own momentum, and once you were in, it was hell to get out until you'd been beaten to a pulp or beaten the other guy to a pulp. Fletcher had been exceeding reluctant to get into this fray and was now adamant about keeping on with it.

Behind Cassidy were the two women who had been among the most passionate ideologues, denouncing as cowards the two men on the jaunting car, one of them black, who had wanted to turn back. An action had been set in motion; it must be allowed to continue until it bore fruit, no matter what that fruit might be. It was not a matter of courage or cowardice; it was aesthetics. One didn't run the curtain down in the middle of the second act. Even if one got killed in the process, the show must go on.

They were taking the long route around to Kaska's, much farther than the direct route through the woods that the marchers took, but, on the other hand, faster. Joseph was in the lead, driving the Dover coach in which sat the silent men, their dark thoughts fermenting in the thick silence that Fletcher had demanded.

What is foreseen does not happen, and what happens is not foreseen. That is the rule of combat operations, all of them. We have no idea what we're getting into, thought Cassidy, or how we'll survive it or if we'll survive it. We cannot guess the ending of this Greek tragedy except that we know it will be tragic. This is not high comedy, it is low tragedy. Tragedy with much buffoonery.

The soldiers were taking another break while Arguello rounded up the stragglers and counted heads. In this interval Roberto's gold watch sounded its two musical notes—C and G—which meant that it was half after the hour—or 12:30. It was a gold pocket watch, very thin, its gold outer face and back heavily embossed with the figures of trumpeting angels. Roberto always wore the watch on his military campaigns as part of his élan, taking it out of his watch pocket (how many people had watch pockets anymore, alas?) while bullets whizzed about his head to see what time it was. It made an indelible impression on the junior officers—or at least Roberto hoped so.

Now the two silvery notes—C and G—reminded him sharply that the platoon had been on the march for a full hour, up hill and down dale, across streams and through heavy woods, and the men were becoming exhausted. Roberto summoned Arguello to his side.

"How much farther, *capitán*?"

As if on signal, the light blazed forth at that very second, high up the hill. A good half mile away but still a beacon that startled Roberto into whispers. "What is that?"

"Kaska's floodlight. He has one outside the cabin in order to repair the antenna at night." This, too, in whispers.

It was time for strategy, but first Roberto, good officer that he was, took time out to congratulate Arguello on his unerring accuracy in leading the men through these dark woods to their destination, a superb bit of guidance which would duly be rewarded.

Then to business. The men were to be dispersed in a full circle around the cabin so that no one could slip through the cordon. "You are to take each squad to its place because you are the one who knows the ground and who can see in the dark. You must remind everyone that they are not to shoot but to take prisoners. We are here to gather information. When you have done that, return here."

It took Arguello half an hour to disperse the men in a circle around the cabin and well out of the circle of brilliant light. The two men, Roberto and Arguello, crept tree to tree up the slope to the very edge of the clearing, still in the shadow of the great trees.

In whispers Roberto said, "I suspect a trap has been laid. We will try a little guile."

He raised his voice to a shout. In English: "Victor! Victor! It is I—Roberto."

Whoever came to the door would not be Victor. That much he knew. But who would answer the shout, that he didn't know.

No one did.

The brilliant light shone on the old cabin, revealing the plaster falling from the chinks in the logs, which were themselves dark with age and weather.

Roberto raised his voice again with its deep baritone machismo: "Kaska! It is Roberto Garcia come to pay a call at Victor's invitation. Are you home, Kaska?"

Silence.

"Something is very wrong," whispered Roberto. "Perhaps we should rush the place."

"No," said Arguello. "I'll go. You stay and cover the door."

"No," said Roberto. "You are too valuable. We need your guidance and your night vision. Get Georgio."

Georgio was pure cannon fodder. A vast hulk who had joined the army (as had so many others) for the food and then eaten himself into tremendous size and brawn.

Georgio was summoned and instructed. He came out from behind the tree into the circle of pure white light and marched, quaking, up the slope toward the house.

Armand on Leatherstocking had been circling to the west of the cabin in a little glade whose every tree he knew well. His heart was singing as had Pierre's at the marvelous battle scene in *War and Peace*. Ah, adventure! Or perhaps not adventure but Aardvron. He'd taken the last of the yellow tablets ten minutes ago and felt a warm flood of good feeling, just short of bliss, though very close.

At the very first shouted "Victor," he had closed his eyes and felt the thrill clear to his toes. This was *Danger*! How piercing the elation!

He opened his eyes and saw Georgio emerge from behind a tree and walk up the slope toward the cabin. Georgio looked very scared. Armand leveled the Hosford and took a deep breath which, of course, was the proper beginning of a good sighting. The Aardvron was humming in his veins, making every red corpuscle dance.

He had killed in Grand Central Station with the man's own gun, but it had been a battle—a battle he had won by superior cunning (beautifully coached by Kaska). He had killed Kaska, although that had been entirely accidental. Surely a third killing should not bother him, since he was now clearly a killer of considerable experience.

But the fact was it did. Sighting down the rifle at the porcine face of this Latin, Armand suffered a revulsion so strong as to make the rifle shake. This killing would be in coldest blood, something he'd been instructed to despise.

He lowered the rifle. This man was not Roberto. Armand had never seen Roberto, but he had had dealings with him by radio, had had intelligence reports on his elegance, his style. This man had no elegance, no style.

A trick. I am being played for a sucker.

That angered Armand (the Aardvron still humming in his veins but turning him toward choler as sometimes happened with Aardvron).

He leveled the rifle again. He would not shoot the man, just shoot off his cap as a flippant way of telling Roberto that he was onto his little game. He squeezed off the shot carefully after a very long and meticulous sighting, and it was not altogether Armand's fault that the shot went wrong. Leatherstocking moved slightly, and Armand had to correct his aim a little too rapidly. Also Georgio was on rising ground and Armand hadn't accurately allowed for that. The shot caught Georgio between the eyes, killing him instantly.

"Oh, I *am* sorry!" Armand called out.

Always apologizing.

The shot rang through the quiet night like the crack of doom. Anne and Lucia heard it on their horses, both of which jumped a little and reared back as horses will.

"Shooting!" said Lucia. "I'm scared."

Armand and his Hosford on that horse Leatherstocking, Anne was thinking. He could be shooting at cans again. Or at something more substantial. "Come on," she said and urged Faun ahead with her knees. Lucia followed on Ariel, and a few minutes later they could see through the trees the brilliant white light in front of Kaska's cabin above them, as they were still on the slope of the mountain facing up.

They were to the east of the cabin, going up toward it on a diagonal. Lucia was leaning forward, her head next to the horse's neck to avoid the branches. She never saw the brown arm that reached out and encircled her waist and pulled her off Ariel, but she felt the strength and the menace of the arm to the bottom of her soul, and she screamed a blood-shattering scream that resounded for miles in the quiet woods.

Pure terror. She screamed and screamed.

Spurred by the screams, Ariel bolted.

Lucia was still screaming only moments later when another brown arm got Anne Falk by the throat and hauled her off Faun, who trotted off.

There there were two of them screaming, high mezzo-soprano in the black night.

19

Cassidy had actually given Lucia lessons in screaming. Lucia—Cassidy thought—was too well brought up to scream properly. Too many nannies, too many governesses. Cassidy had taken her out to Central Park and instructed her on the fine art of letting go with full-blooded howls loud enough to freeze the blood of rapists, hoods, murderers, and had succeeded in unleashing her so well that she attracted a patrol car with two furious cops. It took a lot of explaining.

And here it was, Lucia's well-coached scream, splitting the blackness, freezing Cassidy's own blood. The scream, in fact, transfixed the whole cavalcade. The horses pulling the Dover coach tried to bolt and were stopped only by Joseph's expert handling. Behind him Amanda reined in the Lancia, as did Cassidy with the jaunting car and Keefe with the circus coach.

When the second scream came and when Anne Falk added her own high screech, Cassidy hurtled off the driver's seat of the car into the woods in the direction of the action. Fletcher, a younger, quicker man, caught him in three strides, pulled him to earth, and sat on him. "Cool it, man!" hissed Fletcher. "You'll get us all slaughtered." Cassidy, heaving and glaring.

Keefe materialized out of the blackness and put his big hand on Cassidy's head. "Our only advantage is surprise," he said quietly. "You'll get us all killed—and the girl too."

Cassidy panting: "Get Rattigan—and his knife."

"We all have knives," said Keefe and went to get the little clown.

Cassidy was on his feet now, murderously calm. Got the shoe polish out of his jump suit, began blacking up, the whiteness shimmering through the trees like mist.

"What is it?" whispered Fletcher.

"Kaska's searchlight. Over his door. Maybe half mile." He passed the shoe polish. "Black up. It's Indian warfare from here in."

The others came through the gloom in twos and threes, Fletcher handing around the shoe polish.

Keefe said, "We'll need a password so we don't go killing each other."

"Spit," said Rattigan. "No word like it in Spanish. No *sp* words at all."

The white cop faces disappearing under the shoe polish, changing their nature, invisible cops, with all the magical properties. No more jokes. Reeking of sobriety. With a little fear to sharpen the mind.

"We'll go first," said Cassidy, very low. "Keefe and Rattigan and me. Squads follow at five-minute intervals."

"Ten," said Fletcher. "We don't want to run into each other."

"Quiet is the word. We know they're there. They don't know we exist." Adding as an afterthought, "No prisoners." As if it needed saying. Coming from Cassidy, it was a wholly new statement, flaring like a match, changing the play.

After the shot—and his apology—Armand had turned Leatherstocking 180 degrees, the Aardvron singing in his veins. Musically. All very high chords. The chorale of Beethoven's Ninth Symphony roaring in his mind with the full orchestra, Toscanini conducting.

Expecting answering fire and turning away as he'd learned from his guerrilla studies. Roberto was a clever man. He must have had some plan, and therefore it was sensible to reverse direction, the Aardvron symphony and chorale crashing its mighty chords in Armand's head. All an accident, don't you see. I didn't mean . . .

The two soldiers, Fulgencio and Guillermo, lying in the grass at the edge of the blackness could have shot him, but the orders were: Don't shoot. Take prisoners. It was Guillermo who leaped and encircled Armand's waist with his strong arms. Armand, intoxicated with the Aardvron symphony, smashed the butt of the Hosford into the man's face almost absently, scandalized by the interruption.

It was just then that Lucia's screams—to be so shortly followed by Anne Falk's—split the night like rifle shots. To Armand, already in the grip of his symphony and chorale—all those mighty chords—it was sensory overload. Scream upon scream upon scream.

Leatherstocking had bolted up past the cabin to the very crest of the rise—Armand's mind beginning to explode with the screams, the music, the sublimity, a thousand angels singing contrapuntal reproaches.

Armand pitched headlong off the galloping horse and rolled over and over into the drainage ditch where he lay very still, facedown, blending into the foliage like camouflage.

Amanda was holding the heads of the lead horses of the Dover coach, crooning, "There, there," calming them after the screams. Joseph going from carriage to carriage, saying, "Woo woo," patting rumps, the soft familiar voice quieting the horses. Grumbling nevertheless: "Shouldn't be in the shafts, standing still all this while. Leavin' us two wi' twelve horses. It ain't right."

"Well, it's not often, Joseph, not often," said Amanda, crooning so the horses would think she was talking to them, stroking the lead horses' faces.

In the rest of the woods, silence like ink. Leaf droppings clamorous in the immensity.

"That was Lucia screamed," said Amanda Shotover softly.

"Miss Falk too. Miss Falk scream."

Whatever it meant.

Joseph going softly from carriage to carriage, calming the animals.

Roberto had seen the horse Leatherstocking galloping on the very edge of the light and disappear with its rider into the darkness of woods about a hundred yards to his left. This was the man who had shot Georgio—who lay facedown in the pool of white light. The killer, Roberto guessed, was alone. There was unmistakable aloneness about that single shot.

"Now," Roberto said to Arguello, "make a dash for it."

Now he was willing to risk his invaluable Arguello. Now the odds had shifted in favor of risking Arguello's life but not yet of risking his own. Not yet. It would be a long night.

Stooping low, Arguello sprinted for the cabin door under the naked effulgence of light.

The screams came just as Arguello was in the midst of this move. Roberto, connoisseur of screams that he was, quivered with appreciation. A child in terror. A woman in terror. Not pain, terror. The plot thickened and Roberto, a minimalist, frowned. He was not one of those aesthetes who thought all plot was obscenity; he liked a little plot, but plot within manageable limits, and he hadn't been aware that a woman and child were in the script. Unless . . .

Arguello had long since ducked into the cabin. Roberto was left with his thoughts, which were pointillist. The great hulk of Georgio lying in the white light so *eloquently*, shrieking to the high heavens that he was *dead*. No getting around it. Death was so *unmistakable*. The thing has begun, thought Roberto. How marvelous!

Arguello came out the cabin door in the glare of light and waved his right arm toward the house, meaning come along, the coast is clear.

The screaming had stopped, leaving an aftermath of unearthly silence with its memory of the screams like footprints in the brain. Roberto rose and walked up the steep slope toward Kaska's door. Then came the sound of galloping hooves again. Armand, his veins whistling with Aardvron, was on the move (just before he fell off). Roberto hurtled up the slope (not liking the indignity of this haste) and threw himself into the cabin, there to confront the deeply skeptical dead face of Kaska with the single word *Bienvenido* written on his forehead.

Roberto was affronted. "You think I don't speak English?" he said to the corpse. "How very unkind!"

The white light was penetrating the foliage now, carving unimaginable monsters out of the leaves. Cassidy, Keefe, and Rattigan had gone down, first to their knees, finally to their bellies, contributing their rustling and scratching to the other night noises. Approach like foxes, fight like lions, disappear like birds. As the French used to say of the Iroquois. That is our objective, Cassidy was thinking. We are imaginary. That is our strength. We don't exist. When we do ...

Shutting his mind down hard on the absence of screams. There is only one thing worse than a scream. The silence that follows it.

Cassidy crawling on his belly, hearing the rustles on his

right and slightly behind him of Keefe: on his left and slightly ahead of both of them was Rattigan.

They had a bit of luck. A soft whisper in the dark: "Rodrigo?" It was a question. The questioner was Rodrigo's partner, Perez. He had heard the rustlings and assumed (since, as Cassidy had said, there was no enemy there, the Americans being imaginary) the rustlings had been caused by his friend and fellow soldier Rodrigo, who was lying twelve yards away and might have been expected to whisper back: *"Qué?"* Or something like that. But Rodrigo was sound asleep and here was the other great advantage of the Americans over the Hispanics in this encounter. The Americans had come five miles by carriage, grumbling and jeering at the slow pace, in discomfort, but nevertheless riding all the way, at rest. The Hispanics had walked the five miles, up hill and down dale, the branches and roots catching at them, walking into the trunks of trees, stumbling across streams. Rodrigo was not the only one who, when the forward movement had ended, had fallen asleep. No enemy about. Where's the harm?

So instead of his friend Rodrigo answering *"Qué"* it was Rattigan who answered Perez with a soft *"Sí"* and then crawled over to Perez. Just before Perez discovered Rattigan was not, in fact, imaginary, Rattigan cut his throat, his hand over Perez' mouth so that any gurgling sounds which always accompanied the slitting of throats would be muffled and, please God, sound like ordinary night noises.

It was Cassidy who had crawled the extra yards and come upon the sleeping Rodrigo. There, his night vision sharpened by hours of blackness, his face was four inches away from the brown face of Rodrigo, cherubic with sleep which is always a return to innocence. But one couldn't have thoughts like these with Lucia's screams resounding in his mind and with his own "No prisoners!" hanging there in the darkness like a witch's curse. He shot the sleeping soldier in the back straight through the heart with the silenced .25. *Sppplp*, like that. Two down and thirty-eight to go.

Not two minutes later Keefe came upon another sleeping Hispanic and put his stiletto delicately through his ribs into the heart. Regretfully, because Keefe harbored a theory that each death diminished his own vitality by a measurable degree, that he was allotted only so many deaths and that after the last one, he, Keefe, would gutter out like a candle. Irish hobgoblin nonsense, Cassidy had said, himself as Irish as they come.

Kaska with the *Bienvenido* written across his forehead, lifelong skepticism imprisoned in his features, had been lifted from his chair, his body frozen in the sitting position, and deposited in the kitchen out of sight. Roberto Garcia now sat at the RD-11 toying with the keyboard, watching the lights flash off and on, the gibberish appear on the screen. He didn't understand computers nor sympathize with them.

Over his shoulder he said to Arguello, "It was that man on horseback shot Georgio. Get him. And tell Maurello to bring me the equipage."

That's what he called the torture equipment—the equipage, which was both a Spanish and an English word. Roberto was not sure what it meant in either language, but it had a nice modern sound, calculated to strike awe in the hearts of the simpleminded.

Arguello was behind the front door now, gun drawn. "Someone is coming."

The door opened and in came two *soldados,* staggering slightly under the weight of the two females, who were over their shoulders, trussed like mummies. The two men put them on the floor feet first, standing them up like floor lamps.

"Prisioneras," explained one of the *soldados.* They had been instructed to take prisoners. Here were prisoners.

Their mouths tightly gagged.

"They were screaming," explained the *soldado*.

"Yes, I heard," said Roberto. "Remove the gags, please."

He lit a cigarette. It was always best when first confronting *prisioneros* (or *prisioneras*) to light a cigarette. It gave one a bit of authoritative silence in which to contemplate the captives, to establish one's dominance, to strike a little fear.

"Good evening," he said pleasantly, brimful of Latin charm. "You must excuse the rough stuff. We are soldiers. What are your names?"

Furiously, Anne Falk snapped at him: "*Your* name is Roberto Garcia. You're here on a CIA special training mission and you ought to be in the bivouac area five miles from here. What are you doing snatching us from our horses?"

"You frightened the horses!" To Lucia the worst thing anyone could do.

Roberto laughed pleasantly. My goodness, this ice maiden spitting like a cobra! What a beauty she was! Especially when angry. Knowing his name and everything. Well! well! He took a long puff on his cigarette, inhaling the smoke and contemplating the tip, letting them wait.

"What did you say your name was again?" he asked.

"My name is Anne Falk and I'm a CIA clandestine services special officer and I want to know what the hell you're doing dragging us off our horses in the middle of the night?"

"And what are you doing wandering around these woods in the middle of the night?" Roberto Garcia's manner had changed abruptly from Latin charm to total military authority. "I was invited here by this machine," tapping the RD-11, not revealing Victor's name because he didn't know how much this woman knew, "which is our authorized communication channel with your esteemed organization, the CIA. When we got here, we found Señor Kaska shot dead in this very chair."

"No!" Anne Falk, astonished.

"One of my men was shot and killed when walking to this cabin by a man on horseback. . . ."

Oh, dear God! Armand and his gun on Leatherstocking, high on drugs! Anne's face cold as stone.

Roberto continued, looking at her with the heavy gravity of a Spanish grandee. "Not a nice welcome at all for soldiers who are, after all, your allies. And that is by no means all. Several of your CIA operatives have invaded my country and killed twelve of my men, including one of my nephews. I believe there is a man named Cassidy involved in all this. Do you know this man Cassidy? I would like to question him."

She would never have answered that, but as a matter of fact she never had a chance. From outside a shrill, full-bodied whistle, something like a police whistle, high and imperious and alarming, pierced the silence.

It was followed almost immediately by the sound of a shot. Not the thin, high resonance of the Hosford or any other rifle. This was an explosion, a *wumpf* sound, like a large-caliber pistol.

Roberto put out his cigarette in the ashtray and rose to his feet. In Spanish he said, "That's not one of our guns. Arguello, put out that searchlight. I think you'll find the switch right there at the door." In English now: "Señora and señorita, if you'll step this way." He ushered them into Kaska's bedroom with great solemnity. The room smelled of solitude, dank, untended, solitariness imbedded in the very walls. In the center of the room was a neatly made double bed with Kaska's shoes underneath it. A small wooden bureau stood against one wall and a chair beside Kaska's bed on which reposed a lamp. That was all. It was chill and dark, the air heavy with man smell. There were no windows.

"Make yourself comfortable," said Roberto absently. He closed the door and locked it.

Each encounter in the blackness of the deep woods was highly personal, cunning and cold-blooded. The cops on their fat bellies counted on their invisibility, their nonexistence, and they had a high degree of success against the exhausted Latins, many of them sound asleep, who they came upon blindly and dispatched with their knives or strangled with their bare hands silently, each engagement a little different, some of the *soldados* going to their finish without a murmur, others struggling and gurgling and threshing but all within the limitations of noise which seemed reasonable and unalarming. Vengeance was the motivation, the strongest of all motivations.

No prisoners.

Pasionara and her friend Anna (which was not her name) were crawling in tandem quieter than mice (who are not very quiet), on elbows and knees, their hands free to hold weapons, pistol in the left hand, knife in the right, three yards apart. Pasionara had been blooded twice, looking for—as the song says—satisfaction. Not finding it. She had come upon her first sleeping Latin, herself breathless with astonishment, five minutes after she had taken to knees and elbows, and using both hands had stabbed him through the back ribs straight through to the heart, her arm about his neck, hand in front of the *soldado*'s mouth to dim the gurglings, telling herself: That's for *him*, the murdered helicopter pilot, her husband whom she had not liked all that much after all and perhaps therefore not feeling the elation she expected and, she felt, damn well deserved. Or perhaps it was just that killing was not her game, not a woman's game at all and damn the feminists. Like killing chickens, which she had also done and not much liked. Damned hard work, boring, banal, empty.

It was this feeling, this emptiness, that made Pasionara on the next approach a bit careless. She had been—with elbows and knees—quiet as a cat (who are much quieter than mice), putting each elbow, each knee down softly, experimentally feeling out the ground below for rustle and snap. A slow business. But now drugged by success (and, yes, the banality) she picked up the pace a bit, enough to outdistance by a yard or so her partner and wingman, Anna, who would have liked to protest but, with the exigencies of silence, couldn't.

A twig snapped. Leaves rustled. Unacceptable noises. Too loud, too regular, *suspicious*.

Hugging the ground ten yards ahead of her, Vincent Morales, one of Roberto's best sergeants, heard and stiffened. Morales had survived a half dozen of Balisario's miniwars with its neighbors, its uprisings, and civil strife. He was a jungle veteran and now he hunkered low, eyes—he had excellent night vision—straining toward the snappings and rustlings, biding his time, jungle knife in hand. He had been ordered to take prisoners, but like all *sargentos* (those that stayed alive anyway) disobeyed the silly orders of his superiors when that most precious commodity, his own life, was at risk. In the blackness he couldn't see Pasionara until she was almost upon him; he saw first the right hand and arm bearing Pasionara's knife as it reached forward not two feet away from him. Good hand-to-hand man that he was, he sprang instantly for the knife hand before the knife hand sprang at him. His left hand grasped Pasionara's right wrist, smashed it to the ground, as his right hand with his jungle knife snapped forward, neatly slitting Pasionara's throat, so swiftly, so expertly that she—with no vocal cords left— made no outcry and had nothing to do, pinned as she was during the few moments while her life ebbed away, but to feel astonishment that this was the way it was to end, so swiftly, so unexpectedly, so *unfairly*.

She was, however, a big woman, and she threshed a bit, her legs kicking about, making small noises, and this covered the approach of Anna, who was crawling five feet behind her, much less than infantry procedure dictated, very unorthodox, and for that reason not foreseen by Vincent

Morales. Night vision sharpened by hours of blackness, Anna saw her friend in the grip of the *sargento*, the blood gushing from her throat.

She dropped her knife and transferred the .38 to her right hand. In that interval, Sargento Morales, who had not yet seen her, had put his sergeant's whistle to his mouth and blew a long screeching note that shook the very branches to warn his fellow soldiers of the danger at hand. It could be heard for miles through the silent woods, waking up the sleeping Hispanics.

It also notified the cops that the silence game was up, that something had alerted the enemy because no cop had brought his whistle along. The cops were no longer imaginary or invisible. Very bad news indeed.

The whistle blast was Sargento Morales's last act. Anna shot him between the eyes from a distance of four feet, the service .38 sounding like a cannon for miles throughout the dark woods, waking up the squirrels, startling a pair of deer drinking at the forest pond a half mile away into flight, arousing in the stomachs of the combatants of both sides bottomless dread.

The whistle and the pistol shot ended the first phase of the battle of Shotover Hall and ushered in phase two, which defied not only all the rules of war but of sanity itself.

20

Cassidy was thirty yards from the edge of the clearing on which Kaska's cabin stood, Keefe five yards away from him on his right, Rattigan slightly behind and four yards to the left of him, when the whistle, then the revolver shot shattered the peace. Cassidy froze, face to the earth. Ten seconds later the floodlight over Kaska's door went out. The darkness was now absolute.

Cassidy called a conference, clicking his front teeth with his fingernails. *Clk. Clk. Clk.* A meaningless sound to anyone except Keefe and Rattigan, who'd heard it before when the need was dire. They crawled to Cassidy's side. Cassidy found Keefe's right hand in the darkness and spelled out on the palm of it with his forefinger: KAL. Short for Kalashnikov. They were badly outgunned and the automatic weapons on the three soldiers they'd killed would come in mighty handy. It wouldn't be easy to find them in the dark, but then, nothing that night was easy.

On Rattigan's palm he spelled out four letters GREN for grenades. Soldiers would be presumed to have them on them. The pair to stay together for mutual support in case of enemy action.

That meant Cassidy would be left alone to handle whatever was out there. Neither Keefe nor Rattigan liked that, but Cassidy was boss man. Off they crawled.

A sliver of light, triangular, showed the cabin door and vanished. Someone had opened the door and come out. Cassidy could feel the presence a hundred yards away, palpable with menace.

Came now gunfire scattered around the woods, not general but sporadic. The war was assuming new dimensions and going badly for his side because everywhere it was automatic fire. The cops had no such weapons. An automatic opened on Cassidy at that moment, twenty yards away to his right, raking the area three yards in front of him.

Cassidy took his time, aiming five feet behind the flash, squeezing off a single shot. A yelp and silence. No more automatic fusillade. Cassidy crawled silently on knees and elbows until he found the dead soldier, the wrong half of him hidden behind a tree. He took the Kalashnikov.

In another part of the woods, Anna lay bathed in tears beside Pasionara's body, swallowing the sobs to keep the noise level down. Around her flashed gunfire, some of it police weapons. The *soldado* who had killed Pasionara lay himself dead on top of Pasionara in the rape position. Occasionally bullets thudded into one or the other of the two bodies, which formed—at least on one side of Anna—a nice bulwark. She screwed her face into the dirt, the firing getting closer. On one side a blast she thought must be a police .38. Someone crawling toward her, not too quietly.

"Spit," she hissed.

Out of the darkness came an answering "Spit." A moment later she was joined by a cop named Mulvaney. A comedian, always making jokes, this guy. Even in ordinary times she didn't like comedy cops much. Still he was alive and breathing and on her side. He patted her on the ass to tell her how much he sympathized, having seen even in the nothing light the dead face of Pasionara whose eyeballs gleamed. Too much. Mulvaney reached a finger forward and pulled the lids down.

Both of them hunkering down now behind the protective shield of bodies, a fortunate thing because a burst of fire thudded into bodies. A vicious noise. *Crmp. Crmp.* It misled the *soldado* who had unloosed the burst into thinking he had hit live bodies, and he crawled boldly forward right into Mulvaney's police .38. Mulvaney shot him in the head and reached forward to get the man's Kalashnikov. A bad move because the *soldado* had a buddy who almost cut Mulvaney in half with his automatic weapon.

Anna fired at the flash, right head on *at* it, blindly, instinctually, her subconscious screaming, *self-defense. He shot first, your honor.* (So brainwashed was she by idiot judges who insisted that cops never fire until the victim has had time to call his lawyer.) A bull's-eye at very close range. Right between the eyes. That made her second score. Anna dried her tears and felt better. She reached out from her shelter and took two grenades from the belt of the dead *soldado*, put them in her shoulder bag and crawled away. Her boy friend, a Nam veteran, had reiterated again and again: Never hang around. Keep moving—or they'll zero in on you. She moved now toward where the light had been and no longer was. That light on the cabin had been their original destination, and Anna crawled toward it now because she had no place else to head for and because, above all, she needed companionship.

She found it within twelve yards.

"Spit," she hissed and "Spit" came back to her out of the black maw like a blessing from heaven. Out of the blackness crawled a Polack named Kuskiusco who called himself for this operation Wolfpack. He too patted her ass, presuming a

217

familiarity he had never before had, but she forgave him; she was very glad to have his presence in this dark night of the soul.

They crawled together toward where the light had been and no longer was and almost immediately encountered a hail of fire from their right, two guns opening up simultaneously, a bad mistake. Wolfpack fired his .38 from a crouch, rolled, and fired again. Two bull's-eyes. Deadly at short range was Wolfpack, a born snapshooter, once a very good basketball player.

Wolfpack helped himself to the AK-47 off the last corpse and patted Anna on the ass again, feeling entitled. She felt he was entitled too. The camaraderie of war. A bullet had grazed her shoulder, tearing open the cloth, and she felt mortal, vulnerable, overjoyed to be alive. Thanking God (Anna was very religious) for each additional minute.

Wolfpack was taking the shoes off the corpse, listening hard all the while, because something was crawling his way from his rear. He hunkered down next to the corpse. "Spit," he said into the earth. For answer a burst of flame. Wolfpack threw the shoe in a gentle basketball arc to his left and it splatted into a bush, drawing fire away from Wolfpack, who was up on his knees instantly firing this time the AK-47 first into the *soldado* straight behind who had been making all that noise, then into the companion at his left who had been giving the *soldado* covering fire, silencing both.

Wolfpack was having a very good evening, enjoying himself as he hadn't since he left East Rutherford Tech. Why was killing against the law when it was such *fun*?

This action was happening forty yards from Cassidy, who was glued to the redolent earth like a fallen leaf, some of the bullets passing directly over him. It was interfering with his thinking. He had been concentrating on that man—or group—who had for some reason left the cabin and were out there in front of him doing . . . what? He got his answer—

three sharp blasts on a whistle. From the sound, the man had pulled way over to the right. Why?

Regrouping the troops, Cassidy guessed. The three blasts were a signal of some sort. Bad news. The other side had discipline, they had signals; we have . . . *spit*.

Where were Keefe and Rattigan? Where was Lucia? In the cabin? Meanwhile, the bullets getting uncomfortably close.

Two more blasts—one long, one short—from the whistle out there. Sounded like a leader. Would that be Roberto? No, Roberto was higher staff than whistles. (Hard to conceive him on this expedition at all.) He'd be inside the cabin. That was a noncom, that whistle—maybe the man with the demonic face whose name Cassidy now knew was Arguello.

Arguello had picked his assembly point carefully just on the basis of the noise of the firing. The action was, he figured, there, there, and *there*—and so he picked a site where the action wasn't and whistled his men to get to the assembly point out of the line of direct fire where he could orchestrate some kind of encircling action. He had the troops and he felt—and Roberto agreed—that whatever was out there wasn't soldiers.

Therefore the first three short blasts, which meant break it off, pull back, and circle in the direction of the whistle. Very sound strategy.

But the second blast of whistle was something else. Bullets were coming from all directions, and Arguello prudently took refuge in a drainage ditch. There he encountered what he first took to be a corpse. It wasn't a corpse. It was, Arguello quickly learned, breathing, and what's more, appeared to have no wounds at all. Very peculiar. Next to him Arguello found the Hosford .307.

The man on horseback who had killed Georgio?

Hence the long and short blast of the whistle. That was a signal for Cabo Maurello and his three *soldados* to come to him at once. Maurello and his three men were in charge of the equipage. Arguello was going to accomplish two things at once.

Anne Falk and Lucia were flat on the floor in Kaska's bedroom, Lucia listening to the gunfire, *enjoying* the gunfire. Well, perhaps not *enjoying* it exactly. Appreciating it, living it. Eyes dilated, breath coming quickly. An occasional bullet smacking into the log walls. Very exciting.

Lucia smiled at Anne Falk—and then quickly stopped smiling. Anne Falk's face was knotted with fear, skin ashen, eyes like forest pools. "It's *quite* safe," Lucia whispered. "Those are oak logs. No bullet can get through oak logs."

Anne Falk closed her eyes. *I must pull myself together. She sees!* It wasn't the bullets she feared. It was Roberto Garcia, the torturer. Feared pain worse than death, worse than bullets, worse than anything. *Mustn't let on about the torture. The child mustn't suspect about the torture.*

"I'm all right." Putting on an agonized smile. "You're a marvelous child, Lucia . . . to be so brave."

The agony showing like an inner light. Lucia was thunderstruck. This goddesslike woman with the marble brow whom she worshiped (Lucia being at the age where worship was the common affliction, like pimples) to be so . . . ashen with fear. It humanized Anne Falk, brought her down to earth from her Olympian heights. Lucia crawled over toward her, flooded with thirteen-year-old love and compassion, kissed her on the cheek, put her arms around her, gave her a big hug, and said (something she wouldn't have dared to say before this night): "You're a very mysterious woman, you know. You're supposed to be a companion for Mrs. Shotover but you're *never* around Mrs. Shotover. I spend more time with Mrs. Shotover than you do. I think you have some other function besides companionship."

Anne Falk smiled, the fear in her unknotting a little. "I'm Armand's fiancée."

"Why?" asked Lucia.

That made Anne laugh. "You must never ask an engaged girl *why*. None of us knows why. I think it's because he asked me."

"Lots of men must have asked you."

"No, he's the only one."

Bullets thudding into the oak walls.

"I don't believe it!" said Lucia passionately. "You're the most beautiful woman I ever saw."

"It just scares the men away."

The fear altogether vanished now, the two of them on their stomachs, hands under chins, just having a good talk in the midst of the gunfire, which was now very intermittent. Presently it died away altogether.

"He's out there somewhere, high on drugs—if he's alive." Anne Falk sat up, tossing her blond hair, frowning, getting hold of herself.

"Sssh!" said Lucia.

They heard the front door of the cabin open violently and then slam, shaking the cabin. Someone had come in, the two females pressed flat against the door.

"How's your Spanish?" whispered Lucia.

But they didn't need any Spanish.

Robert Garcia's mellifluous Oxford-accented English came through the door distinctly: "Señor Shotover, what a pleasure to make your actual physical acquaintance after this long, unsatisfying communion by electronic devices. Was it you then who wrote *Bienvenido* on the forehead of poor Kaska after first having shot him?"

Anne Falk's eyes closed as if in prayer. Lucia owl eyed, listening for Armand's reply. There was no reply.

Roberto Garcia in Spanish: "He doesn't seem to have any wound or injury, Arguello. Get a little water from the kitchen. I am very anxious to speak with this man."

A rattle of Spanish from Arguello. He had to get back with his men. He had assembled the *pelotón* to the east of

221

the cabin in preparation for encirclement and assault. He had to get out there to lead the *pelotón*.

Anne Falk's Spanish was rudimentary but enough to comprehend what was said. Lead them? Where? Against whom? Why? How? When? And so forth.

Roberto in Spanish: "Maurello and Jorge will stay with me. I need them. Go with God, Arguello."

An ominous note, Go with God. Roberto didn't know why he emitted so portentous a farewell. It just escaped him, like breath itself.

Anne Falk heard the front door open—the door always gave a little screech as if the stout oak paneling had warped and swelled; another slam, shaking the cabin. Arguello had left.

Roberto in Spanish: "Maurello, put the equipage on that table there and then get me some water. We must bring Shotover to his senses before we use the equipage."

The equipage? What was this equipage?

Oh, dear God!

Body pressed to the dirt, Cassidy saw and heard that telltale screech. The cabin door opened and in the sliver of light he saw four men carrying . . . what? Two burdens. A body? A box? The cabin door slammed and the darkness was again absolute.

Keefe crawled out of the gloom on elbows and knees, his arms full of Kalashnikovs. Rattigan came behind him, holding his left biceps where the bullet had knicked him with his right hand apologetically. "A scratch," he intoned. "Nothing."

There was no need for such excessive quiet anymore. Cassidy could feel the absence in his bones.

Keefe put down the rifles. "They've pulled out," he said quietly. "We could hear them all around us. That way." Pointing to the right of the cabin.

The cabin door opened—again that sliver of light and

222

telltale screech—and slammed shut. One man stood outlined for a moment and then vanished.

Everyone holding his breath, hunkering down.

Minutes passed.

"Spit!" came out of the darkness. Low.

"Spit!" said Cassidy.

Anna crawled out of the murk, and with her companion Wolfpack, the two loaded down with rifles and grenades.

"We've got to get out of here," said Wolfpack, low. A Nam veteran who'd seen it all before. "They're going to be coming at us from the rear unless we move."

Cassidy put his head on the ground, face first, closed his eyes, and agonized. The ultimate, irreversible decision.

Lucia was in that cabin. . . .

Nevertheless . . .

Rushing the cabin was insane. Get himself killed. Get her killed too. Then, of course, there was that other business—his responsibility toward Fletcher and the cops he'd got into this mess.

He took a deep breath and faced up to it.

"Keefe," he said, low. "Take the group back to the carriages. Round up any of the others you see, but don't go looking. I'll catch you up."

"What are you going to do?"

"Tell the gang to beat it back to the carriages."

"How?"

Cassidy showed his teeth, partly grin. "The carriages are *that* way. Get going."

Cassidy on his feet now, moving quietly to the biggest tree. He pulled himself up on the lowest branch, climbing quickly, the branches tearing at his face, his hands, the darkness swallowing him up.

He had better be at least twenty feet up, he figured, and he had to guess when that was. It took five minutes during which Keefe would have time to get the hell out of here. He took a deep breath and let it all out—at the top of his lungs:

"Fletcher!" he bellowed. "All you men in blue! Back to the carriages! Immediately! Get moving! Now!"

He let go and felt himself falling, bouncing down branch by branch, thrown this way and that, trying to protect his face and his balls, letting the rest of him suffer, BLAM, BLAM BLOOIE—ricocheting down the tree. The firing had started instantly—*machine gun* fire, saints preserve us (Cassidy not believing in saints but liking the rhythm of that incantation), tracers going over his head—reds, blues, greens, beautiful and deadly—in that strange curved flight tracers have in the dark, seeming to veer off in long, deceptive arcs when actually the bullets are headed straight at you. Mercifully above him because he was falling. Even in his rough fall Cassidy could not help but think: The son of a bitch is very confident, giving away his position like that. The bastard thinks we're a bunch of hopeless amateurs, and he is absolutely right.

He hit the ground—*wump*—the breath going out of him, the noise of it covered by the roar of the machine gun. The tracers still way over his head. Cassidy picked himself up and took off, crouching, going too fast. Within ten yards, he tripped and fell headlong.

Up again he took it slower, crouching hands in front of his face, still running into trees and bushes, occasionally falling flat. On one of these falls he looked at his watch. Three-thirty. Jupiter! In an hour it could be getting light and they'll encircle us and cut us into little pieces. . . .

It was 3:40 before he got back to the carriages. Cops wandering around drinking whiskey from bottles or coffee from thermos bottles Amanda Shotover had pulled out of thin air. Nobody saying much, an air of demoralization in the atmosphere, some of the cops with blood over their shoe-polished faces, some limping, all quiet.

The black man named Snoops, the man with the bamboo cane with the razor blade stuck into it, handed the whiskey bottle to Cassidy, who took a deep swig.

"How you make out with that thing?" asked Cassidy.

"Got a couple. My buddy didn't make it."

Cassidy emitted a little sigh, patted the man on the arm, and went down the line.

Keefe was counting and doing the arithmetic. "Twelve," he said bitterly.

"Fletcher?"

Keefe shook his head, frowning. Cassidy was stabbed with guilt clear to his toes.

"He could be out there lost," said Keefe, low. "I think a lot of 'em got lost. Christ, man, these are *city* cops used to signposts on every street corner. You throw them into these dark woods in the middle of the night! It may be days before we find all these guys."

Keefe bit it off because this was not the time for reproach.

"The twelve include you and me and Rattigan?" asked Cassidy.

Keefe nodded gloomily and showed him the figures. "Here's the score of the other side, near as I can make out. That girl's done damned well—two—and Wolfpack got four. Snoops thinks he got two certain, one probable. . . ." They went down the list, Keefe and Rattigan and Cassidy tossing in their scores. Even giving the soldiers every benefit of the doubt, it looked as if the cops had just about halved the original forty of Roberto's men.

"How about weapons? What we got."

Twelve Kalashnikovs. Automatic weapons for everyone, which would help. And eleven grenades.

"We got maybe forty minutes before it starts to get light. We got to move." Cassidy directed Keefe and Rattigan and Snoops to the storage bin not two hundred yards away for the gasoline.

"*Gasoline?*"

Cassidy's mouth was twisted and taut because this would be the last throw of the dice. "The Spaniards used this one on the Carthaginians and it worked very well."

"Isn't it fortunate we have a historian in our midst?" snarled Keefe. "You'll be writing up the history of this lamentable expedition, will you? I want to do the footnotes."

Off he went with Rattigan and Snoops. Cassidy set the rest of them to collect dried wood, which in the dark would not be easy. And told them where to put it.

Cassidy took another belt of whiskey to fortify himself and went off to confront Amanda Shotover. She would loathe the operation.

He found Amanda still holding the lead pair of the Dover coach, soothing the horses, petting them, all four feet six of her. Without looking at him, she said: "Where's Lucia? That was Lucia screamed."

"And Anne Falk," said Cassidy. But of course, she was interested only in Lucia. Cassidy wasted no time. He outlined the plan. As he expected, she blew sky high.

"Not with my horses!" she snapped. "Not with my carriages! Not with me! Not with Joseph! Absolutely not! It's obscene!"

"If you want ever to see your son alive again," said Cassidy, very tired, the moral muscles in him stretched to their outermost. He was not at all sure she gave a damn about her son. "If you want ever to see Lucia again . . ." He knew how badly she wanted to see Lucia again. "If you want any of us to get out of this alive . . ."

But in the end it was none of these arguments that swayed Amanda Shotover; it was the events themselves, as in all wars, that shaped the action, molding the destinies of the players inextricably, reducing all the mortals on the scene to insignificance.

Through the black night came a long, loud, lingering howl like the baying of a wolf except that this howl was quite recognizably human. There was agony in the howl but much else—mysticism, exultation, even a note of high glee. A very strange howl. Cassidy had no idea who could make such a noise, but Amanda did.

"Armand!" she said and closed her eyes tight but not quite tight enough. The tears forced themselves through and down her aged, reluctant cheeks. It was as if, Cassidy thought, she suddenly assumed the responsibilities of motherhood after an absence of thirty years, as if that long, loud, lingering howl had awakened in her the capacity to feel again her own humanity.

21

Anne Falk put her hands tight around Lucia's ears, but of course it was no use. Those howls would have penetrated stone walls. Lucia, rigid as a board, pounded on the locked door, screaming: "Stop that! Stop that! *Stop that!*" Protests of such innocence as to be undecipherable, almost inaudible to the modern mind, like bat cries. At one point Lucia even said—over the general tumult—"You're *hurting* him!"—a declaration so fraught with simplicity that it would never occur to anyone over the age of thirteen.

The pounding and the cries upset Roberto's concentration; he unlocked the door and confronted the two females sternly. Roberto was a dedicated torturer and this behavior of Lucia's was, to put it mildly, unseemly. "You must be quiet," he said in his best Spanish grandee manner. "You are interfering with the questioning. This man has stolen a great sum of money from us and we are endeavoring to get it back. It's a matter of simple justice. The moment he tells us we will stop the questioning."

Quick as light Anne Falk said, teeth chattering with fear,

"He has mental and emotional . . . blocks that prevent him from . . . answering questions. You are going about it in the worst way. . . ."

But of course she was hurling this argument over a cultural chasm four hundred years wide. These were arguments that Roberto not only could not understand, he couldn't even hear. He said only to Lucia—with great dignity, for he was a very dignified man—"If you persist in this unruly conduct, you may have to take this man's place in the chair."

A very big threat that was actually hollow since Roberto would never torture a child. There was no point; children simply died on you almost immediately. There was no gratification in children, very little in women. Men were something else.

Roberto closed and locked the door and went back to his chair. The equipage was on the table next to the RD-11. He took a deep breath, collected himself, and then—his good humor restored—smiled pleasantly up at Armand, who hung in the chains, arms outstretched like a crucified Christ. Armand's eyes were open, but there was no recognition; they were very deep pools, full of light. The mouth hung open with great expressiveness—a bit of mischief, almost mockery in that mouth. Very interesting.

"Now, where were we?" asked Roberto pleasantly. He was trying to establish some form of communication. So far, there had been none at all.

Armand had simply screamed. But what screams! Roberto had never in his very wide experience heard screams of such timbre, such depth, such purity. He had, of course, read all the musings of the great torturers of the past—Ghiardelli of Milan (one of the greatest); Monsignor Ybarra of Castile, the Inquisition master of them all; Friar Esteban of Guelph—and each had spoken of *soul screams* of such intensity that one could all but see the naked soul hanging in the air like a religious experience. (There was always a bit of religious nonsense in these musings which Roberto disregarded, concentrating instead on the philosophical insights, which were immensely rewarding.)

Here it was, for the first time in his researches (as he called them), the Great Experience itself. But these screams—magnificently soul-stirring though they were, collector's items beyond price, unforgettable—were nevertheless yielding no information at all. Reluctantly, Roberto lowered the voltage on the equipage to the tiniest prick, trying to bring Armand down from the sublime to the commonplace level of mortality.

"I don't think I've quite got through to you, Armand. I am only attempting to learn the whereabouts of the money you have taken from us, which belongs to the Republic of Balisario." In tones of mild reproach, as one would speak to a wayward child who knows not what he has done. The gifted torturer always assumes a stance of moral superiority over the torturee. It is one of the great truths that the torturee is racked with guilt for having got into this position. Truly, he must have done something awful to deserve such pain. In the end the torturee submitted—no other word so carries the sense of it—*submitted* to torture as if offering the gift of himself, his body, his soul, his everything.

That is, most of them did. Not Armand. Armand was not following the script. As the low voltage seeped into his body, his inward-looking eyes, with the strange golden light in them, were cast heavenward, not looking at Roberto at all, ignoring Roberto (there can be no greater humiliation for a torturer, especially the *serious* one Roberto considered himself to be, than to be ignored by the torturee). Armand spoke—or perhaps spake—in this wise:

"Hear my prayer, O Lord, and let my cry come unto thee. Hide not thy face from me in the day when I am in trouble; incline thine ear unto me: in the day when I call, answer me speedily."

Roberto didn't recognize Psalm 102. He was a Catholic

231

but not a well-educated one. What he recognized was the religiousness of this cry, its biblical nature. He was in fact scandalized by the peremptory tone of it—Armand telling God just how to behave. It was bad enough to get a religious one in the chains, but far worse to get a dictatorial religious who marched to his own drumbeat.

Armand, beyond pain, spoke softly now, "For my days are consumed like smoke, and my bones are burned as an hearth. My heart is smitten and withered like grass ..."

Roberto interrupted, trying to interject a word of sense in these religious ravings. "The money?" he said softly. "What have you done with the money?"

Armand went right on, unheeding. "O, my God, take me not away in the midst of my days; *they* shall perish ..."

They seemingly aimed right at Roberto and his men—a curse. ...

"... but Thou shalt endure and *they* shall be changed. ..."

Again that *they* like a knife at Roberto's throat.

In the next room Anne was weeping proud tears, breathless with admiration that Armand could so confound his torturer with his own indomitable weakness.

Through her tears she said to Lucia, "You want to know why I'm engaged to Armand; *that's* why. He never fails to surprise me. ..."

Snoops, Wolfpack, and the man who called himself Peanuts (a great big unpeanutlike man with tired eyes and a gentle manner) were Cassidy's scouts. Nam veterans all. Cassidy laid down the law: "No killing. Not even knives. Observe and stay out of trouble and get back. They're not to be forewarned that *we're* forewarned. Otherwise you'll blow it all."

"Suppose one those guys try kill us? asked Snoops, playing it for comedy.

"Die quietly."

"Yeah," said Snoops.

"I must know which direction they're coming from." The logical direction would be straight down from the north, from the cabin, but they might be trying to encircle them and come from the rear. Or they might not even know where the carriages were and not start the encircling action in time, in which case . . .

Peanuts spoke up softly. "They be scoutin' us too. You ready for that?"

Cassidy nodded. "We'll take care of that here. We're hoping they haven't time. Time is what it's all about." Looking at his watch. "We have maybe half an hour before it starts to get light."

"More'n that," said Snoops. "It's real cloudy. Ain't gone get light till five anyway."

The fatalism of battle.

"Snoops, to the right of the track. That way." Cassidy pointing, keeping voice down. "Wolfpack, straight ahead, right down the track—but be careful. Don't walk into 'em. Peanuts, in the woods to the right. You got half an hour to find 'em and get back."

Off they went into the dark night.

The others were gathering wood for the carriages, which wasn't easy. They had plenty of twigs and small stuff, but the big stuff was hard to find. The Dover coach was toughest to fill because it was biggest, Cassidy pitching in to help load it up. Little by little all four carriages were piled high with brush and timber. Afterward Cassidy tried to get Joseph and Amanda to go back to the house. Or anywhere. They wouldn't.

"Desertion would besmirch my sacred honor," said Amanda.

You had to be eighty-five to *say* such a line. "I wouldn't have you besmirch your sacred honor for anything," said Cassidy.

Keefe and Rattigan returned from the supply box bearing two five-gallon cans of gasoline. Too much. Cassidy put the cans next to the carriages, showing his teeth with the pain of it. Timing was all—and he had to guess about that. The Spaniards had worked this lark on Hamilcar, Hannibal's father, in 228 B.C., routing the Carthaginians. But they had wagons rather than carriages, oxen in place of horses, and pitch in place of gasoline. The same lark but with high technology might blow up in his face.

The waiting began now, and this was most terrible of all. The screams had long ended. There was no sound at all coming from the cabin, which lay half a mile ahead of them in the clearing.

No screams from Lucia. Was that good news? Or bad? Perhaps she was beyond screaming. Cassidy closed his mind down on that and thought of other things. The two-thousand-year-old ruse he was attempting was one of the early examples of true guerrilla warfare, *guerrilla* itself being a Spanish word. But while the Spaniards invented the word, they hadn't invented guerrilla warfare itself, which went all the way back to the Scythians against Darius, the Persian warrior-king, in 512 B.C. Hispanics were playing victim to their own trick. Could I work *that* into my lecture at the New School—if I survive this night to make any more lectures. . . .

Looking at his watch. Four-forty. The scouts already ten minutes late. Ah, the waiting. The waiting! How often had he had to wait for Keefe and Rattigan to report back from some mission or other while Cassidy tried to occupy his mind with ironies and self-criticism, back when the world was young?

Snoops crawled out of the blackness. "Nothing," he reported in a whisper. "Half mile on my knees. Not even a groundhog."

Five minutes later Peanuts came in loping because he was late. He shook his head. "Some bodies, some of 'em ours. Nothing that breathes."

The soldiers must be coming straight down the track. For

exhausted troops, the easiest way. Two minutes later Wolfpack arrived in a low crouch, his hands making a jagging motion straight behind him, then drawing a line over his lips. No noise. They're back that way. Holding up both hands with seven fingers outstretched. Seven minutes back, pointing again down the track.

It was all hand signals now. Cassidy had worked out the drill in advance and coached each man in his part. Now he patted and pointed. Keefe and Rattigan doled out the grenades frugally because they had only so many and they were the artillery. Two each to Anne and Wolfpack, who'd be behind trees to the left of the track down which the *soldados* were advancing. Dugan and Scipio would be flat on the ground to their rear, covering the flanks with the Kalashnikovs.

On the other side of the track, behind trees—and they would have to find good stout trees to protect themselves against their own grenades—would be Snoops and a thin young man who called himself Hellfire, each with two grenades. Covering their rear would be Peanuts and Pear Tree.

Everyone had automatic weapons.

Cassidy whirling his right forefinger around in a big circle now, which meant hurry, hurry, hurry.

They would be stationed a hundred yards ahead of the carriages. Cassidy gave them five minutes to get there. Again a guess as to time and distance. May the god of war be with us. Dumb luck, the greatest of all generals.

Cassidy, Rattigan, and Keefe would guard the rear. They had much to do first. Cassidy made a last silent effort to get Amanda and Joseph, both in their eighties, out of the line of fire, waving his hands at them because he couldn't risk speech. They simply shook their heads. Amanda still holding the lead horses of the Dover coach, Joseph going down the line patting the horses pulling the other carriages, who had been very quiet throughout the night.

Cassidy going now from carriage to carriage, drenching

the loads of wood with the gasoline, splashing the stuff over the brush and lumber, over the splendid interior of the Dover coach, that masterpiece of eighteenth-century coachmaker's art, over the Lancia with its magnificent satinwood inlays, its basketwork; over the circus coach, that unique piece of coachmaking, only one ever made; over the Irish jaunting car, sharing the smelly stuff out equally, trying not to breathe the damned fumes.

The five minutes were up.

Cassidy lit the pinecone with a match and laid it on the ground. With his gloved hand he lit another pinecone from the first one and put the burning cone into Keefe's leather-gloved hand. Keefe had played cricket long ago for Trinity in Dublin and he had never forgotten the overhand pitch of the cricket bowler. Keefe ran with it three steps and over-handed the burning cone into the Dover coach.

WHOOSH!

Flames exploded in all directions. The terrified horses bolted straight forward, screeching with terror. Amanda hurled herself to the left, barely getting out of the way as the burning coach and four horses shot past, flames lighting up the sky.

Cassidy handed the second cone to Keefe, who hurled it into the Lancia.

WHOOSH!

This time it was Joseph who had to dive for the bushes to get out of the way of the screaming horses, four of them in full gallop, flames shooting skyward, singeing their rumps.

Rattigan was hanging on to the pair of horses hitched to the circus wagon who had reared straight up and were doing their best to bolt into the woods. Keefe just managed to light the gasoline on that coach in the nick of time. Rattigan was propelled into the brush by the force of the horses bolting forward at full gallop after the other carriages.

The jaunting wagon was lost to the action. With no one

holding the horses, the team turned clear around and bolted down the track in the wrong directon—unlit.

Cassidy had counted on chaos. Organized chaos (if there is such a thing) is what warfare is all about, but the chaos he got was beyond anything he imagined, beyond anything he could imagine.

The Dover coach with its four terrified, screaming horses (a sound so fearsome that no one who has ever heard it can ever forget it) covered the seventy-five yards down the track to the advancing Hispanics in 4.6 seconds, which gave no time for reflection or even reflex action. (In 228 B.C. Hamilcar's Carthaginians had had a much longer time to react against the slow oxen, but they hadn't managed to get out of the way either.)

The *soldados* were advancing in twin lines, one on each edge of the track, when the inferno of blazing carriages and screeching horses sprang at them, the gasoline-fed flames now thirty feet high, illuminating the soldiers like bright sunlight but throwing the surrounding woods into even greater darkness.

Wolfpack was quickest off the mark. He lobbed his grenade into the center of the track and ducked back behind his tree. The explosion rocked the earth and six of the Hispanics went down. Anna tossed her grenade three seconds later and from the opposite side of the roadway Snoops' grenade went off a few seconds after that. The carnage was less because the soldiers had dived to the ground (as planned by Cassidy), but the grenades caught the lead horses of the onrushing Dover coach right in the chest. The lead horses went down, piling the following pair and the coach itself into one huge untidy heap, flames leaping twenty feet, all of it right on top of the first soldiers. Into this mess Hellfire threw the fourth and last grenade.

The four horses pulling the Lancia at full gallop were panicked by the grenades and tried to avoid the flaming Dover coach by circling around it to the right. There was not room for any such maneuver. The left wheel of the Lancia caught the right wheel of the burning Dover coach. The lead horses of the four-horse team went to their knees; the second pair rearing up behind them came down with their forelegs caught on the haunches of the lead pair in a great tangle of horseflesh.

The soldiers meanwhile were lying in the full glare of the flames, the Kalashnikovs of Wolfpack, Anna, Scipio, and Hellfire opening up on them from both sides of the roadway, firing out of the darkness into the bright light.

The circus coach and its pair of horses ran right off the track to avoid the burning mass ahead and overturned.

The flames now lighting the trees themselves.

The screech of the surviving horses—powerful, unearthly, shattering—could be heard for miles.

Under the glare of flames the Hispanics lay sprawled and still, a jumble of outflung arms and legs.

Only one had got away.

Arguello himself.

Arguello had turned the lead over to his deputy, Carlos, and was bringing up the rear. This was not cowardice—no one had ever accused Arguello of that. Arguello brought up the rear because he knew his men inside and out, knew their limits, their weaknesses, and their tricks. It had been a long night. Faced with another march through the dark woods, Arguello knew that his troops would melt into the darkness for a bit of sleep (great sleepers they were, like foot soldiers everywhere) if given any opportunity. He was bringing up the rear to forestall this, and his men, terrified of Arguello, marched meekly to their doom in front of him.

When the flaming carriages had burst on the scene, Arguello was immobilized by astonishment for a second or two. The first grenade would have caught him but for the fact he was out of range. By the time the second grenade exploded, Arguello had dived into the woods and hunkered as close to the ground as he could to avoid the other grenades and the defilading fire.

He recognized an *emboscada* when he saw one, having worked the business several times himself. After the firing stopped he crawled through the dark woods in the direction of the cabin to tell Roberto what had happened and to figure out what to do next.

The ambush was swift, devastating, demoralizing even to the victors. Cassidy, Keefe, and Rattigan came up the track cautiously, not quite believing it was over so swiftly, the flames roaring now through the trees but beginning to die down because the trees were green and covered with dew.

Wolfpack and Scipio had come out from the sheltering trees and were shooting the few *soldados* who still drew breath, putting them out of their misery. No prisoners.

The horses still screaming their god-awful screams.

Then came a strange sight. Amanda Shotover, erect and grim, carrying a Kalashnikov in one hand and a knife in the other (Cassidy never found out where she'd got either of them), walked straight down the roadway, smoldering with fury.

She went through the flames to the circus coach where a horse lay screaming with a broken leg—the bone sticking out white as paper—and shot the stricken animal between the eyes. With her knife she cut the other horse free of its harness. The horse shot into the woods.

She went on to the next overturned coach, the Lancia. The two lead horses of that coach had perished in the flames from the Dover coach. The second two horses she cut out of their harness, and they went off into the woods, one of them limping horribly.

The Dover coach in the lead had got it worse. The lead two horses had died in the first grenade blast and the rear two were grievously wounded by the other grenades. Amanda shot them both.

Silence descended on the woods, an enormous, shattering

silence, an earsplitting silence after the gunfire, the grenades, and the screaming horses. Only the crackle of flames was heard and that, too, was dying away.

Cassidy was going down the line, inspecting the bodies, counting corpses, and looking for one particular demonic face with its centuries-old ferocity, not finding that face.

Amanda walked up to him and said, "You killed my coachman."

"I'm sorry," said Cassidy. Amanda had already walked away back to where Joseph lay in the roadway, a bullet in his forehead, himself a hundred yards away from the action. Amanda crouched down and closed the eyelids of her oldest servant.

Keefe came up to Cassidy, jubilant. "Not a scratch on our side. I can't believe it."

"Joseph got killed. The old coachman."

"Ah, hell!" said Keefe.

Cassidy rubbed his red-rimmed eyes, felt the stubble of his beard, the weariness in him. "Arguello got away. We got to be careful of that son of a bitch. And it's not over yet. We got to crack that cabin."

The first faint glimmerings of the gray dawn now lighting up the eastern sky.

They went up the track in two widely spread files so Arguello couldn't make a quick killing. When they got to the edge of the clearing, it was 5:10.

Cassidy on his belly with Keefe next to him looking at the cabin outlined against the approaching dawn.

Keefe said, "Rattigan's a monkey. He could get on that roof, put a couple grenades down the chimney to stun 'em, and we'll rush the front door."

Cassidy shook his head. "Lucia's in there. So's Anne Falk. No grenades, no rifle fire."

"What then?"

Cassidy closed his eyes, his brain going round and round, flooded with the weariness.

Lucia in there with that torturer and that killer and the dawn coming up, *ee-yi*. . . .

A long silence. His eyes fell on Kaska's beehives at the left of the cabin.

"Bees," he said finally, showing his teeth in a glare of a ferocious smile. "Ask around if anyone's handled bees. The bees will be asleep until the sun is well up, so we have lots of time."

Keefe lit up. "Bees, is it now, Thucydides? Where in hell did you get this one?"

"The Corsicans, you uneducated Irish ape! Every schoolchild in Corsica knows about it. The Corsicans threw beehives into the ranks of the advancing German soldiers in 1732 and routed them. You bloody Irish think you're the only underdogs ever won a battle."

"Look who's calling who bloody Irish, you Hibernian tosspot."

Out of nowhere Fletcher appeared full of apologies. "Sorry. Got lost in the damned woods."

"You're in the nick of time. We're about to attack that cabin with bees," said Keefe. "The newest wrinkle in high-technology warfare."

22

Armand hung now in his chains, eyes closed, unconscious, out of reach. Roberto sat beside the RD-11, suffering failure. No one, he reflected sadly, knew the pain the torturer suffered when he failed, the torment of frustration. He, Roberto, had exhausted his wiles on this *religioso*—high torture, low torture, persuasion, guile—the whole body of his very great expertise and he had got exactly nowhere. What was even more painful was the thought that he didn't know what else to do. To turn up the power beyond where he had gone would simply kill the man, and what good would that do? Then he'd never find the money. He would have to return to Balisario and confess failure to El Presidente, who was himself quite a torturer. Not, of course, in Roberto's league in the matter of sophistication, intelligence, and technique but in gusto and brutality perhaps even his superior. And in his rage who would El Presidente torture? . . .

Roberto shook himself away from that awful thought to concentrate on the problem at hand. Armand was shivering now, waves of trembling shaking his chains. A bad sign.

"Maurello," said Roberto. "Take the man out of the chains. Lay him down there on the floor."

If only I had more time. I could take him back to Balisario and spend hours, days, on this matter. But there was no time. He had to get the money and return.

Armand was now on the floor, trembling away. "Get a blanket, Maurello. In fact, a couple of blankets. Wrap him well. We must get him warm again." Always a very considerate torturer was Roberto.

"Where would I find a blanket, *comendador*?"

"In the bedroom," said Roberto, pointing to it and refraining from adding *estúpido* or any other insults. He was invariably polite to his subordinates, who nevertheless feared him as they would the devil himself.

Maurello unlocked and opened the door, banging it hard against the face of Anne Falk, who had had her ear against it, her arms around Lucia.

"Ouch," she said.

"Me pesa," said Maurello.

Anne Falk jumped to her feet and ran to the unconscious Armand. On her knees she took his head into her lap, felt his pulse, stroked his face, pushed up the lid, and looked into the eyeball, all this watched closely by Roberto, his mind churning. He was at the end of his tether.

"Very interesting personality," observed Roberto in English. "He has great depth. Surprising in an Anglo-Saxon. Usually you don't find much depth in Americans. You are his beloved, are you?"

Anne said nothing, convulsed by fear.

Under ordinary circumstances Roberto strongly disapproved of cross-torture—that is, the torture of husbands or wives in front of their spouses in order to elicit some information from the observer in order to stop the torment of the other. Contemptible, that sort of thing. Anyway, it didn't work. But in this case . . .

Maurello was back with the blankets, which he wrapped around Armand assisted by Anne Falk.

What had he to lose? Roberto was reflecting. He had never tortured women for reasons that feminists would hardly find flattering—that he considered them beneath his notice. The well and truly tortured man yielded up his mind, his soul, but with a woman—what was there to yield up?

Still, he had tried everything else. If he got the woman screaming, might not those screams penetrate to the innermost recesses of the *religioso* and bring him out of his trancelike state into something resembling the present? It was worth a try.

"Maurello," said Roberto in Spanish. "Seize the woman. We will try something new."

Maurello signaled his two men, Esteban and Luis, and the two of them converged on Anne Falk, whose head was bent over Armand. She didn't notice the men coming at her, but Lucia did. Lucia had been standing at the door watching all this, and now she uttered a little scream.

It was drowned out by the sound of an exploding grenade that startled everyone in the cabin. There had been no gunfire for quite a while and no grenades at all. The first grenade was followed by another and another and another in rapid order, and after that came a chatter of rifle fire.

Roberto had risen from his chair and stood listening, scowling. Very familiar, those sounds. His men's weapons. But what was the meaning of this fusillade? He had not expected organized opposition. After all, the U.S. was his country's ally and it was a country mercifully free from the guerrilla warfare that so plagued his own country. Roberto didn't like the sound of this business at all.

Luis and Esteban had seized Anne Falk and brought her to her feet. Lucia screeched the single word: "No!"

Wearily, Roberto wrapped his arms around Lucia and put his hand over her mouth. "You are interfering with my thought processes," he said to Lucia, who kicked him in the shin and bit his hand. Really, these American children were so ill-mannered! Maurello was helping him now, the two of them binding the struggling thirteen-year-old with wire—there was miles of wire in this most electronic of cabins—gagging her with one of Kaska's towels and depositing her on Kaska's bed, still kicking and trying her best to scream through the towel.

Anne Falk, on the other hand, was offering no resistance at all to Luis and Esteban as they put her into the chains. She was immobilized by fear and it shamed her, the fear, her mind three thousand miles and five hundred years away. *I fear the fire.* Joan of Arc, the indomitable, had feared the fire and had died in what she most feared, so there was perhaps historic respectability and precedent in fear; it was not altogether shameful. . . .

All of this took a little time. Lucia, a little wildcat, had not been easy to subdue. Roberto nursed his bitten hand, his kicked shin, and tried to reassemble his thoughts while Luis and Esteban were stringing up Anne Falk and putting the clamps on her two legs. Maurello came out of Kaska's bedroom, closing the door behind him. Roberto, who was still panting from the struggle, reached for one of his remaining cigars, intending to calm himself with the blessed smoke. Both of the remaining cigars had been crushed during his battle with Lucia. Roberto pulled out the remnants of his shattered Havanas from his breast pocket and laid them on the top of the RD-11.

Arguello came into the cabin, opening the front door and closing it behind him very fast, the motion itself an alarm bell. Arguello leaned against the door, every lineament of his brown face a harbinger of disaster.

"Emboscada!" he said. *"Somos extirpatos!"*

Unimaginable, all of it. Not a tremor, not a blink out of Roberto. Disaster was a Hispanic tradition, response to disaster so ingrained in the Hispanic character that Roberto dwelt not for a moment on the details. Arguello was too much the veteran of past wars to be wrong about catastrophe. This was no time to go into causes or assess blame. Roberto's mind leaped over all these impediments to the paramount concern: what to do now?

Somos extirpatos.

Not quite. He had Arguello, Maurello, Luis, Esteban, and himself. Five soldiers.

Aloud he said, "We have hostages."

The Americans did not have guerrillas but they *did* have the CIA, which frequently acted in a manner directly opposed to the policies of its own State Department, so he'd heard. A military action such as would wipe out forty of his best trained men—there would be a court of inquiry about *that* when he got back, *if* he got back—could be orchestrated only by the CIA.

"Put the woman over there directly in front of the front door. They will not fire into the room where one of their own compatriots is suspended in chains."

The woman had said she was a CIA covert-action operative, had she not? If those out there were CIA . . .

"Someone's on the roof," said Arguello. "Turn out the lights. We're under siege."

Roberto now could hear it too, moving softly but not softly enough. Not one person but several people. . . .

Pear Tree had indeed kept bees on Staten Island and was, like all bee men, an idealist, a naturalist, and a gentle man (as opposed to a gentleman, which is something else). He was, of course, outraged by Cassidy's idea and not mollified by Cassidy's historical footnote. Even if the Corsicans had pulled this on the Germans in 1732, it was no way to treat a hardworking colony of bees. Like all bee men, he ascribed to bees all the virtues—thrift, industry, self-discipline, teamwork, self-sacrifice, honor, courage, decency—he found so conspicuously lacking in modern man. In short, no. It was a replay of the scene with Amanda Shotover with her horses.

Cassidy said, "My daughter, who is thirteen years old, is in that cabin with Roberto Garcia, who is the most infamous torturer in all Latin America. Keefe has already been tortured by this man. Tell him, Keefe."

Keefe, that eloquent Irishman, laid it on. After two minutes, Pear Tree had had enough. "All right! All right! I'll need some muslin to stop the entrance." There wasn't any muslin but there was a blanket hanging on Kaska's clothesline. At the rear of the cabin was a lean-to and in that they found Kaska's bee gloves, which came clear to the elbow, and his helmet with its veil of gauze. Only one pair of gloves, one face mask. Cassidy took them. He'd be going into the cabin alone and he'd need them most. The others would just get stung.

Pear Tree gently wrapped the sleeping bee colony in the blanket and carried it to the rear of the cabin where Rattigan, already on the roof, hauled it up with Kaska's clothesline. Pear Tree joined Rattigan on the roof.

Gray light was coming up fast now, the men red-eyed, sweaty, their clothes covered with dust.

In low tones Cassidy gave them the word. From now on it was unarmed combat. They were not to use their guns except to save their lives. "We have to take Roberto Garcia alive. I want to talk to that son of a bitch, and I don't know which one he is. Knock 'em out. Don't kill 'em."

Wolfpack and Anna joined Rattigan and Pear Tree on the roof, stationed on the overhang over the front door. Anna, who was terrified of bees, had to be prepared to hurl herself off the roof on the backs of any fleeing Hispanics, whether or not covered with bees. Wolfpack too.

Scipio and Hellfire were placed backs to the wall next to the two front windows (the only windows the cabin had), prepared to run down and tackle any fleeing *soldados* who were to be clubbed into submission with the butts of their police .38s.

Snoops and Dugan and Peanuts were stationed on their

bellies in the cover of the woods before the front door, in case anyone got through the circle. They, too, were instructed to capture, not to kill.

Cassidy and Keefe crept on their knees under the front windows to the very edge of the front door, Cassidy wearing the gloves, the bee hat and veil on his head.

He had the whistle to his lips—he'd taken it off a dead *sargento*—when the front door opened.

Huddled next to the front door, neither Cassidy, Keefe, nor any of those on or near the cabin could see the extraordinary sight, but the three cops on their bellies at the edge of the woods got the full view—and it was dazzling.

There, hanging in chains in the crucifixion position, eyes downcast in the maidenly way one hardly ever sees anymore, looking in the pale light of the encroaching dawn like an El Greco in a poor light, hung Boston's most beautiful debutante of 1975.

In the dim light of the cabin, Arguello supervised the arrangements of which he totally disapproved, himself a soldier, not a torturer. Anne Falk was suspended on the steel frame, arms outstretched in an attitude of total submission, herself beyond fear, in a state resembling catalepsy. She had lived, she thought, a thousand years in the last ten minutes.

Roberto, seated now next to the front cabin wall with his hands on the equipage, was also in a state of trancelike resignation. His *pasión* had obscured his military judgment. That is what they would say at the court of military inquiry. It was a charge that had been leveled before in Balisario, often by Roberto Garcia himself against various military commanders who had let their *pasión* for polo, for girls, for other extravagances get in the way of their competence. Rather than be put in such a disgraceful position before men he despised (among others, El Presidente himself), it would be a far, far better thing to die gloriously leading his men in a last charge, taking along a few gringos in the process, leaving his descendants honor rather than shame.

What was he doing here with his hands on this equipage, about to torture a *woman*? Should he not instead have his hands around a rifle, charging the gringos? Or was that sentimentality? Then there was the matter of that man Cassidy. Roberto wanted to meet Cassidy. He wanted to put this man (who seemed to be at the root of all his difficulties) in the position now occupied by Anne Falk. Was that why he was seated there, hands on the equipage rather than on a rifle?

All these thoughts chewing up a lot of time while Arguello, the demon-faced one, scowled and looked at his watch and wondered what in hell had come over his commander to waste precious minutes while the enemy scurried around on the roof.

"Comendador," he said.

Roberto sighed. "I know. I know. You may open the door, Arguello."

Arguello stood well back under cover of the heavy front door. Anne Falk was framed in the doorway.

"Señor Cassidy," Roberto called out in his best Oxford-accented English. "I will offer you a trade. This delightful lady, who like yourself is employed by the CIA, in exchange for yourself. Señor Cassidy, are you out there?"

Just to add point to the message, Roberto, the artisan of torture, delicately turned the rheostat to produce not a big jolt, a very small jolt; he wanted to bring forth only a small feminine wail, a sort of hors d'oeuvre of what was to come.

Nothing happened. Nothing at all. Anne Falk hung there, eyes still downcast in that maidenly way, quiet as a sleeping bat.

Roberto turned the rheostat further. Still nothing. Still no sound, no movement from Anne Falk. He turned the rheostat all the way. Nothing at all.

"They've cut the wire," said Arguello, the old campaigner. "We had better try something else, *comendador*."

Then came the whistle which galvanized everyone in the room because it was so close, seeming to come right out of Roberto's head.

On the roof with his bare hands exposed to the now awake but still sleepy bees, Pear Tree dropped the brood chamber with its enormous queen bee surrounded by her retinue of worker bees and warrior bees. The brood chamber dropped twenty-two feet down the chimney to the brick floor where it smashed open, sending a cloud of furious warrior bees into the room. On top of the brood chamber Pear Tree dropped, one after the other, the two supers—brood chamber and supers containing perhaps fifty thousand bees.

In warfare nothing works out as one expects. This applies both to defender and attacker. The bees were a two-edged weapon, attacking both defenders and attackers in unexpected ways. As in 1732, the bees produced first and foremost surprise—that greatest of all military advantages. The band of remaining Hispanics were brave men all against the usual rain of discomforts—shot, shell, mortar, bayonet—but bees, especially bees in such enormous quantities, were beyond anything they'd ever experienced. It has been said many times that all is fair in love and war, but whoever said that didn't have bees in mind.

The bees unhinged Arguello, a very brave man, from his reason. The noise alone of fifty thousand angry bees is enough to separate a man from his senses and on top of that the swarm headed right at Arguello and landed on arms and face. He bolted past his commander and into the open air, too frightened even to cry out, his very vocal cords throttled with fear.

The worst possible example to set for Maurello, Esteban, and Luis. If their own revered *sargento* was to behave in such a way... The three of them followed him out the door, screaming Latin epithets. *Exeunt*, pursued by bees.

If they had been in the cabin, the cops might also have been demoralized, but they weren't. Anna leaped on the fleeing Arguello's back from the roof, bees or no bees, and clubbed him senseless with her .38. Wolfpack leaped on Maurello, also from the roof, Scipio on Luis, and Hellfire on Esteban and knocked them cold. All of them were badly stung.

But the number of bees outside were as nothing compared to those inside. Inside was madness. Libraries have been written about bees and their behavior. Maurice Maeterlinck in *The Life of the Bee*, his masterpiece, apologizes at the outset for adding more prose to a subject which, he says, has already been thoroughly covered by Aristotle. Still much remains to be said. Nobody has ever explained why bees will attack some people (some men will be attacked by every bee that flies and spend their lives in dread of bees) and will leave others strictly alone.

Some beekeepers can cover their naked bodies from head to foot in affectionate bees and will not be stung once, while others are pursued the moment they leave their front door. Kaska's bees were as selective and as puzzling as any. They went for Arguello and, of course—because they will always pursue a fleeing man—after Esteban, Luis, and Maurello.

Anne Falk, hanging in her chains, was stung on neck and face and hands, perhaps twenty times—a serious amount of bee venom—but nothing next to what could have been.

Armand, lying unconscious, was not stung once. Quite a few of the bees settled on him, to rest perhaps (though when you venture into bee motivation, you are getting into the farthest reaches of higher mathematics). Bees have a sense of smell six hundred times ours and perhaps about Armand there hung an odor of sanctity (or maybe insanity) that gave the bees pause. Perhaps they just liked the man. About bees you can never tell.

Roberto they didn't like. Just as the odor of sanctity (or insanity, which is sometimes the same thing) might have emanated from Armand, so its opposite—the smell of evil—might have risen from Roberto's flesh, inflaming the bees. Whatever it was, the bees settled on Roberto, on his hands and neck and face, all the exposed parts, and stung and dropped off to be replaced by other bees who stung again.

The behavior of Roberto was as incomprehensible as that of the bees. He might easily have flung himself out the door after the first sting or even before it. He didn't move at all. He didn't even rise. He sat immobile to be stung and stung.

The reaction to bee venom is as mysterious as the likes and dislikes of bees. Some men can be stung again and again and over the years become almost immune to bee stings. With others it can get worse until one sting alone is fatal. To some persons bee venom is so toxic that a single sting can paralyze them.

Something like this happened to Roberto, a paralysis due not entirely to bee venom. He had had this vision of dying gloriously at the head of his troops (the legend to be handed down to generations of Garcias). The first bee sting immobilized him and, at the same time, astounded him. His limbs were incapable of movement, partly a paralysis of will as well as bee venom, but his mind remained hyperactive, his brain flooded with most unwelcome thoughts, painful thoughts, agonizing thoughts.

Far from dying gloriously, he was, he realized, dying ridiculously, stung to death by little angry insects. What a legend to hand on to generations of Garcias! And it would be handed down, he was sure of it. The humor of it had a very Hispanic ring to it, the kind of ludicrousness that would appeal to the author of *One Hundred Years Of Solitude*. The Garcia name a butt of ridicule for hundreds of years!

All these thoughts flooding his brain while being stung to death by bees, bee venom acting as always in peculiar ways, never more so than in its action on Roberto Garcia. His limbs paralyzed, his mind hyperactive. Very odd.

Cassidy had waited outside as long as he dared after Arguello and the other three had come out. He was as scared of bees as anyone, but he had the only gloves and the veil. He walked into the cabin, silenced .25 in hand (because he had no idea how many Balisarians remained there), looking for Lucia and not finding her.

"Lucia!" he called.

"She's in the bedroom," said Anne Falk calmly. "Don't open the door. She's safe as long as the door's closed."

Cassidy found a chair and got Anne Falk out of the chains and carried her out to the gray dawn and lay her on the grass. He went back and carried Armand, still unstung, out into the open air followed by bees.

Lastly he went back for Roberto.

He had wanted Roberto alive, almost above all else, but clearly that wasn't going to happen. Roberto was a parody of the sitting human shape, all of him covered by bees—the face a solid mass of bees from hairline to neckline, covering forehead, nose, eyes, mouth, every inch.

Still, there was life there or why else would he be sitting there? What was holding the man on to his chair? Even as this thought crossed Cassidy's mind, Roberto slowly tipped over to the left and collapsed to the floor. (Ever after Cassidy was to speculate that Roberto was still alive when he first came in, still alive when he came back in for the third time, and died before his very eyes.)

A cloud of bees arose from the body and Cassidy got out of there fast.

"The smoke!" he yelled up at Pear Tree. "Give us the smoke!"

Pear Tree had already set the blanket to smoldering. He cut off a bit of it and dropped it down the chimney, smoke billowing out into the room. With the rest of the smoldering blanket, Pear Tree came off the roof and went into the cabin, not even bothering with the gloves and veil. (He was one of those whom bees leave alone.)

The smoke calmed the bees. Pear Tree went to the brood chamber and rescued the queen, took her out to the open air, where he released her to the upper air, her faithful followers swarming after her. After that Pear Tree went first to Anne Falk, whose eyes were closed.

Amanda Shotover rode out of the woods on Leatherstocking, grim as death under the gray sky. She rode right up to her unconscious son, leaped off the horse, and knelt next to him. Armand lay, eyes closed, his mouth twisted into an ironic smile as if he were above all this commotion.

Keefe said, "He's alive, Mrs. Shotover. The bees didn't touch him."

Amanda was bent over her son, studying that ironic smile. "He's a survivor, my son. Always was."

A very odd thing happened then. Armand opened his eyes, the gaze golden but opaque, looked right through his mother, unseeing, and said very distinctly, declaiming it: "I have done one braver thing than all the worthies did. And yet a braver thence doth spring, which is to keep that hid."

Whereupon he closed his eyes and went right back to wherever he was.

"John Donne," said Keefe, the scholar from Trinity. "But don't ask me what he's trying to tell us because I don't know."

Amanda Shotover shook her head slowly in wonderment and exasperation. She leaned over and kissed Armand on the lips, not a loving kiss, rather an admiring kiss. The kind of kiss, Keefe felt, that General de Gaulle might give a soldier after pinning a Croix de Guerre on him.

Pear Tree spoke up sharply. "This woman has to be taken to the hospital. Fast. She's in shock."

Anne Falk's cheeks were grotesquely puffed, her lips swollen, her forehead and eyelids lumpen, all of her monumentally unbeautiful. Amanda Shotover gave the unconscious girl a long, flinty look and said:

"Put her on Leatherstocking on the rump." She mounted the horse. Keefe and Pear Tree draped Anne behind the saddle, facedown, and tied her securely. "I'll take her to the garage, but someone will have to come along to drive the car and to get her into it. I can't drive a car."

It was Rattigan who trotted along at her side the five miles back to the garage, and Rattigan who drove Anne Falk to the hospital in Marietta. But Amanda Shotover went along to the hospital and she stayed there all that day and well into the evening until Anne Falk regained consciousness and was pronounced out of danger.

Everyone's behavior was a bit off center that day. After all, Amanda's own son lay in a coma on the ground. She left him to attend a woman she couldn't stand. It was almost as if she knew Armand would be all right without her. Or perhaps she knew there was nothing much she could do for Armand, whereas to Anne Falk she could be very useful.

Cassidy missed all this. He'd gone into Kaska's bedroom and sat on the edge of the bed where his bound and gagged daughter lay looking up at him rebelliously. He gazed down at her ironically and said: "You look very well trussed. I like you like that. I can speak my piece without fear of interruption."

"Mpf. Mpf. Mpf," said Lucia.

"Oh, absolutely," said Cassidy. "I thought you were under strict orders to stay in that upper bunk until I came back."

"Mpf. Mpf. Mpf."

Cassidy sighed and shook his head. "You missed the worst of it, and it's not over yet."

Keefe came in then and closed the door carefully after him. He surveyed father and daughter. "Aren't you going to untie her?"

"Why?" asked Cassidy.

The shot was loud, clearly a police .38, but not close.

"What's that?" asked Cassidy.

Keefe sucked his bottom lip. "The dawn comes up like thunder in these parts."

"Oh, Christ!" said Cassidy.

Three more police .38 shots, with their peculiarly hollow boom.

"It's none of our affair," said Keefe. "I didn't approve or disapprove. I just walked away."

"Yeah," said Cassidy.

No prisoners. Vengeance was complete. Like a Shakespearean play, every last detail was worked out. Except this wasn't the sixteenth century.

"You and I would have done worse if we'd been given the chance," said Keefe, reading Cassidy's mind, not for the first time either. Cassidy didn't want to hear it, but there was no stopping Keefe, who wanted it off his chest.

"We were saved by the bees, you and I. The bees took the matter out of our hands, a fortunate thing. We should be very grateful to the bees. It would have been a very bad thing for our immortal souls to have done what we had in mind."

None of this had been discussed, but Keefe knew his man very well, knew his mind inside out.

"Shut up," said Cassidy.

He didn't want it even hinted at in front of his daughter.

But Keefe was right. It would have been very bad indeed for his immortal soul (Cassidy believing neither in souls nor in immortality) to have done what they had in mind. What Cassidy had in mind was to wring out of Roberto Garcia the one thing that had baffled him from the first day when Armand had invaded his apartment: the identity of Victor. To do that he had intended to put the torturer in his own torture rack and let Keefe, who had a score to settle with Roberto, turn on the juice. That had been the plan. It had not been so much as mentioned, but they both knew it. They had been saved by the bees.

But now how would he ever find out who Victor was?

Cassidy untied his daughter's hands and she tore the gag off her mouth and said violently, "I bit the son of a bitch on the hands and I kicked him in the shins. I wanted to kick the bastard in the balls but I couldn't reach."

The language from his thirteen-year-old daughter shocked Cassidy to the marrow. She'd never used language like that, not ever. He opened his mouth to protest and closed it firmly. Instead of protest he leaned forward and kissed her on the cheek.

"Good for you," he said.

23

Lucia was sound asleep on Kaska's bed. Cassidy covered her with a blanket and joined Keefe in the kitchen. Kaska lay neatly on his side, his legs rigor mortised into the sitting position, *Bienvenido* inscribed on his forehead.

"Alas, poor Kaska, I knew him well," said Keefe. "There he lies, Cassidy, the ultimate survivor—except that he didn't survive. If Kaska can't survive, what chance has mankind?"

Cassidy was on his knees inspecting the little round hole. "Single shot through the heart—and him the fastest gun in the West. Now, who could manage that?"

"The KGB."

"The KGB doesn't write *Bienvenido* on their foreheads. It's not their style—nor Roberto's either." Cassidy straightened up on his knees, his hands in the small of his back, trying to get the stiffness out. He felt diminished. Kaska was one of the few who'd been in the game from the outset, on the other side, of course, but nevertheless part of the ever-narrowing circle. The death of old enemies left a hole in his private world not so very different from the death of old friends.

"I think he was in on this lark, Keefe. He may even have been running it. I never believed in that defection. If you cut this man open, cut right down to the bottom of his soul, you would find Karl Marx written on the inside of the inside—in code, of course. This whole caper, including Kaska's defection, has been orchestrated on Dzerzhinsky Square—some grand humiliation for Uncle Sammy that may still come to pass unless we forestall it. You think that's too paranoiac, you Irish Hamlet?"

"No more than usual, Thucydides. It's reading history does it. Destroys the brain cells—like absinthe."

Fletcher hobbled out of the woods, eyes bloodshot, face grimed with shoe polish and dust, mouth hanging open as if he hadn't the strength to close it.

"Where are the others?" asked Cassidy.

"Looking for the rest of the team. Christ, they can't *all* be dead." Fletcher sat heavily at the kitchen table and closed his eyes. Keefe poured him coffee.

"How the hell am I going to explain this to twenty grieving widows, Cassidy?"

"Get some sleep. I'll think of something."

It was 8:30. No one had slept that night.

Fletcher opened his eyes, in which there was a trace of wry humor. "I've got to get the *bodies* back to New York. The Irish revere dead bodies. You know that, Cassidy. You're a fish-eater yourself."

"Was," said Cassidy.

Rattigan drove up to the cabin in a pickup truck. "I've been sent back to get Armand and take him to the hospital."

"Where's Amanda?" asked Cassidy.

"At the bedside of Anne Falk, maintaining a vigil, which is something only the upper classes know how to do." Rattigan's face twisted into his clown smile. "They own that hospital outright, Cassidy. The Shotovers built it and maintain it. In the old days the very rich had their own chapel and their own priest, but now they have their own hospital, their own doctors."

"Aah," said Cassidy. "That will make things a bit easier. Did you see Alison?"

"He's gone back to Washington in that monstrous CIA limousine which is nuclear powered and doesn't have to be refueled for twelve years."

"I'll drive," said Cassidy. "Rattigan, stretch out in the back and get some sleep. Keefe, get some sleep yourself. I'll be back in an hour or so."

"When are you going to get some sleep, Herodotus?"

"I've given it up," said Cassidy. "It's a very bad habit."

The hospital was of latticed oak painted white with green shutters, elm shaded, and looked as if the twentieth century had passed it by altogether. Cassidy found Amanda at Anne Falk's bedside, stiffly upright but sound asleep in a chair. Dr. Wentworth, who was eighty-five years old, white-haired, and big bellied, was injecting Anne Falk with Diphen.

Cassidy said, "Armand is to be admitted under the name Joseph Dunn and kept under lock and key at the very end of the top-floor corridor under twenty-four-hour nursing. You're to tend him yourself and tell nobody anything, the nature of his illness, treatment, anything at all."

Dr. Wentworth, who had known Armand Shotover since he was a baby, glared ferociously at Cassidy. "Are you trying to give me orders, young man?"

Only a man of eighty-five would characterize Cassidy as a young man. Cassidy said, "If you don't hide him, the CIA is going to spirit him away to one of their own hospitals again, where they'll put him under the same drugs that drove him out of his wits the last time and like to killed him."

Amanda Shotover slumbered on. Dr. Wentworth was putting his needle into a stainless-steel pan with a lot of other needles. He didn't look up.

"There are specialists for his condition," said Dr. Wentworth. "I don't know how to treat coma."

"Neither do the specialists," snarled Cassidy, whose contempt for doctors was only exceeded by his contempt for lawyers. "His vital signs are strong—pulse, lungs. Leave him alone, Doctor. He'll come out of it when he feels like it."

"Medicine by superstition," snapped Dr. Wentworth.

"That's all medicine has ever been," rasped Cassidy, "bloody superstition! You damned sawbones killed people for three hundred years by bleeding them in the name of science. Now you're giving them cancer by X-rays, murdering them with unnecessary operations, and making drug addicts of them by prescribing every quack nostrum the rotten drug industry invents. Witch doctors, all of you!"

"Get out of my hospital!" roared Dr. Wentworth.

That woke up Amanda Shotover. Or perhaps she'd been awake all the time. "It's not your hospital, Dr. Wentworth. It's *my* hospital. Do what the man says."

Dr. Wentworth huffed and puffed and glared, struggling with his professional pride. In the end he said *"mmmm,"* which doctors have said for centuries when they'd rather not say anything at all. At eighty-five he could hardly find another hospital, so he had to say *"mmmm."*

Cassidy turned on the charm because he had to. "Doctor, the CIA will use all sorts of pretexts, all kinds of trick questions and stratagems. Armand must not be on any records, either under his own name or anyone else's. Warn the nurses not to say anything to anyone."

Later Cassidy sat awhile with Amanda, who looked at him with her vinegary smiled and said, "Cassidy, you look like something written by Tennessee Williams—decayed, mildewed, rotton to the core."

Cassidy smiled. "I need a few things, Amanda, that only an old autocrat like yourself can provide. Are you ready?"

"Now what?"

"Twenty body bags. The hospital should have 'em."

The old lady's eyes were deeply sad. "*Twenty*, Cassidy?"

"We may not need them all," said Cassidy. "We hope." The other thing he needed was a bit more embarrassing. Cassidy sighed and sucked his front teeth. "To put it bluntly, Amanda . . ."

"Let's have it, Cassidy."

"Do you own the coroner as you own this hospital? I need twenty death certificates. Signed and stamped with the official seal. Hunting accidents, all of 'em. . . ."

Rattigan took his turn at the wheel as Cassidy slumbered next to him on the way back to Shotover Hall. He was still asleep when Rattigan pulled up in front of Kaska's cabin, and Rattigan let him sleep on. Inside the cabin Rattigan found them all asleep—Keefe snoring away next to Lucia on Kaska's big bed, Fletcher asleep on the kitchen floor. Rattigan went back to the truck and closed his own eyes.

Cassidy woke an hour later to find Fletcher counting the body bags. "We don't need twenty," said Fletcher. "We found eight of the boys in the woods, some of them sleeping it off, some of 'em hopelessly lost. Well, they'd had a bit to drink."

Cassidy showed Fletcher the death certificates—signed and sealed. Fletcher was outraged. "Jesus, Cassidy, I thought we were crooked in New York, but you couldn't get a death certificate signed and sealed. The Mayor himself couldn't do it."

Cassidy said, "Shotover Hall is almost half of Alester County. The Shotovers own not only the coroner but also the sheriff, one U.S. representative, two state senators, and about a third of the Governor." He smiled evilly at Fletcher, who was—for his size and weight—quite virtuous. "You're a city boy, Fletch. You don't understand the country. *Life* magazine once ran an article listing twelve homicides in each of which the finger of suspicion pointed directly at a very rich man or woman. In every case there was enough evidence certainly to indict and probably to convict. None of them ever stood trial. If the coroner says it's an accident, the investigation never starts."

Fletcher hated the idea, even if it got him off the hook. Partly off the hook. "The widows'll never buy it," he said gloomily. "Hunting accidents, my ass. What'll I tell the widows, Cassidy?"

"The truth," said Cassidy. "There's nothing more healing than the truth. Tell them their husbands were the avengers of eleven murdered cops in a very noble but highly illegal operation. So illegal that if even a whisper of the truth got out it would severely endanger their widows' pensions. Nothing will silence a grieving widow quite so completely as a threat to her pension."

Nobody said anything for quite a while.

Keefe spoke up. "You have a devious mind, Cassidy. Fancy suggesting the truth. You could get drummed out of the CIA for a thing like that."

"They've already thrown me out," Cassidy said. "For exactly that reason."

24

Cassidy was packing for both of them. Lucia's jodhpurs
that Amanda had given her. (When would she need those
again?) Her French grammar she hadn't opened for a week.
His silenced .25 wrapped in one of Lucia's old wool socks,
scrunched in under Lucia's jeans, and his old gray sweater,
intertwining old worn garments, daddy's and daughter's.
His *History of the Crusades* on top of pile. He hadn't
opened it once.

Lucia came in wearing her scruffiest jeans and an old pair
of sneakers, filthy even by her standards, eyes in that plain
face dark with woe. "Letitia's leaving. She wants to say
good-bye." Lucia opened the door for her and Letitia, a
bone-thin black girl of about eighteen came in, her face
streaked with tears. All the black women in that household
were either emaciated or fat as hogs. "Bye, Professor. It
been a real pleasure knowing you." Cassidy folded the
twenty and slipped it to her. He couldn't think of anything
to say.

They were all leaving. Yesterday Gravity, who did the

halls and the bathrooms of the cavernous upstairs. Today Letitia, who had done all the bedrooms. "None of 'em have been paid for weeks, Daddy," said Lucia, who knew every last one and the names of their children. "The place is falling apart. We're deserting just when Amanda needs us most."

What could he do about that? Pay Amanda's bills? He couldn't pay his own. "We've got to get back before you flunk out of eighth grade," said Cassidy. And while he still had some students left at the New School for Social Research.

"Geoffrey's doing all the cooking. He can't clean the house," cried Lucia.

Cassidy folded his red plaid shirt and put it on top of the *History of the Crusades.* "Are you ready?"

Lucia nodded miserably. "I'm very sad, Daddy."

"It shows," said Cassidy. "Come on."

He left the suitcase on the bed and the two of them went down the vast hall, down the wide front stairs that had been built for the nineteenth-century parties where girls in hoop skirts sat on the steps with their beaux.

They found Amanda in the sun room seated in her usual white wicker chair, fiddling with the silver tea things on the little painted tea wagon. With her was a heavyset man with dewlaps overhanging his white collar. Around his belly and the seat of his chair were official-looking documents, legal size, that had spilled out of a briefcase at his feet.

"Sidney Dorp," introduced Amanda between her teeth. "Professor Cassidy and his daughter, Lucia. Sidney is a *banker.*" The last word pronounced with extreme distaste, as if she were saying: Sidney is a rapist.

"Lucia and I are going for a last ride, Amanda. We hoped you'd come along."

Amanda uttered a bark of pure pleasure and shot out of her wicker chair. "What a marvelous idea! I'll get my jodhpurs."

Sidney Dorp looked extremely unhappy. "Mrs. Shotover, we haven't even begun to ..."

Amanda was already out of the room.

Sidney Dorp looked thunderous.

"She's a very spry octogenarian," said Cassidy.

Sidney Dorp was gathering up his documents carefully, reverentially, as bankers will. "Mrs. Shotover," he barked, "considers the discussion of money beneath her dignity. Like the Queen of England, she never soils her hands with money."

Dorp was assembling the litter of papers in his lap. Cassidy caught a glimpse of "DEED OF TRUST is made this 27th day of May 1981 ..." That old piece of paper. With it were other papers, other loans....

"Unfortunately," Sidney Dorp was saying, "Mrs. Shotover is not the Queen of England. She is a mortal like the rest of us." Dorp put the last of the papers in his briefcase, snapped shut the clasps, and stood up, a round, disheveled, angry man. "Would you kindly tell Mrs. Shotover that the bank will be forced to accelerate the deed of trust as of Monday. Good day, sir." He marched out.

"What does that mean—accelerate the deed of trust?" asked Lucia.

"It means they set it to music and dance to it. Like this." Cassidy did a little two-step, his only dance step.

"Daddy!"

Geoffrey glided in in his noiseless way, immaculately turned out as always, white gloves on his black hands. He picked up Amanda's teacup and put it on the painted tea wagon, picked up Sidney Dorp's teacup, still full to the brim, picked up the silver teapot as if it were a sacred object, and placed it softly, carefully, on the tea wagon.

"Are you leaving like the others, Geoffrey?" asked Lucia.

"Where would I go? This is my home. I been here forty-five years, Miss Lucia." Geoffrey pushed the painted tea wagon out of the sun room, through the gun room, the music room, the sitting room, and clear back to the kitchen where he took off his frock coat, put on an apron, washed the tea things, and put them away.

Sunlight was dappling the forest floor as they picked their way through the woods, following an old trail that Amanda had ridden with her husband forty years earlier. Amanda was on Leatherstocking, Lucia on Faun, Cassidy on Ariel.

"Have you heard from Mr. Fletcher?" asked Amanda, low to Cassidy.

Lucia was riding ahead. They didn't want her to hear any of this.

It was Amanda who had come up with the old school bus, a Reo, that dated clear back to the days when Shotover Hall had its own school and the bus had picked up black children dotted around the twenty-seven thousand acres and brought them to the school and then took them home. The Reo was an immense antique with leather seats that had been kept running by Shotover mechanics as a kind of challenge. In it went the living and the dead in their body bags. That way Fletcher and his crew could drive back to Manhattan with no annoying permits, the cops taking turns wheeling the ancient bus down I-95. In Manhattan Fletcher had arranged to take the twelve bodies, separately, to twelve different undertakers (because it's easier to explain one body than twelve, or even two). After that Fletcher had taken on the widows, one by one. And that was just that.

Three days ago. Sunshine glistening on the leaf mold of the forest floor from the immense trees that were blotting out the little trees because that part of the woods had not been forested for years. Eventually those big trees would die and topple and there would be no medium-sized trees to take over and continue. Much of Shotover Hall existed in limbo, a land that time forgot. No one had set foot in much of the land for years.

Now it was all coming apart at the seams, which was not so surprising. What *was* surprising, Cassidy thought, was that it had held together so many years, impervious to land speculators, economic change, sloth, and all the other forces that nibbled away at great estates. The other great estates were barricaded behind lawyers, fortified by unbreakable trusts, shielded by accountants. But Shotover Hall had been held together by a childlike man of forty playing house with the CIA, paying Shotover Hall's bills in cash, week by week, as if banks had never been invented. Now Armand lay in a coma and the golden flow had stopped. Somewhere there was twenty-six million dollars in cash. But where?

Cassidy sighed and told Amanda what the banker had said.

Like Lucia, Amanda asked what *accelerate* meant.

"It means the whole loan is due, principal and interest, on Monday. A million and a half. Have you got a million and a half?"

"I haven't got two dollars," said Amanda with a little moue of distaste. To Amanda, talking about money was like talking about one's bowels. Very poor form.

"You mean they'll foreclose on Shotover Hall," said Amanda, Leatherstocking picking his way delicately between the great trees.

Cassidy explained deeds of trust. The bank didn't have to go through foreclosure. Foreclosure was a long process that could be delayed in the courts. With a deed of trust the bank could take possession immediately, if it wanted to, though why it would want to, Cassidy didn't know.

It was a CIA-owned bank and the CIA always operated behind fronts. There was no better front than an aristocratic old family that had owned the place for a hundred and fifty years. The Agency was trying to bring pressure for some obscure reason of its own, buried behind layers of secrecy, layers and layers like an onion's many skins.

Somebody in the Agency wanted to know where the twenty-six million was. Why? Twenty-six million was chicken feed to the CIA. Unless . . .

Cassidy shook off the thought and yelled up to Lucia, who was riding ahead: "Not that way, love. This way...." Cassidy turned his horse, Ariel, leftward through the forest glade under the huge beech trees and spurred the horse up a little grade, looking back to be sure Lucia was following.

He didn't want Lucia going the way she was headed because that way lay the mass grave under the naked red earth. For two days he and Keefe and Rattigan had gone through the woods with the front-loading tractor, picking up bodies one after another, forty-two in all, and taking them to the deep ravine in one of the most godforsaken bits of the twenty-seven thousand acres. The hardest part had been getting the bulldozer through the woods to the ravine. Keefe had driven the bulldozer because Keefe could drive anything, and over the deep ravine the bulldozer had piled the red earth on top of forty-two bodies.

The final humiliation for Roberto Garcia—to be buried with the enlisted men.

Hugh Alison's most secret telephone didn't ring often and when it did Alison always answered it personally, with the single word "Yeah,'" with a rising inflection. "Yeah," like a question mark. No one else was allowed to answer it, though Grace used to pick up the most secret phone from time to time out of simple old-fashioned wifely defiance. (Cassidy had once promulgated as Cassidy's Law the proposition that a rich wife could be told to do things with some expectation she would do them, but to tell a rich wife *not* to do something was really asking for it.)

At 10 A.M. that morning the most secret telephone rang. Alison was shaving with the electric shaver. He turned it off and reached for the most secret telephone. Usually he had some premonition. Pyotr in Stockholm. Hugo in Lisbon. This morning his mind was blank, foreboding. "Yeah," he said with a rising inflection.

The voice on the other end rocked him.

"Ali Baba is not in place," said the lady who was known as the Iron Butterfly.

Using cryptonyms even on his most secure phone. She had never called him. Never. He had always had to call her. Alison was both astonished and alarmed.

"Mrs. Van Fleet?" he said. One had to use the *Mrs.* Harriet Van Fleet was an old-fashioned woman who intensely disliked *Ms.* She had once had a husband, though no one knew what had happened to him. Cassidy's theory was that she ate him.

"I flew in to the airstrip this morning. There's no one there. No one at all." The voice cold, accusatory. "There are forty-one packs on the ground at the northern end of the runway—but no soldiers, no Ali Baba."

Ali Baba was Roberto's cryptonym.

Alison's mind in turmoil. What in God's name was Harriet Van Fleet doing at the Shotover Hall airstrip? And where were Roberto and his forty men? (Ali Baba and his forty thieves. What a cryptonym to pick!)

Alison said, "Ali Baba arrived three days ago. I assumed they were training. . . ."

"You assumed wrong, Mr. A," said the cold, deadly voice. "I suggest, Mr. A, you go to never-never land and find out what has happened and report back to me personally by eight o'clock this evening."

Alison had a dead phone in his hand. He hung up slowly.

He could get a CIA plane to take him there. Half an hour. But if there was no one there to meet him, he'd be miles from the house. . . . Armand had always met him, but Armand was . . . wherever Armand was. As for Kaska . . . Alison had tried the radio telephone to Kaska the night before and got no answer, not even a recorded answer. Something very wrong there.

There was no alternative but to drive to Shotover Hall. Three hours. Christ!

Alison drove himself in his own car this time and all the

way one question burned in his mind: Why had Harriet Van Fleet, the President's personal aide, the most powerful person in the administration, flown to Shotover Hall? It was hard to get the damned woman out of the White House at all. She ate there, slept there, lived there.

Why? . . .

A quite different question was agitating Cassidy. What in hell did the CIA want with Shotover Hall beyond what it already had? The place was a great convenience as it was. A huge supersecret estate that was masked behind its own aristocratic pretensions. Why change things? What reprehensible activity would be concealed there? Perhaps a school for guerrilla warfare whose lessons the United States, like all nations, had to relearn painfully war after war.

Perhaps he could teach there those always forgotten lessons about the nature of guerrilla warfare passed on by the Scythians and Attila and Sun Tzu, to say nothing of Pancho Villa, Aguinaldo, Lawrence of Arabia, Lenin, Mao, Ho Chin Minh, and our own Red Indians Sitting Bull and Crazy Horse. What an idea—that the Agency would ever listen to him again! Or that anyone would. . . .

They came out of the trees unexpectedly into the brilliant sunshine in the clearing behind Kaska's cabin. It caught them by surprise, the cabin. They had not intended to visit the place—but there it was, demanding attention.

They rode quietly around to the front door. Lucia slipped out of the saddle to the ground and put Faun's reins behind her saddle, securing the reins by slipping the stirrup leathers over them.

Cassidy scowled. The place stank of death—Kaska with *Bienvenido* on his forehead, Roberto covered from head to foot with bees. (A sight that would haunt Cassidy the rest of his life.)

"I want a drink of water," said Lucia, the lament of all

thirteen-year-old girls since the beginning of time. She went into the cabin.

"Where is that delightful Russian who talked literature to us?" asked Amanda, sitting her horse like a dowager empress.

"He was retired," said Cassidy crisply.

Kaska, too, lay with the enlisted men under the red earth.

"Perhaps I shall come live here if they evict me," said Amanda with a glint of humor. "They'd never find me here. Is there a room for Geoffrey?"

The old lady slipped out of her saddle and went into the cabin after Lucia. That left Cassidy with the horses. He slid off Ariel and grabbed Leatherstocking's reins just as the horse was about to step on them and secured them behind the saddle as Lucia had. He did the same with his own reins and left the horses to graze.

Inside, Lucia was wandering around the central room of the cabin, a tin cup of water in her hand, touching things, her eyes bright with a thirteen-year-old's curiosity, sniffing the air as if it held secrets, fairly exploding with naked energy.

"He seems to have left all his toys," said Amanda.

The RD-11 still sat on the table, looking very twentieth century in that eighteenth-century woodsman's cabin.

"What is it, Daddy?"

"A radio with a computer in it that does everything but tie your shoelaces."

Lucia was fiddling with it, pushing this button and that to ON.

"It won't work," said Cassidy. "Keefe cut the electricity to the cabin."

Even as he said it, the RD-11 came alive with a very computerlike sound—*whup whup whup*—and the roll of white paper turned over and shot forward. Cassidy remembered that the RD-11 worked on its own batteries when the power was shut off.

Lucia was still fiddling with the dials.

"Leave it alone, Lucia," said Cassidy. "It's a very complicated gadget. It's likely to bite your hand off if you do something it doesn't like."

"Daddy!" said Lucia gleefully.

Whatever button she had pushed had set the RD-11 to typing away at very high speed.

All three of them—Amanda, Lucia, and Cassidy—watching now as the words spilled out on the white paper

YOU WANT TO KNOW WHO VICTOR IS? YOU WANT TO KNOW WHERE THE TWENTY-SIX MILLION IS? WELL, LISTEN, MY CHILDREN AND YOU SHALL HEAR . . .

It went on like that for four feet of single-spaced childlike prose, full of exuberance, sweetness, and innocence, as if this were Dungeons and Dragons they were playing. . . .

Signed ARMAND.

Alison was furious.

"You're not supposed to be here," he sputtered. "You were taken off! That was an order, Cassidy! You are violating your trust. . . ."

"I'll drive," said Cassidy very gently, because that was the way to handle Alison when he blew up like that. Underneath Alison's anger Cassidy detected a lot of fear. Cassidy pushed Alison ever so softly into the leather passenger seat of the Jensen. (An English car of which there were only about four in America and wouldn't you know Alison had one of them?) "You must be very tired from the three-hour drive down, and I realize it's very boring to ask you to turn right around and go back but that's the way it's got to be because we haven't got much time."

Cassidy put the Jensen into gear and started down the mile-long drive underneath the immemorial cedars, talking away.

"Incline your seat back and close your eyes and I'll tell you the whole scam. You and I are going back to confront the Dragon Lady together because I don't think I can get into the White House without your number four clearance and I don't think you can confront the Dragon Lady by yourself, Hugh, because you haven't the quality of irreverence that this confrontation is going to require."

Irreverence was a quality Cassidy had more of than almost anyone. Alison listened to all of it without saying a word. Alison had always been a good listener, one of the reasons he had hung on so long in an agency where palace coups were not unusual. Cassidy ran through all of it and then there was a long silence. When Alison finally spoke, it was in a low murmur, as if talking to himself. "Hardly anyone realizes how dangerous she is." He started to say something else and then trailed off.

When they entered the city limits, Alison insisted on making a phone call. Cassidy wanted very much to listen in on that call but he couldn't because the car was double-parked. Anyway, Alison made it very fast, and when he came back he was quieter than ever. A bad sign.

It was after nine when Cassidy pulled the Jensen into the west entrance of the White House, and they had trouble persuading the guard even to make the phone call. They were all afraid of the Dragon Lady. The sight of Alison's number four clearance did the trick and the guard made the call. "Mr. Hugh Alison to see you, Mrs. Van Fleet. He says he's expected."

The guard listened for quite a while, then turned to Alison. "Mrs. Van Fleet says you were expected an hour ago. Now it's too late. You'll have to reschedule in the morning."

Cassidy had no intention of waiting. The idea was to catch her by surprise, before she got her defenses up.

Cassidy said, "Just say the word Victor to her."

"Victor?" said the guard.

"Victor," said Cassidy.

"Victor," said the guard into the telephone.

In the White House service elevator to the private quarters, Cassidy said, "Let me do the talking, Hugh. I know the score better than you and, anyway, I'm tougher and I have less to lose."

Alison said, "You'll have to blow her out of the water, Horatio, or she'll blow us out of the water. She's solid steel, this lady. Keep your left up and your eyes open."

Harriet Van Fleet met them at the door of her small sitting room wearing a floor-length dressing gown imprinted with large angry red roses which looked, Cassidy thought, as if they'd bite your nose off if you smelled them. It was a small cluttered room full of books, including the one that Harriet Van Fleet had apparently just been reading, which lay open face-down on the coffee table: *Russia Since 1917* by F. L. Schuman. Nice light reading.

Cassidy took the T-4095 out and started sweeping the room. "This isn't for our protection, Mrs. Van Fleet," said Cassidy politely. "But for yours. You won't want any of this conversation recorded."

"It's already been swept." Harriet Van Fleet's first words, soft but malevolent, eyes venomous as a cobra's. A little too self-satisfied, Cassidy was thinking. How could she be up to anything? He'd given her no time.

Cassidy put away the T-4095. There were no microphones. Harriet Van Fleet remained standing in her flowery floor-length dressing gown so Cassidy stood too. Only Alison sat down, on the little sofa, eyes on the floor, fiddling with his silver-headed cane.

Cassidy began his recital as he did so many of his lectures at the New School, diffidently, the very offhandedness of his manner contributing weight to his information. "As you must know, this country has had an arrangement with the Swiss government for monitoring Swiss bank accounts that they and we have reason to believe are of criminal origin. Your bank account number 2985648739 at the Credit Suisse has been under scrutiny for some time. . . ."

Lies all of it except the account number, which Cassidy had got from Armand's revelations. He had to throw the book at her because it was going to be difficult, very difficult. . . .

"You somehow found out Harburg had sent out not only your Swiss bank account number but also the exact amounts of cash Roberto Garcia was sending you each month. You got in touch with Garcia—probably through the diplomatic pouch—and told him to silence Harburg, but first to find out—by torture—who he'd sent this information to. You found out it was Armand Shotover and you tried to have him killed. But he's not dead, Mrs. Van Fleet, and he's told us a great deal, including how much Roberto sent you— eleven million dollars. . . ."

None of these damning accusations had put the slightest dent in the Dragon Lady's composure. She was looking at him almost with indifference.

Cassidy kept going, now pacing back and forth, something he did in New School lectures, except that here there was very little room to pace in.

" . . . all of this cash coming from the sale of cocaine in this country, which is a felony. . . ." Cassidy gave a litle deprecatory cough. He was at the room's one window, now overlooking the side entrance. A car's headlights out there. The President that night was playing host in the State Dining Room to the President of Costa Rica and at that very moment was probably telling Irish jokes in dialect, at which he was very skillful. Still, no one should be arriving at the White House that late. . . .

Cassidy's recital went on quite separate from these side observations, a trick he'd long learned as a college lecturer—to have his mind busy with other thoughts while lecturing away.

"Kaska [he was saying] was never what he seemed, Mrs. Van Fleet. He was never a defector. He was planted here to make mischief; the nature of that mischief, at the time he was planted was unknown to the KGB. He was—as it were—to invent his own mischief, which is why they planted one of their best men to improvise an embarrassment for the United States. Mr. Kaska has been dealt with, but the information he fed the KGB lives on in their files. When it explodes, the scandal will come from abroad, where we can't control it. A cocaine ring centered in the private quarters of the White House. . . ."

Harriet Van Fleet had her back to him now and was facing her front door. She seemed hardly to hear what he was saying. What the hell was the damned woman up to?

Cassidy plowed on because there was nothing else for him to do. "That is why you have to resign, Mrs. Van Fleet, not only for honor of your country but for your own protection. If this scandal breaks while you still inhabit these quarters, it will create so great a furor that an investigation *must* be made—and frankly, Mrs. Van Fleet, you are in no position to withstand investigation. The facts are too damning. Whereas if you are out of the White House . . ."

That's as far as he got. The door opened and they poured in—half a dozen of them, far too many for the job at hand, and among them Cassidy had time only to notice his old colleague Brendan Vogel, who now had Cassidy's arm twisted in a hammerlock and his own arm around Cassidy's neck, whispering, "Easy, Horatio, or I'll break your fucking neck."

Alison barely moved. He handed over his walking stick with its concealed single-shot .38 without protest. Then there were the handcuffs. The Dragon Lady was saying, in that silky voice of hers, "I thought you'd never come. Where's Ben Riddle?"

"He's gone to see the President, Mrs. Van Fleet," said the gray-haired man who Cassidy belatedly recognized as Philip Hinds, the number two man, an even slicker survivor than Alison. Hinds seemed to be in charge.

"Highest national security," Harriet Van Fleet was saying. "There must be no record at all of their even visiting the White House. Mr. Alison was last seen on his way to Virginia on a top-secret matter when he vanished. Mr. Cassidy vanished in the same area weeks ago."

"It's already taken care of." said Philip Hinds.

They were to disappear from the face of the earth. It had happened before. Agents had simply evaporated, their disappearance blamed on the KGB, their families taken care of.

They were all out of the room and into the little self-service elevator which barely held them.

"Thanks, Philip," said Alison. "Hated to trouble you at this time of night. Do you think she bought it?"

They were taking the handcuffs off both of them.

"No," said Philip. "She didn't like the fact that Riddle wasn't there. She's on the phone right now, trying to find Riddle but she can't because we cut his phone."

Alison said to Cassidy, "Riddle is her personal fellow at the Agency. She put him in there to watch out for her interests, and we've had to be very careful with him."

Philip Hinds said, "We've got to hurry because she's a clever dame. She won't be fooled for long."

Cassidy was massaging his sore wrists and keeping his mouth shut.

They went through the White House kitchen, which was the fastest way to get there, came through one of the swinging doors behind a waiter, and lined up along the wall of the gilded room, trying to look like Secret Servicemen. The President was on his feet reading from the teleprompter as if ad-libbing the stuff, telling that one about the fat lady who wanted to go to heaven but they had no wings to fit her size. It got a good laugh, the President himself laughing at it. (Some of these jokes he'd never heard before he read them on the teleprompter, and while they tried to get him to read the stuff in advance, he frequently didn't.)

Hinds was whispering to Alison, "We call this the Alexander Haig curve because a President threw it at him first."

Cassidy was counting the house. It was a middling White House dinner, which was still fairly big news. All the important Latin American ambassadors were there with a few European ones that had strong ties with the South Americans, like the French and the Italians. There were at least four of the better known syndicated columnists, and one national network anchorman so the affair would be well commented on.

The President was a marvelous performer, looking his audience right in the eye, even while he was reading off the teleprompter so genially, so informally, with such a sparkle in his eye that he looked as if he were making it all up as he went along, so full was it of hesitations and little deprecatory shrugs, enjoying himself to the full at the same time and taking his audience along with him.

The Alexander Haig curve was at the very end.

"It is with extreme reluctance that I have had to accept the resignation of Harriet Van Fleet, one of my most valued advisers. . . ." Right there the President became aware of what he was saying. There was a small hesitation (but then, there were all sorts of small hesitations in his delivery) detectable only to the band of men lined against the wall.

The President was booby-trapped by his own professionalism. Like the old pro that he was, he kept reading the lines as if improvising them while his mind was busy on assessing their meaning.

"Mrs. Van Fleet has been asking to be relieved of her very heavy responsibilities for some time now in order to return to the halls of academe, which is her true love. . . ."

Malarkey, all of it. Harriet Van Fleet would *hate* to return to the halls of academe from the halls of power.

The President keeping his bright smile pinned on his face while underneath—to the band lining the walls—there was just a hint of the desperate struggle going on inside him. He was truly trapped. He couldn't admit to having read something he had no prior idea of, which would mean admitting that everything that came out of his mouth was put there by someone else.

He went on with it: "If you are wondering why I am announcing this at this dinner, it is because—as you all know—Mrs. Van Fleet is the architect of many of our Latin American policies, and I thought that you diplomats from the Southern Hemisphere should be the first to know. Mrs. Van Fleet will be sorely missed on your continent."

Like hell. Harriet Van Fleet was the gringo they loved to hate in South America. There would be dancing in the street from one end of the continent to the other.

The President told a few more jokes, still smiling, and sat down—but the very way he sat down told the little band of men lined up against the wall that he was angry. Someone would have to have a very good explanation.

In the Oval Office waiting for the President, Alison said, "She would never have resigned, Horatio. Never! She told me that Nixon made a very great mistake resigning—that he could have toughed it out—and of course Haig never resigned. He *threatened* to resign, which is something else again. Reagan *accepted* his resignation before it was offered."

Which is why they called it the Alexander Haig curve.

"How did you get the stuff on the teleprompter?" asked Cassidy.

Hinds said, "We've always had a man on the teleprompter—not to put things in but to take things out that some of his nuttier advisers write for him, not least, Harriet Van Fleet herself. Again and again she would have got us into severe hot water with this government and that if we hadn't tampered with the teleprompter."

When the President arrived well after ten, it was Cassidy who had to do the explaining. "You've got to get her as far away from the White House as possible, Mr. President, because she will be seen to be, not only a crook, but a tool of the KGB."

That was the clincher—that this administration whose religion was anticommunism could be seen to have a tool of the KGB in the White House.

"Lunacy!" muttered the President. "If she wanted money, she could have set up a consultancy like Kissinger. She'd have made millions. Honestly!"

Cassidy said, "It is what is known as the thrill of illegitimacy. It's what keeps the Mafia going although they have quite enough loot to invest it in honest enterprises, many of which are just as ruthless as the dishonest ones. But the thrill of cheating someone isn't there with the honest stuff. It's more fun to embezzle, even though it's much harder and riskier."

Later at Alison's Georgetown house over a drink Alison asked, "Where's the twenty-six million, Horatio?"

Cassidy said, "What twenty-six million?"

A great line he owed to Jimmy Durante.

In the show *Jumbo* there was a scene in which Jimmy Durante is trying to steal an elephant. Someone catches him at it and says, "Where you going with that elephant?"

Durante said, "What elephant?"

What twenty-six million? No one had reported twenty-six million missing. It had never appeared on any complaint, on any police blotter, on any official memorandum. It had never officially existed.

What twenty-six million? Cassidy smiled as innocently as Jimmy Durante had smiled in that long-ago show when he said, "What elephant?"

Epilogue

Getting the stuff from Grand Central Station to Shotover Hall was something else. A major problem in both logistics and covert spookery.

The surveillance was massive.

Even when Cassidy walked Lucia to school from Thirteenth Street, there would be two of them doing their transparent shuffle, trying to look innocent. While spotting the tails was easy, shaking them wouldn't be. It was an A-1 twenty-four hour tail, very expensive and almost impossible to shake—so Cassidy didn't try.

What he did try to do was drive them nuts, and he did pretty well at that. He and Lucia played hopscotch on the sidewalk; they dawdled through Eighth Street bookshops; they stopped for cups of coffee in sidewalk cafe's. They took about and hour and a half to do the ten-minute walk from school to Thirteenth Street.

Wasting the taxpayer's money.

On Friday, the important day, Lucia and Cassidy actually took two hours killling time between school and Thirteenth Street, and when they got there they didn't even dare talk about it because Cassidy was sure they were being filmed, taped, transcribed. It was very boring not only for the tails but for Lucia and Cassidy because of course the real action was elsewhere.

That was the day a little bent white-haired lady, accompanied by a very erect elderly companion who had a bristly white beard and piercing blue eyes, walked through Grand Central Station in one of its busiest times, 5:30, through a sea of commuters and wives getting away for the weekend, to the bank of lockers on the mezzanine floor. The man opened the big locker with a key and took out the two very large canvas suitcases. Staggering a little under the load, he carried the bags down the stairs, down the long ramp to the East Side subway, where the elderly couple pushed through the rush-hour crowd to the Lexington Avenue express. They stood up, the two old ones, all the way to Eighty-sixth Street, where they got off and padded up the subway stairs, down Eighty-sixth street to Second Avenue and from Second Avenue up to Ninety-first street where the Reo was parked.

The military man drove down Manhattan, through the Holland Tunnel, across the wastes of New Jersey to Virginia. When they got to Shotover Hall, they entered through the new drive and drove the Reo clear to Kaska's cabin up on the mountain, the Reo puffing and wheezing on the steep slope but its high axles clearing the sharp ridges of the roadway.

In Kaska's cabin, Keefe and Rattigan stowed the two bags under Kaska's bed and only then did they take off the wigs, the beards, the dress, and the rest of it. Both of them were too exhausted to talk much.

Amanda had left bread, butter and eggs, and bacon in the refrigerator and there were beans in the cupboard. Rattigan cooked up eggs and bacon and heated the beans.

"I suppose we ought to count it and steal a little," said Keefe.

"I'm too hungry and too tired for that nonsense," said Rattigan.

After supper they both went to bed without even looking at the money.

Sunday night Cassidy unloaded Lucia, very much against her will, on Deborah and flew alone to Marietta where he hired a car and drove to Shotover Hall, openly defying the tails to follow him up the mile-long driveway. Shotover Hall was much too big for surveillance.

Monday was the day they accelerated the loan and on that day Amanda and Cassidy appeared at the bank in Marietta with a suitcase full of cash—a million and a half plus interest. "Count it," said Cassidy to Sidney Dorp, whose dewlaps looked even more outraged than ever. "I'll want a receipt for it, and Mrs. Shotover also wishes the return of the deed of trust marked paid in full."

It wasn't usual but, as Cassidy was delighted to point out, "cash is still legal tender in this country."

If there was anything a bank hated it was cash.

"They're just lucky we didn't pay it in pennies," said Cassidy as they drove away. "They'll report it, you know, so you must expect a visit from the IRS."

"And what'll I do about that?"

"Pay the man what he wants."

They picked up Anne Falk at the Marietta Hospital. The puffiness had disappeared from the cheeks and the forehead, but some of the statuesque proportion of cheek and bone, the symmetry of outline had been lost to the bee stings. She would never be as beautiful as she once was, but then, Cassidy thought, no one needed to be *quite* that beautiful. The gray eyes had a touch of sadness that would be there forever, the legacy of the bees and the torment she hadn't suffered but had feared.

The three of them went up to the sixth floor to the room at

the very end of the corridor where Armand lay face up, eyes closed, wearing that faint ironic smile—just out of reach of the world.

Anne Falk kissed him on the lips, felt his forehead, fussed over him for a bit. "I'll be back tomorrow," she said to the nurse.

"It could be a long vigil," said Cassidy. "The sawbones don't know what they're dealing with—as usual."

"I'll wait," said Anne.

As they turned into the mile-long driveway, Amanda, who had said very little up to that point, turned to Anne and said, "Welcome home."

That night Anne Falk again visited Cassidy's room, wearing the same red wool sensible dressing gown she'd worn the first time. Otherwise, though, it was a different woman.

She sat on the edge of the bed, looking Cassidy in the eye crisply. "Armand ran the place like a toy train, paying the bills in cash the way you do in Monopoly. We can't go on like that. Anyway, Armand isn't here to do that. We can't keep the money stashed under a bed indefinitely. We've got to invest it. I have a friend in Boston Commonwealth who knows how to launder cash into proper investments without attracting the feds . . ."

This was the girl who had been trying to persuade Armand to give the money back. Cassidy was at the window looking out at the moon turning the trees into artworks. Without looking at her he said, "I don't want to get involved with that money anymore. I'm a puritan soul, Anne. I don't know whose money it is, but I know it isn't mine." He shut up right there before he started running on about money. Cassidy had a theory that all money over, say, ten thousand dollars, was inherently evil, which he used to bore his friends with after too many Wild Turkeys, but he didn't want to get into that monologue now. What he said instead was:

"Anyway, we'd never get it to Boston. We'd be raided

before we got ten miles. The money would be taken by unidentified men driving an unmarked car."

"You didn't know I could fly?" asked Anne Falk. "You do know we have our own airstrip here. It's very hard for an unmarked airplane to stop another airplane in the sky."

What struck Cassidy hardest about that hardboiled solution was the little word "we."

"We've got our own airstrip."

And she wasn't even married yet.

Much, much later he was discussing it with Keefe. "She's a new woman. Do you think it was the bees did it?"

"The torment," said Keefe

"But she was never touched. You'd cut the wires."

"She was in the chains. Once you've been in the chains with the fear in you . . ." Keefe grimaced as if he were in the chains himself again. "It does something to the soul. Armand will find out when he wakes up—if he ever does."

"I had gone through my little black book twelve times, considered every number there, but I couldn't make the connection—a *woman*." Cassidy and Keefe were in the back room at Spumi's in the semidarkness Manhattan drinkers love. "And of course Armand knew who Victor was. She'd been dealing with him because he was easier to dupe than Alison. What she didn't realize is she was dealing with an old-fashioned patriot. He was outraged by this corruption in high places."

Keefe growled, "What in holy hell was Harriet Van Fleet's White House telephone number doing in your black book, Cassidy? I didn't know you dealt on that level."

"I don't. Alison does. I had to call him there once—Alison was showing off what a big shot he was—and I kept the number because you never know when you'll need a White House number. Naturally, it was the last number in the book I thought was the right number."

Keefe said, "If Armand was such an idealist, what's he

doing with twenty-six million in two very heavy suitcases I had to carry?"

"He shot the spic with his own gun," Cassidy said. "Kaska put him up to this play. The guy's hands were full of suitcases and Armand reached in his side pocket, got out the silenced gun, and shot him. Put the dough in the locker, locked it, walked downstairs to the subway, and took it to Fourteenth Street to see me, closely pursued by those two goons. It's all on tape. He was going to hand over the money to Uncle Sammy to prove what a crook Harriet Van Fleet was, but the affair took a nasty turn."

"Will he ever come out of that coma?"

"Your guess is as good as the doctors'. Anne Falk goes to see him evey day and sits there looking at him. The rest of the day she spends running Shotover Hall—all twenty-seven thousand acres. A great joke on the CIA because they put her down there to keep any eye on it and she winds up stealing it from them. And now she's got twenty-six million bucks to run the place with—or, rather, twenty-four and a half, after paying the rent. You've got to watch these Boston debutantes very carefully. Their ancestors were all buccaneers."

At the New School Cassidy was even more savage and sardonic than ever to his class of twelve, a very bright group of extreme right-wingers whom Cassidy delighted in baiting. In riposte, they threw at him hard right-wing questions he suspected they got out of *Partisan Review*.

That day, as his own ironic commentary on American foreign policy in Vietnam, Lebanon, and Central America, Cassidy read to the class some of the reports, made to King Philip of France about his own disastrous war against the Berbers in 1833: "We have profaned graves and mosques. We have sent to their death on mere hearsay and without trial people whose guilt is extremely doubtful. We have killed off on mere suspicion whole populations who have since been found innocent. We have surpassed in barbarity the barbarians we came to civilize—and we complain of having no success with them."

Cassidy liked that sentence so well he repeated it. *"We have surpassed in barbarity the barbarians we came to civilize."* He would never forget how close he came to torturing Roberto with his own torture equipment . . .

"In our efforts to spread democracy, shooting sixteen-inch shells into mud villages, destroying communities in order to rescue them from communism, raining death on them from gunships in an attempt to woo them to the delights of capitalism, we have never succeeded in selling our virtues; we have only succeeded in acquiring *their* vices."

This provoked an uproar of dissent from his right-wing students, which Cassidy listened to with a good-natured grin because he was rather fond of these young people (especially one sexy virago with bare, muscular legs she kept crossing and uncrossing while voicing opinions slightly to the right of Torquemada).

Cassidy listened well but always gave himself the last five minutes—the final word. "I'll leave you with one last thought. Fifty percent of the expensive armament we provide to those right-wing dictators in Central America to slaughter their peasants with wind up in the hands of the Communists. There's nothing unusual about this. In Vietnam half our guns and our cannon found its way to Ho Chi Minh's forces until the end, when they took the rest of it. Fifty years ago this country spent a fortune arming Chiang Kai-Shek, whose crooked generals sold much of it to the Communists, and in the end, of course, the Red Chinese got all of it. In the last fifty years the right wing in the United States has armed more Communists than Lenin, Stalin, Bhrezhnev, Chernenko and Gorbachev added together.

"When I was last in South America, there were four different sets of Communists—Stalinists, Trotskyites, Maoists and Castroites. They all hated each other's guts—

until we unified them by our actions in Central America. Look at Cambodia now that we have left. The Red Vietnamese, backed by the Red Russians, are fighting the Khmer Rouge backed by the Red Chinese—four different sets of Communists cutting each other's throats. Every time we intervene against the Communists anywhere in the world, we succeed in accomplishing exactly the opposite of what we set out to do—unifying the communist hordes against the democratic world. Why don't we just leave them alone to kill each other?

"But that's enough of that. Next week we get back to the Crusades, where four hundred years of Christian intervention succeeded only in entrenching the Muslims from one end of the Middle East to the other. Good day."

Cassidy was strolling down Fifth Avenue, enjoying the spring sunshine, when the woman with the bare, muscular legs fell in step, shaking her tawny mane at him like a weapon. "You're counseling *weakness,* Professor, as a foreign policy. How can you admire *weakness*?"

"Actually I admire strength," said Cassidy. "Where did you get those muscular legs—basketball? Field hockey?"

That made her even angrier. "That's not the important end of me, Professor."

Cassidy took her elbow and steered her into Weber's where they were serving on the sidewalk. "Wild Turkey," he said to the waiter. "And for the lady—what? Grapefruit juice?"

"Wild Turkey," said the young lady grimly.

"Mercy," murmured Cassidy. "You mean we agree about something?"

An hour later they were at her place, a vast loft in the West Village. There was no bed, only a four-inch-thick pallet on the floor, which had to do.

"My legs," said the tawny-haired one bitterly, "are the attraction."

"Well," said Cassidy, "I'm working my way up. Your breasts are very nice too. Someday . . ."

"Someday you'll get to my head—and you'll be horrified."

Cassidy kissed her on the lips, "It's a very nice head. Actually. You mustn't think convictions are all that important. Some of the men I've most admired"—he was thinking of Kaska or, as he used to be, Yuli "—harbored pretty dreadful convictions, but they had other qualities—wit, taste, originality—that attracted me. I can overlook a man's religion but his taste in neckties, never."

"You're beginning to sound like Oscar Wilde."

"Then it's time to go home." Cassidy started to pull on his trousers.

"Really, you're the most irritating man I've ever met!" Cassidy was putting on his shirt now. "When will I see you again?"

"In class," said Cassidy, "when each of us will try to change the other one's mind about the nature of the world—and we'll both fail."

By the year 2000, 2 out of 3 Americans could be illiterate.

It's true.

Today, 75 million adults… about one American in three, can't read adequately. And by the year 2000, U.S. News & World Report envisions an America with a literacy rate of only 30%.

Before that America comes to be, you can stop it… by joining the fight against illiteracy today.

Call the Coalition for Literacy at toll-free **1-800-228-8813** and volunteer.

Volunteer Against Illiteracy. The only degree you need is a degree of caring.

Ad Council   Coalition for Literacy